B!TCH
ON HEAT

RICHARD TONG

Published by
O GROUP LTD

FIRST EDITION AUGUST 2013

ISBN 978-988-12563-0-0

BITCH ON HEAT
© 2013 BY O GROUP LTD

Written and directed by Richard Tong.
Layout, design and typography by Iain Richardson.
Graphic characterizations and illustrations by James Ng.
Cover by Iain Richardson, from an idea by Nicholas Angel.

Comments, enquiries and information?
ogroup.com.hk

There are six million stories in the neon city. This is one of them.

BITCH ON HEAT

BITCH ON HEAT

1. HEADLINES & HEMLINES

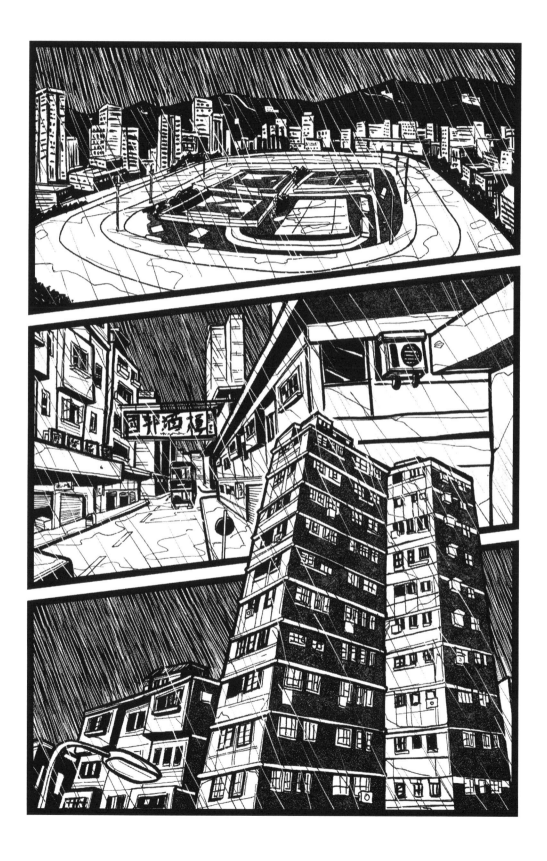

IT'S HUMID. HOARY. Twelve shades of bleak. And will probably get worse before it gets better. I'm waiting for my Macintosh to reboot. I've been assaulting the beige tower for three weeks, only recently elevating it to a status slightly above novelty typewriter. I reboot it half a dozen times a day. I dig the sound of it. Rebooting. I like to tell people I'm rebooting my computer when they ask what I'm doing. I'm rebooting my Apple Macintosh, I say. It makes me sound current. It also gives me something to do. While I'm up here, waiting.

Waiting.

I prefer to sit up, vertically speaking. Three or four feet off the ground. When people come to me I want them at see-level. Eye to eye. Sitting down, on a chair, makes me feel vulnerable. Like I've surrendered the high ground. And it's hard to concentrate, express coherent opinions or articulate emotions when someone is hoisting their block and tackle in my face. If I had a car it would be a Range Rover, so I could preside over the traffic as well. You won't find me cornered in a booth at pubs or clubs, or squatting on some faux-leather footrest either. I'll be at the bar, keeping an eye on the door. Ditto restaurants.

Only the paranoid survive.

Sitting up is just one of my things. Like sleeping with the bathroom light on, even though the illumination is undetectable from bed. Like being unable to put down a crossword until all the blanks are filled. Even if my answers are wrong. Like getting angry with people who smoke while they walk. Not with smokers. Just those who smoke while they're walking. Like not eating long grain rice. Short grain, please. There is a difference. I'm sure this kind of autism has a name. They're just keeping it from me. I don't know why. I can't be the only one uncomfortable with a fabric if it's more than ten percent wool. It's no big deal. Everyone has crosses to bear. Little tics and traits. It's not like my penchant for an elevated position inconveniences others. Some even appreciate it.

Angel Fuk, for instance.

My extraordinary PA, administrator and director of client services, Angel is grateful she doesn't have to stoop when she brings invoices and cheques for me to sign. Or faxes and phone messages for me to ignore. She doesn't have to sit down to discuss her briefs. The briefs that herald the start of a new job, that is. Not the kind that gird her feisty loins. Although we've had discussions on those too. There's not much of her I haven't considered. She has a predilection for A-frame miniskirts and six-inch heels. Along with a cavalier approach to décolletage. These are a couple of her things. You don't hear me complaining about them. That's just the kind of person she is. Liberal and liberated, with a licentious sense of humour. Her turn of phrase, in Cantonese and English, is quite rich. She employs enough colourful adjectives to make Scorsese blush. Her oratory skills were honed during teenage years, boarding at a Methodist Ladies College in Australia. Rhythm Methodists, she says.

The Three Rs: riding, rooting and a-rogering.

Here she is now. Arriving. Throwing her umbrella in the corner. Stamping the water from her slender pins.

Saturated in sexuality, she pulls at the open neck of her white silk blouse. And shakes off the dampness.

Every cloud has a silver lining, I think, admiring the astonishing legacy of bone structure bequeathed by the northern roots of her family tree.

The elevated geography of her fundament says Shanghai. Porcelain skin and dignified gait suggest Beijing. The overall effect would ruffle a vicar's vestments. And blow the beads off a cardinal's cassock. Congregations worship at her divine altar. No false idols there. Her physical presence could engorge a corpse.

Arise Lazarus.

I once mentioned her coquettish carriage and confabulation could lead to relationships based only on sexual attraction. What's so *only* about that? she said, with a smile that punched me in the pants. And left me to wonder when Altenberg had crept onto the Methodist curriculum.

At five-foot-seven Angel Fuk is the embossment of the classic China doll. Her long, dark hair is frequently pulled back in a ponytail, exposing small pocilliform ears, studded with one-carat diamonds. Cherry mouth and fleshy lips make Angel more fukable. Beneath this vivacious exterior lies a layer of minx and fox-like cunning. She's a pert example of Hong Kong's cultural cornucopia. A biomedical mélange.

Like me.

I'm part Mongolian, part American and nothing in particular. Just another of the displaced masses. This city is built on a bed of dislocated humanity. Erected on their bodies. Paved with their outrageous successes, spectacular failures and pathetic dreams. This year there's more of them about than ever. Year Of The Rabbit? More like Year Of The Rat. Maybe it's the return to mainland sovereignty. Thatcher stamped an expiry date on Hong Kong's underbelly a few years ago. Opportunists are looking to extract what they can, while they can. In case it disappears altogether. No doubt many of them are impatient, illegitimate by-products of interracial disharmony too.

We're all waiting.

2. PARTNERS

SITTING AROUND doesn't bring out the best in me. I don't have a sunny disposition at the best of times. Intense. Cacogenic tendencies. The legendary patience of the Chinese wasn't patched into my DNA at conception. Neither have I absorbed any via osmosis in the decades since.

My birth straddled Year Of The Cock and Year Of The Dog. If the ovules of The Cultural Revolution were sown in 1957/58, as many think they were, then I was part of that too. The Great Leap Forward's first step back, according to my mother.

Bastard son of Genghis Khant, says Angel, on bad days at Black Rock. She's probably not far from the truth. The Mongol warrior spread his seed so wide I've heard his genes are hot-wired into eight percent of the population.

It's the Mongol in me that came close to conquering Angel more than once upon a time. I was a subscriber to Wilde's belief that the only way to get rid of temptation was to succumb to it. The thought crossed my mind many times during the three-month trial period that began her engagement with the agency. Opportunities to violate her probation and reprobation abounded. Now there's about as much chance of dipping my pen in the company ink as there is my wife walking through the door. Angel and I are aware of this. It's a major factor in the candid, brutally frank nature of our relationship. And one of the reasons I formally wed her to the company. Incorporated her as a stakeholder in So Fuk Yu & Partners. Angel Fuk is, in every sense, vital. The same cannot be said of the third leg in the body of our enterprise.

Benny *The Fish* Yu.

He's my other half, professionally. A necessary evil that makes our primary business concern possible. He creates layouts for half-assed ideas. Prepares artwork for watered-down executions. We've known each other a long time. He accepts the dynamics under which I operate. Not a lot of people can tolerate that. It cuts him a lot of slack. The problem is he knows it. And takes advantage of it. This gives me the shits because I know, with all that extra rope, people like Benny end up hanging themselves. And get others lynched with them. Benny thinks he has that covered too.

A self-deluding ladies man, he wears gold Saint Bernadine and Saint Fiacre medallions on a thin gold chain around that neck he's always sticking out. They're a handy combination, as far as patron saints go. Bernadine watches over compulsive gamblers and people in advertising. Saint Fiacre looks after cab drivers, florists, gardeners, tile makers, box makers, pewterers and hosiers. He also prevents haemorrhoids, sterility, syphilis and assorted venereal diseases. Saint Fucker, as Benny refers to him. It's the reason he never bothers with condoms. What Saint Fucker can't fix, Dr Salk can, he insists. Why he drags the man responsible for the polio vaccine into it, I have no idea. He probably has him confused with Fleming. The jury is still undecided as to whether AIDS, the latest scourge of the world's underpants, is part of Saint Fucker's remit. Angel awarded Benny his piscean *nom de plume*. I thought it was because *fish* is one of the meanings of *yu* in Cantonese. She said it's because he's got lips like a garoupa, slippery skin and a penis that would taste worse than anchovy pussy.

Benny is supposed to work for me. Lately, however, he always seems to be working on something else. I don't mind that so much. Something else is usually a woman, barely out of her teens. Young women dominate my life as well, although for different intents and purposes. It's not Benny's fault my world view has altered dramatically. But he is starting to grate more than usual. The things he finds amusing. His flirting with Angel. A possible prelude to less honourable intentions and intra-office turmoil.

Hey Angel, he said the other day. You got a mirror in those jeans? 'Cos I can see myself in your pants.

It's getting to her too. And it takes a lot to ruffle Angel's wings. *Gweilo* clients, the *white ghosts* who make up an indecent percentage of our business, often pass indiscreet lowbrow entendres, following encounters with her.

Is that where you get the Fuk from?

I would've found these exchanges amusing once. Not any more.

It's not that I've grown weary of tenuous puns or phonetic tomfoolery. Our business is indebted to it. Neither am I riding the wave of political correctness that's sweeping the planet and threatening to destroy Asia. I'm not even particularly sensitive to the way it objectifies, demeans or could be considered disrespectful. Angel can handle herself and gives as much as she gets. It's simpler than that.

Much of the humour in me has died.

More often than not, I find myself sitting here like this. Waiting for Benny to get back from fucking whatever. Leaving Angel to field calls from clients and suppliers who want to know where their artwork is because the fucking deadline was yesterday.

The walls of the agency have long been sprayed in blue language. Most of it in the direction of our previous employer. Some of it toward each other, in the high-spirited and good-natured way that friends do. When we pencilled Angel's name into the company charter, and flew our new name up the flagpole, everyone saluted.

So Fuk Yu & Partners.

We liked the nugatory nuance. It made us sound like a goombah law firm, instead of struggling advertising agency. It was better than Yu So & So, which I thought sounded a bit soft. My wife liked it though. General consensus was that So Fuk Yu better reflected our dogmatic approach to work. Our attitude to the industry for which we were going to be the blunt weapon of choice. With retrospective clairvoyance it was, like much of my life, one of those things that were funnier at the time and you really had to be there. Still, as we like to say, fuck 'em if they can't take a joke. It's kind of the company's unofficial mission statement. A prevailing mind-set that catches the uninitiated by surprise. Particularly when expressed in the presence of my two-year-old daughter.

Mei is my constant companion and honorary fourth member of the creative hub. Better she learns how and when to use expletives from me, than some kid in the playground. The way to diffuse the power of these words is by decriminalising them, I say, borrowing from *Lenny Bruce's Guide To Parenting*. Use them more often, not less. My job isn't to shield her from life but to equip her for it. Blah, blah, blah. Probably not the approach Bill Cosby advocates in *Fatherhood* but, well, fuck him if he can't take a joke.

Mei sits across from me, by the door, at a pint-sized table. Armed with crayons and a huge stack of paper. When that becomes boring I introduce her to the television. And transform the irresistible force of youth into an immovable object. She sits in her beanbag and watches pirated Sesame Street videos. I'll get one of those laser disc players as soon as a few more titles become available. I got burnt on 8-track cassettes and Betamax. I'm not going to get fooled again. When it's time for Mei's afternoon nap, or if I'm working late, I take her to our flat on the fifteenth floor. We live there with my ancient Chinese mother-in-law and God fearing Filipino domestic helper. Architecturally, the unit is on the thirteenth floor.

But the fourth and fourteenth storeys were removed to avoid the bad *feng shui* associated with the number that comes after three and before five. I hope it worked for others. It didn't do much for my family's prosperity or my wife's good fortune.

She left the building a year ago.

I was waiting for Benny that day too. The phone rang. Ba-ba? a tentative voice inquired at the other end of the line.

It was Por-por. My mother-in-law.

Everyone in our house has a double-barrelled term of endearment. I'm Ba-ba. My daughter is Mei-mei. The maid is Bing-bing. My wife was Ling-ling.

Por-por never rang. We barely spoke at the best of times, getting by on grunts, whistles and mime. There was no animosity. We simply had no catalyst or common basis for conversation. My Mandarin, her preferred language, was stalled in its infancy. Pound for pound, we were evenly matched when it came to Cantonese. Cruiser Weight division. I can get myself into an argument and out of trouble. It's a coarse language. I usually find its directness refreshing. On this particular day, however, I graduated to a new level of comprehension. Simple. Crushing. Por-por's voice decimated.

Ling-ling is dead, she said.

My wife had been to the doctor. She was waiting to cross Nathan Road when the #4 Public Light Bus changed the trajectory of her life. Just like that. It jumped the curb and ploughed the crowd. Ling died instantly. And so did the fetus she was carrying. Her soul was vaporized. This was the first I'd heard of Ling's latest maternal machinations. And the last time I answered a telephone. Ever.

I have no memory of how the call ended. Or what happened after. How I made it up fifteen flights. Thirteen flights. Wouldn't matter if it were a hundred. I still wouldn't know how I made it home.

I rejoined the world twelve hours later, on the cold living room floor.

I would never
leave Mei alone
that long again.
Ever.

Ling's funeral was a well-attended outpouring of grief. A menagerie straight out of Hong Kong's human zoo. Every level of the food chain was represented. It was the only time I've been on the business end of sympathy.

Since that day, Por-por, Mei and I have been terminally bound together by the holy trinity of Ling: mother, daughter and wife.

This is the insoluble truth of my life.

Luck has never been a lady to me. Until the birth of my daughter, women have rotated through my life at 45rpm, like novelty singles.

My mother died of cancer. It ate her to the bone just in time for my 18th birthday. She worked the nightclubs of Tsim Sha Tsui. Hostess bars and karaoke joints. Before that she was part of The Cultural Work Troupe Of The Central Garrison, Beijing. Entertaining at the highest level. She danced with Mao, on more than one occasion. I don't think she traded physical thrills for financial and geographical gain, but it's hard to think of your Madonna as a whore. Her final years were spent corralling girls who truly worked at the coalface of humanity, bodies to the grindstone. She helped make ends meet, so to speak. She took care of them when they were returned in less than original condition.

Damaged, commoditized women populated our Sham Shui Po flat. They were the tapestry that clung to the idiocy of my infancy, the folly of my youth and the sins of my teenage years. Littered about like the books I stole from the library. These girls were my aunties. Their pragmatic, volatile owner-operators were my primary male influences. Along with classic literary characters, popular movie stars and a select group of law enforcers. The latter arriving to investigate beatings, reports of theft or illegal workers. They'd look the other way, if the cooze was physically willing or financially able. Society frowns on those plying this biological aspect of the hospitality industry but, from where I sit, it's the well-heeled who commit the most reprehensible acts. Operating lives of greater dishonesty, duplicity and depravity.

On the rare occasion feminine fortune did smile upon me, something inevitably managed to fuck it up. That something was usually me. Until Mei came along Her birth gave me more than just a soiled diaper to pin hope to. It was Fate's way of telling me I should've been nicer to women. To underline the point, She took Ling away. And relegated me to the punch line of The Cosmic Running Jape. The latest version of which is about to be rebooted.

I look up from the Macintosh and see a windswept Micki Tse.

This is funny, for all the wrong reasons.

3. TYPHOON SEASON

HER FIRST NAME is one of those naïve bastardizations of English that prevail in Hong Kong. It's what happens when children are allowed to choose their own appellation. It also means you sometimes get biblical with people called Creamy and Winkie. Idot. Floral. Melpomenade and a Polyhymenia (twins). Blowie, Mucus, Wagina and Propane. Micki's choice of moniker was an unimpeachable, phonetic translation of her traditional Chinese name. Mei-chi. It was also, in all probability, the only innocent thing about her. Guilty pleasures took on dangerous new dimensions in Micki's quiddity.

I'm shocked, yet unsurprised, to see this precarious blast from the past before me. Micki Tse doesn't wait in reception. For anyone. You know when she has arrived. She charges the air with her presence. It feels, smells and tastes different when you're in her orbit. She's a potent *deciso* force of nature with the power to make men, and open-minded women, adjust their priorities. In an instant. For that reason Micki could be equally unpopular with less confident females. They consider her a predator. Maybe she is. Micki has been in the hunt and enjoyed her share of kills. It is not, strictly speaking, a fair or accurate assessment. It's just her nature. The way she is. The way she's built doesn't hurt either.

Micki Tse is the personification of Freud's anatomy-is-destiny. Men, and the aforementioned women of liberal disposition, see their futures entwined with her soma the moment they lay their glazzies on her.

The sharp, Vidal Sassoon bob of jet-black hair is an affront to the big-haired Whitney Houston perms favoured by the general population. Large almond eyes sit wide above high cheekbones, dark pools on her alabaster complexion. Like an oriental Eva Marie Saint, with fleshy comforter-cushions. You could pop those puckering pillows on the end of a tug and fend off the QEII. Those of cheiloproclitic persuasion would have glass-door fantasies about her lips, dreaming of the day she walks into them. And those suckers attach themselves. The elegant neck, straight shoulders and rigid spine give her 5'11 extra impact. As do a firm set of curves. Small breasts, highlighted by a sleeveless, white Lycra turtleneck, sit high on her chest with the audacity of youth. Defying the maturity of her years. The way she carries them, *nobilmente*, combined with an enviably slim waist, so evident in high-waist pinstripe slacks, give them heroic qualities. Narrow hips and the graceful contours of her peach suggest it would be rude not to take her roughly from behind in the kitchen.

This is not to say, as Shakespeare put it, she was an easy glove. Going on and off at pleasure. It's just that for the few who know her intimately, it's not out of the question. There was a time when I knew it to be a welcome certainty. As sure as I know her thighs can crack walnuts at Christmas. As true as those disproportionately long legs go all the way up. And back again.

Micki, most are equally stunned to learn, holds degrees in Physics and Psychology from Oxbridge. She operates a successful PR company too. Carpe Per Diem. Ask why a person with her qualifications is in PR and she'll tell you.

Her clients embrace everything from luxury automobiles to expensive champagne, high fashion labels, blood diamonds and Tahitian pearls. They are businessmen, politicians, cadres, actors and musicians. Exactly what she does for them is not always clear. Suffice to say she's a shrewd professional who knows success is a bitch that must be bedded on a mattress of corpses. Carpe Per Diem makes good money. Many are forever in its debt and, thusly, hers. For Micki to be in Hong Kong is something of a rarity. She has offices in Beijing, Shanghai, Macao, Singapore and Taiwan. She spends most of her time ricocheting around the region. Giving people the runaround. Running the hapless ragged. Dining with Desai, mixing with Mans and partying with Pangs, *affretando*. For her to be in my lowly purlieux is a bit of a shock for one other notable reason.

Things did not end well between us.

Micki Tse has a younger sister. Esther. She doesn't induce the same spontaneous, glandular reactions as her sibling. She is, in advertising parlance, Avis to Micki's Hertz. *When you're #2 you try harder.* What Esther lacks in aesthetics she makes up for with goofy enthusiasm, dogged determination and spirited performance. She has more horsepower than a rag of colts. Lights your fires and kicks your tires in a different way. You end up in the same place, just via a different route. She is an amusing, picturesque detour.

Some play at love for sex. Some play at sex for love. Esther is one of those women that just play at sex. She uses it like a fly swatter. She'd be a nymphomaniac, if they could slow her down. A philandrist of the highest order, she has an edacious appetite for the possessions of others. Their men in particular. As the Bible would say, she covets thy neighbour's lot. And you don't get lips like that from sucking lemons. If cuckolding were an Olympic sport she'd take the Gold, Silver and Bronze. Then fail the drug test and have to give the medals back.

This I also know to be true. From personal experience.

I first met the sisters five or six years ago, when I was working bars and clubs. Establishing myself as a diffuser of problems. Micki was getting Carpe Per Diem off the ground. Esther just always seemed to be around. I don't think she's really ever done anything other than exploit life. The two girls had found their way into a big apartment on The Peak. And thought they'd feel more secure with someone like me in the house.

What started plutonic soon went tectonic, as Micki and I embarked on a riotous affair. *Impetuoso, forzando* and *risvegliato*.

Esther revealed her true form about eleven months into the lease. She coveted thy flatmate. And thy sister's mate. Took sibling rivalry to a felonious new plane. She had her wiles and her way with me, much to Micki's surprise. I was pretty surprised too. Back then, however, I took what I could and got away with the best of both worlds for almost six weeks. I don't think I'm being disrespectful to either of them when I say, in those Wildean days of yore, I would've fucked mud if it made itself available.

I'm glad we didn't get Venetian blinds. You would've screwed them too, Micki said, as she closed the door on the best sleeping arrangement I ever had.

She was probably right. I really loved that apartment.

Now, here she is. A tellurate tempest, storming back into my life. Breezing past my daughter without even noticing her. Maybe it's faux Catholic guilt and the weathering of time but, as she stands before me, I realize I still have a soft spot for Micki Tse. Although, at this point, it's more like a semi-hard spot. But I'll try to keep that in perspective. And out of view.

The two of us stare at each other. I'm waiting to see if this glorious apparition eventually fades. Micki's drilling right through me, for effect. And personal pleasure. See who flinches first.

Angel floats in from behind. Sorry, she wouldn't wait in reception.

She never does, I assure her. And I'd be disappointed if she did. It's okay. It is okay, isn't it, Mick? Is this going to get ugly? Some latent homicidal urge? Have you come for, what do they call it, closure? Will there be par-boiled rabbits and a horse's head between the sheets in the morning?

Actually, now I think about it, that's a possibility in our house anyway. I've consumed all kinds of gastro-aberrations in the name of bicultural relations.

Micki's expression suggests nothing. It's probably been that way for the last three-and-a-bit years. Fine thanks, Jack, she says. How are you?

I shift my gaze to Angel. Raise my eyebrows and wobble my gulliver in a haughty manner. Well *la-di-dah*. She backs out of the room and closes the door. Almost. It wouldn't be too hard for her to hear any conversation that ensues. And it will save recounting it to her later.

I decide to try and break the staring competition deadlock. Mrs Tse, I say. It's been, what, three years?

Four, she replies caustically.

Four? And still so angry. Shall I have the weather bureau hoist Signal 8?

Micki swivels. Observes. Then turns to face me. I raise my finger and speak in a faux Government Health Warning tone. It is dangerous to smoke while having a child, I berate her.

She puts the paraphernalia away. Smiles. It seems genuine. I heard, she says. Congratulations. She's sweet. Got her mother to thank for that, obviously. Are you going to introduce us?

To her mother? That's going to be a little difficult.

Left you has she? Welcome to the club. You can lay off the Mrs Tse crap. The ink on that divorce is well and untruly dry. When did yours walk out?

She left us all, I say. Died last year.

Micki observes me silently, wondering if my last comment was meant to be funny. Or have I come to terms with it, gone through the obligatory Victorian grieving period of three months, and got on with it. I'd forgotten how much fun it can be to throw her. If only for a second.

I DIDN'T KNOW YOU SUBSCRIBED.

YOU DIDN'T THINK I COULD READ.

I JUST ASSUMED YOU LOOKED AT THE PICTURES.

THE *HAUTE MONDE* TAKES MY MIND OFF THE STYLIST'S SNOKES WHILE SHE'S DOING MY HAIR.

TELL ME SOMETHING, MICK. WHY ARE ALL THE BEAUTIFUL PEOPLE SO UGLY?

If reason were to judge what is beautiful, Jack, then sickness would be the only ugliness, she replies academically, quoting someone wiser than all of us. Although it's unlikely Lichtenberg was holding Tatler when he said it.

I stand and move around the desk. Cross the room to Mei. I lift her to my hip and take her to the desk.

Micki adopts an aunty-like tone as she playfully pokes her in the stomach. Who's this? What's your name?

Mei-mei! I'm two and a half!

Clearly Micki's conjuration worked on all ages and persuasions. You're too cute is what you are, she says, then smells Mei's hair and kisses her forehead. She looks to me as she holds Mei's hand. She's adorable, Jack. Lovely name too, she says with a hint of a smile. It suits her.

It was her mother's idea not mine, I'm quick to establish. So, what's your excuse for being adrift in the social pages? I guess I'm a hard act to follow.

Apparently so am I, she says looking at Mei.

It's tough for guys who come after me. I think it's got something to do with my roguish charm. The ladies miss it.

Roguish charm?

Well, I am a bit of a scoundrel. Like Han Solo. I can't help it if women hang on to all these romantic notions about me.

Romantic?

Yes. You know. Turner. Blake. Delacroix.

Constable. And So, she completes the list. The great romantics.

That's us.

You could be romantic. Up to a point. The point of ejaculation.

That hurts, I say, as if wounded. You girls put guys like me up on this pedestal and keep making comparisons. It's really not fair.

I take Mei back to her table. Put a fresh sheet of paper before her, grab a crayon and make a circle. Draw me a picture of the pretty lady, sweetpea, I instruct her. Can you run some air cover in here? I call to Angel, walking back to my desk. She enters. Turns up the air-conditioning and sits next to Mei.

I pull a small partition out from the wall. An antique Chinese screen. It creates a temporary enclave. And the illusion of privacy.

Micki's eyes zero in as I return to my seat. She speaks in a controlled, low tone. Yes, Jack. You were a man of classic virtue, she says. A saint. Esther and I were just talking about that the other night. Whatever happened to Saint Jack?

Well, at least you're talking again. I love it when a family comes together.

Blood is thicker than Esther. And any idiot she beds. Including Mr Tse.

Oh dear, I sympathize. A serial adulteress. Don't give up. You know what they say: third time's a charm. Besides, these days, all the married men live like bachelors. And all the bachelors like married men.

How are the widows living? What do they like?

I lift two cigarettes from the pack. And an ashtray from the bottom draw.

Micki fires the Dupont.

4. FUNNY BUSINESS

I HELP PEOPLE. I can't help myself. It's another of my things. I should've been a fireman. A Samaritan. Or a nurse. I might've been a policeman if it hadn't been for that incident at the recruitment centre. And certain aspects of my past. For honest, gainful employment it was be a rozzer, or towelboy at Wang Palace Spa & Sauna. I ended up meeting a lot of the same pricks during my stint at The Palace anyway. There's no shortage of them in this game either.

Most clients come to me if they need ads. Or direct mail. I take care of that. Doesn't matter what's in their budget. I get it done. Catalogues, letters and invitations. Radio spots. TV ads that can't afford to immolate Michael Jackson.

Along with ransom, blackmail and extortion, advertising is the one of the most profitable forms of writing. Which is why, sometimes, people need help with other things. I can take care of that too. If it's the right thing to do. Consider me a not-so-smooth *Spenser For Hire*. A less chivalrous *Magnum PI*, sans khaki shorts, Hawaiian shirt and outrageous moustache.

I talk to people on my client's behalf. Could be a stern word. Or something more. Like a punch to the gulliver. Magnum would agree.

Forcing the issue was like cramming for finals the night before. But you can't be a student forever. Sooner or later, you have to graduate.

The whole pen-is-mightier-than-the-sword thing never really reconciled itself with me. Sure, the pen usually pays better. And offers a healthier return. It's cleaner and can be declared on a tax form. Sometimes, however, resolution comes with a left jab. There's a sense of instant gratification too. The fruits of your labour are immediate. You don't have to wait three months for the cheque. Cash is paid in advance. Or less than 30 days.

You can't go wrong with a trade, lad.

My reputation is okay. Fair. Honest. Expedient. Never unduly rough.

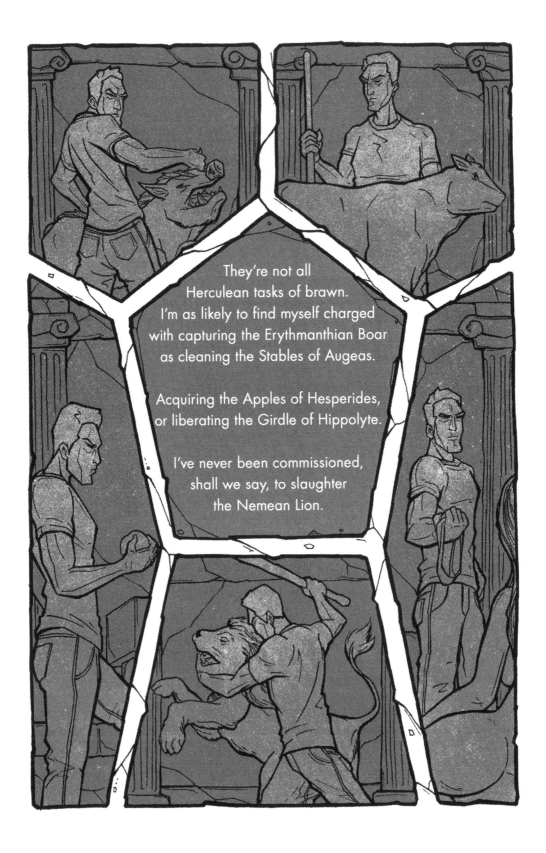

I did shoot a guy in the face with a Makarov 38, once. In my defence, however, that was an accident. It was his fault. His piece too.

Scared the crap out of me.

Him as well, judging by the stunned look on the remnants of his face.

Police found the body where it fell, in Kennedy Town. A cop I knew eventually got around to asking me some questions. There wasn't really anything to pursue beyond that, unless a witness came forward. Or they found the weapon and something linking me to it. None of which was likely to happen. It was a long time ago. And preceded my foray into advertising. It was one of the events that precipitated my entry to the business. That and a couple of other coincidences. Like when I woke up with a knife wound and decided the future for a doorman cum private security blockhead wasn't going to get any better than that. If the communism of our neighbours has taught us anything - and it hasn't - it's that people who work with their hands don't make much money.

Conversation with regulars at the club led to freelance work as a copywriter.

An aptitude for it led to gainful employment. A voracious reading habit meant that whenever I was lost for words of my own, there were plenty to purloin. I caught the brass ring of advertising and was half-shocked to find out it wasn't made of gold. I can't complain too much. It delivered me to Ling and the life I have now. It's just that reputations are like old habits. And wives. They demand things from you. And die hard.

Not everyone knows So Fuk Yu is, to coin an industry term, a full-service agency. It's not the sort of thing you advertise. You don't have to. It's one of those things that are kind of classified, on a need-to-know basis. Certain circles know more about it than others. Micki Wong has leveraged the full breadth of my portfolio before, albeit on more of a *pro bono* arrangement. A long time ago in a galaxy far, far away...

MICKI EXHALES TWO PETITE LUNGS OF SMOKE. Rolls the glowing tip of her cigarette around the base of the ashtray. Unable or unwilling to look directly at me. Is she being coy, or about to unfurl a lie?

Esther is in trouble, she says.

Shituation normal, I reply.

I don't like this guy.

So what else is new? Stop introducing her to your men.

I won't even dignify that, she says indignantly. It's not my husband.

Ex-husband. The ink is dry, remember?

He's a business acquaintance.

Stop doing business with him.

I have. Esther hasn't. And I don't like him. At all. He's dangerous.

So is she. That's what it's about with her. Danger. What makes him different from all the other cicisbeos and brief encounters?

He was connected to casinos in Las Vegas and Atlantic City, which means he probably still is. He arrived in Macao ten years ago. Knows everyone. Everyone. Deals in diamonds with the Russians. And that's just the stuff I know, or can talk about. Unless I want to wake up with a dismembered cock in my mouth and a splintered beam of pine sticking out of my crotch.

Eloquent as ever, Mick. He sounds very entrepreneurial.

I'm not the only one who wishes he would disappear.

So relax. Maybe the Cossacks will solve your problem for you.

I'm worried for Esther. She could get caught in the middle.

She'd love it. And that might untangle another of your Gordian knots too.

She's my sister, Jack. Family. That little girl of yours, no matter what she did, you wouldn't want anything to happen to her. No matter how much she breaks your heart. And, she will, one day. All girls do. That's our thing.

I think about the truth of this for a moment.

Esther's a big girl, I say. She can handle herself. The first thing I'd probably do is warn him about her.

That's what I was hoping you'd do.

Have one of your fireside chats with him, Mick. You can be pretty persuasive.

I did. And here I am. Jack, he's weird. Creepy. Mean. He scares me.

First time for everything. You've got me worried now. What happened?

It was a bee's dick away from rape.

Him or you? I pose insensitively.

Fuck you.

We tried that already. Didn't work out. Why not go to the police?

You can't go to them with something like this, which happened like that. And I can't have the kind of talk it would generate hanging over my business.

So speak to Esther. Tell her what happened.

I did. She thinks this kind of thing is normal. Part of the game. Foreplay. Or an attempt at payback for previous indiscretions. She wanted to turn it into a competition.

May the best snatch win.

Before Micki can return the half-volley there's a disruption at the door.

Hey Angel. What's up? Looking a little moist there, just the way I like it. And good morning to you, little Miss Sunshine. Gonna chase the clouds away?

Angel attempts to warn him off. Benny! she cautions.

Angel is right. He does have fish lips and oily skin. A pudgy, friendly face. It's not ugly, nor handsome. Just generic. He's long and thin too. As for the genital tang, well, that will have to remain an unconfirmed mystery. He speaks quickly, with well-rehearsed sincerity, drawing shallow breaths. As if he may get cut off at any moment. Hey Jack, he says. Sorry I'm late. We get those tent cards to Club Deluxe? His glazzies drift over Micki lubriciously. She's chosen this juncture to apply another coat of lipstick. Tracing the burning crimson around her kisser. Around. And around. One more circuit and she's going to give him vertigo.

Don't know, I tell him. Why don't you go see if the artwork magically completed itself and teleported from your desk to the printer in Chai Wan?

Like a moth to Micki's flame he steps deeper into her space. Sorry, he says. Jack can be pretty rude. Benny sticks out his hand and introduces himself. Actually, I'm not sorry, he says. And I'm glad I'm not blind.

Micki rolls her eyes in my direction as she shakes his hand. Then looks at Benny's chest, as if distracted by something. You've got a stain on your shirt, she says.

Where? he asks, peering down.

Here, she says crisply. And stabs him in the heart with the wax tip of her lipstick. It leaves a red smear on the white cotton. She snaps the cap on the black Chanel tube, tucks it into her purse and nails him with a tight-lipped, condescending smile.

Benny decodes humiliation as a come-on. So, before the pregnant pause gives birth to something unsightly, I figure it's in everyone's interest to attempt an abortion. Micki, however, has a problem. She never knows when to back down, or quit. When your wife asks how the stain got there, she says dryly, you can tell her it was all you had to wipe your dick with. It's a small stain. She'll believe you.

Benny blushes, maybe for the first time in his life. Like an inaugural wet dream it's probably an embarrassing yet not unpleasant experience. He retreats to the back of the room. Rummages through a box of leftover promotional items by his desk. And finds a San Miguel t-shirt. Then enters the bathroom.

Micki and I are picking up where we left off when he returns, sporting a new and improved water-slicked hairstyle. His shirt unchanged. Distracted by the mirror in there he's opted for personal grooming instead. And attempts re-entry. As if the last five minutes never happened. Micki Wong? Your old flatmate? I mean, not *old* flatmate. From the past, you know. No offence. Micki Wong? Wow. All those curves. And me with no brakes.

This line of questioning is as unnecessary as it is uncomfortable. Benny knows of the Golden Triangle that was my relationship with the Wong sisters.

I should kick him, and the conversation, in the nuts before he makes gonads of us all. Can you give us a minute?

Sure, sure. Yeah. Sorry. He looks as sincere as it is possible for him to fake. So glad to meet you, finally. I've heard great things. The three of us should get a drink. Or dinner. Hey, maybe we could grab your sister. Make it a double-

Leave it Benny.

He backs away and pretends to busy himself with layouts on his desk.

I continue the conversation with Micki. I don't know what I can do, I say. It doesn't sound like Esther or this Eddie Player are big on common sense. What's his real name?

Eddie Player.

Was Chip Winner already taken?

It's his name, okay?

Okay. Well, if she's got her sights on him we know where that'll end up. She'll get bored, leap out of bed and jump on the next tram to the CBD. If you can't wait until then, get some of your more discreet associates to look into it.

I can't have my business involved in this business.

But it's okay for my business?

Experience has taught me there's very little you wouldn't consider *infra dignitatem*. Who else is there, Jack? Tell me. I'll call them. And don't say the police. Esther's up shit creek and doesn't know half of it. Or won't admit any of it. Maybe she's scared to leave him. Maybe she needs an excuse. Whatever. There's something not right. He's a sociopathic, psychopathic mieskeit.

. HE GAVE ME A MATCHING SET FOR MY THIGHS.

Ah, hope, I ruminate, as if recalling a fond memory. Desire and expectation, rolled into one neat little emotion.

Have a word with him, please. Or her. Just keep your dick in your pants. She locks her maw tight for a moment, like she means it. They're staying at The Mandarin, she continues. Esther is supposed to be with me tonight. Pay Player a visit. Offer him some solid advice. Give him the benefit of your experience.

Something about this isn't quite right. It's almost too perfect, like a TV commercial. Hitting the right buttons, checking the boxes, yet not entirely convincing. Making whole lies out of half-truths. The suspension of disbelief is having a hard time. Taking a few body blows against the ropes.

Micki re-adjusts her wardrobe and returns to her seat, *lacrimoso*. She must have known Benny was watching. I can hear the blood roaring through his veins. It's the kind of bait The Fish loves. He jumps at it. Sorry, he apologizes, without remorse. I couldn't help but overhear. Maybe-

I raise a hand to ward him off, before his gaping mouth is hooked. And he's floundering on the deck. Gasping for air. Not now Benny, I warn. But there are other forces at play. Immutable. Venereal.

This will not be the one that got away.

Micki looks directly at the catch of the day. And crosses her legs in his favour, *lusingando*. With respect, she says baiting the line, it's a personal matter. And I doubt you possess the skills for the task.

Benny stops in his tracks, as if thinking over her comments. Truth is, he's probably forgotten what he was about to say. I should make another attempt to cut him out of the conversation. And banish him to the corner. In fact, what I should do is fire him. Except that would be redundant. Benny's garoupa has a hard-on for Micki Wong's swimming nymph. He's as good as cooked.

With all due respect, he proffers, I can help. And, Ms Wong, you'll find my credentials stand up with the best of them in a tight situation.

Benny is one of those people that become products of their environment. Who think they're injected with the same qualities as those around them. Like secretaries who believe they're empowered with the same rights and privileges as the CEO they work for. Like assistants in luxury boutiques who reckon they're Coco Chanel. Benny figures many of my qualities have rubbed off on him. He isn't completely delusional. He's prone to exaggeration but you can trust him. Up to a point. The point of ejaculation,as some might say.

He can handle himself, sort of. But he's no Jedi Knight either.

Micki can tell I've seen the futility in protestation. All she has to do is gut and fillet him. She pushes her glazzies wider, encouraging him to swim in them.

I'm not sure why Jack won't get involved, Benny admits. But I know he always has his reasons. His priorities have changed. I can help.

Benny's motivation is obvious as he steps confidently toward his audience. Presents himself. Gesticulating the same way he sells ad campaigns. And the account he's interested in handling today is Micki Wong. I'll meet Player, he blunders on. I'll tell him to step away. Come on as a psychotic suitor. Or I'll weasel her out of his life. I'm married. She probably fancies me already.

He's punching over his weight. And he knows it. He'll have to revise his *modus operandi* and make Micki's tentiginous sibling his final resting place. Right now, however, his appetite is stimulated. It's full steam ahead. Fools rush in where angels fear to tread, but this one believes he who hesitates is lost. *Don't look a gift whore in the mouth.* He'll see this as an opportunity to repeat what he considers my crowning achievement. The carnal quinella. Two Wongs will make it right. On the upside, a whole flock of birds might also be taken care of by this misguided missile. When he screws it up, and he will, I'll have the silver bullet I need to rid myself of him.

I terminate the Macintosh. Adopt a professional monosyllabic tone. Benny, cool your jets for a moment. What's being proposed here is not a solution to anything. Even if Player is the problem she claims him to be.

Micki tries to object. I tell her I know there's something wrong. It took balls to come here, but she's not being straight with me. For whatever reason. She can bullshit Benny all she wants. He won't mind. And if he wants to help out then that's his business.

Great minds think alike, says Benny.

Idiots seldom differ, I retort. And eyeball him as I walk around the desk. I move behind Micki. It's great to see you, I whisper in her ear. I mean it. You know if I can help, I will. A lot's changed. That hasn't. Come back tomorrow. Tell me what's really going on. We'll see what I can do. I take a deep breath of Chanel No. 5 for old time's sake. And lift Mei onto my hip. Come on stinky. Bath time. Today is gone. Today was fun.

Tomorrow is another one! she rejoins, completing the Suessian couplet.

I tell Angel she can cut the lights and lock up whenever she feels like it.

Even if they're still here? Leaving a woman in the dark, with Benny, would be a cruel and inhuman thing to do.

Benny's the one who should be worried. Trust me. She'll kill him.

ANGEL IS FROWNING into the phone. Mei sticks her tongue out, as is her customary greeting. And gets no response. Something must be wrong. I should turn around and leave the building. Maybe the whole country.

The moment passes.

It's probably just a client complaining about something Benny hasn't done. Or someone else wanting to know why we haven't paid them.

I drop Mei into the beanbag, switch on the VCR and regain my centre. The Count begins his numerological shtick.

One! One ring! Ha-ha-ha-haaa!

I boot-up the Macintosh. Look at the stack of layouts before me.

Fibre Trim. *Throw away your fat clothes forever!* Club Deluxe. *Boys drink wine, men desire whiskey but heroes desire Martell!* Jens Munk. *International furniture, lamps and accessories.*

All present and accounted for. No typos. The Fish was inspired by something last night. A note leaves no doubt as to what his muse must've been.

Don't worry. She's in great hands!

It's signed with an illustration. Two hands grabbing a naked female ass. If nothing else you had to admire the penmanship. Very Robert-Crumb in detail.

Angel slides a piece of paper across my line of sight. Her disposition is no sunnier than when we arrived. It fails to lighten when I show her the cartoon. She tells me Detective Oldham was on the phone. Benny is knocked up, at Queen Mary.

Knocked up, as in pregnant? I warned him about not using condoms.

This fails to alleviate her load. I'm starting to wonder if someone hasn't kidnapped Angel and replaced her with a Nexus Six android.

You have to call him, Jack.

Benny?

Oldham. Benny's in a coma. His wife has called three times. She and this Oldpig want to know what he was doing in North Point last night.

At least Angel's form is returning. Oldpig isn't a bad effort for this time of the day. Given Oldham is a cop. And advancing in years. I pull the Carpe Per Diem business card from the Rolodex. Give it to her. Tell her to call Micki. Then look at the message before me.

Oldham's number has eight digits. And starts with a nine. He must be packing one of those handheld portables as well. Probably needs a holster bigger than the one cradling his 38. If he runs out of ammo he can probably take them down with his telephony. Or at least have their eye out with the aerial.

I met Oldham when I was tossing Squaddies out of Disco Disco, and the other rat infested joints of Lan Kwai Fong. I'd done him a few solids as far as the cops, the garrison at Stanley and the locals were concerned. He'd done right by me a number of times too. When I might've taken a few liberties with my discretionary powers as a bouncer.

Like when I was on crowd control for The Clash in '82. And a white riot broke out between expats and locals. He dropped by the Hyatt to get official statements from the band. Just as Joe Strummer and I were making our way through the stately brick of hash I'd delivered. He'd also let sleeping dogs lie when it came to that goon I may or may not have shot in the face. And when I may or may not have been involved in some other things that could warrant, say, being stabbed in the abdomen.

It was during this episode in my life that I first encountered Ling.

She changed the dressing on my wounds, and healed me in so many other ways.

Small world, this island. No wonder I nearly fell off.

Oldham is as straight as any who deal with the crooked tree of humanity can be. Thatcher's pact with Deng meant cops like him - English and relatively honest - were in danger of becoming an oddity, if not extinct. One day soon he'd be as displaced as the rest of us. I hadn't seen him since the funeral. Although I'm not sure he knows I saw him at the back of the crematorium. He has more than a few inches on me. He speaks Cantonese like a native. And is allowed to shoot people.

I dial the numbers. He answers on the second ring. Tells me to get over to the hospital. His tone says this is not a request, but a demand. Given my business partner is grimly hanging onto a slab, and I'm probably a major contributor to his downfall, I feel compelled to oblige. I tell him I'll be there in half an hour. That's about as fast as any taxi can get to Queen Mary from my place. On a good day. With Saint Fiacre watching over him. Although my faith in Him is beginning to wane. I wasn't the only pious prick batting a benevolent eye to my responsibilities lately.

I drop a few extra things into Mei's Sesame Street backpack. A cardigan, because hospitals are cold. An extra diaper, because hospital toilets are riddled with diseases. Pens and paper. Lego bricks. Biscuits. Spoon, fork, scissors. String. Gaffer tape. Batteries. Copper wire. Liquid ammonia. A copy of *Catcher In The Rye*. And a few other essential items. *Perfect for school use, weekend trips or spend-the-night parties, and more!* Ernie, Bert, Grover and Big Bird struggle under the weight. Angel says I have enough shit in there to survive the Apocalypse. No stranger to biblical catastrophe, the prospect of such an event doesn't faze me as much as it might others. The Apocalypse is more than a metaphor for the world-ending circumstances that heralded the birth of my patriarchy. Life has taught me that anything can happen. Particularly when you throw a child into the equation. Better to have something and not need it, than to need something and not have it. Still, as I sling the nylon straps over my shoulder, I'm grateful the good people at Fisher-Price had the foresight to pad them. Come on Mei-mei, I say. Let's roll.

Familiar with the drill these words signal she stands and turns off the TV. We walk through reception, holding hands. I ask Angel to make sure the stuff on my desk gets where it needs to go. To phone Benny's psychotic wife and tell her we don't know where he went on the way home, but we'll find out. And we'll call her when we do.

I won't hold my breath.

Blue's not your colour anyway, I reply. Page me if Micki steps out of the shadows. We'll see you later.

See you later alligator! says Mei, as we depart.

In a while crocodile! sings Angel, still frowning on the inside.

THREE STEPS TO THE CURB is all it takes to deflate us. Defeat us. It's not the heat. It's the humidity. The clouds break for a moment and I can feel the sun sucking moisture from the earth, through the concrete. Extracting life from all living creatures.

A battered, red Nissan Cedric throws open its automatic door. I slide Mei across the rear seat. Overzealous air-conditioning induces hyperthermia, while swirling a sickly sweet combination of dashboard air-freshener, cigarette fumes and musky dampness around the rotting interior. A Canto-pop *Living On A Prayer* crackles through dilapidated woofers and tweeters. I ask the driver to head across the island to Queen Mary. And no shortcuts, Uncle. We're in a hurry.

He laughs. Either at my Cantonese or cynical knowledge of taxi drivers.

I pull a yellow LOOK! OUR NEW BABY IS ABOARD! sign from the backpack. And stick it on the rear window. I don't know if it helps to keep Harbingers Of Doom at bay. I found it amongst the stuff they gave me when I identified Ling's body. It makes me feel better about being in cars.

Mei wants to know where we're going. The hospital, I tell her. To see Uncle Benny. He's a bit broken up.

Who brokened him up?

That's the $64,000 question, I think to myself, as Kylie Minogue bubbles her way through *I Should Be So Lucky*. Fuck Kylie and her petite, perky, antipodean personage. I don't mind her, *per se*. But the song is going to bounce around my gulliver for the rest of the day.

Mei is still repeating the chorus as we walk into Intensive Care.

6. QUEEN MARY

OLDHAM IS SIX-FOOT-THREE, with a Bobby Kennedy side-part. And the self-awareness that comes with carrying half a ton of portable telecommunications. I'm not sure doctors condone the lifting of heavy objects at his age. At least he's in the right place if he gets a hernia when it rings.

You want to see your boy first?

Sure. What are we going to do after?

You might want to leave Pu Yi out here, he suggests, nodding in Mei's direction. It's not exactly The Palace Of Union And Peace in there.

He steps across to the nurse's station and asks a comely caregiver to keep my daughter entertained. The Sister is only too pleased to oblige. I give her a plush Glow Worm and *Go Dog Go!* from the backpack. She leads Mei to some chairs by the window. It's hard to tell who is amusing whom. I press into the ward with Oldham.

PLEASE KEEP WILD LOUD BABES OUT OF THIS SANCTUARY.

Benny would like that. He'd find it funny. If he wasn't doing so badly on the Glasgow Coma Scale.

At first glance he doesn't look that terminal. The bits of him I can see anyway. Everything except a fraction of his gulliver is beneath a blanket, or wrapped in bandages. His garoupa gums look as if they've snagged themselves on a plastic breathing tube. I post a wry smile as I recall Angel's physical assessment of Benny. And the bubble-gum of that song bursts out of my subconscious.

I should be so lucky, lucky, lucky, lucky.

Glad you find it funny, remarks Oldham dryly.

Hey? Oh, no. Far from it. I was thinking of something my PA said. About Benny. His lips. She says they're the only thing she sees when she looks at him. And, well, you know, now it's all anyone can see.

Must be a riot at your place. You talk about all your friends this way?

You should hear what they say about you.

I don't care.

Good thing too. If everyone knew what others said about them there wouldn't be four friends in the world.

Your partner doesn't seem to have many either. Where was he last night?

I left him at the office around six. He must have finished late. There was a bunch of stuff on my desk this morning that wasn't there the day before.

What was he doing in North Point, between two and three?

Getting a lube, like everyone else?

That usually ends with a shot of penicillin. The only head he had has been caved in. And it wasn't the pistol in his pants that blew on his guts.

So not a crime of passion then?

There's wounds on his hands and arms. Know anything about those?

We're lovers, not fighters. I don't inspect his mitts after he's been to the washroom, but I'm pretty sure his digits were intact yesterday afternoon. And there wasn't any blood on the layouts, or the agency walls.

Don't know why you'd pummel someone half to death and then shoot him, he reports, looking down on Benny. Unless you had questions that needed answering. Or got into a stoush and beat around the bush before you could draw your weapon.

Uh-huh.

Uh-huh. That's all you got?

I look at Benny. And figure he deserved better.

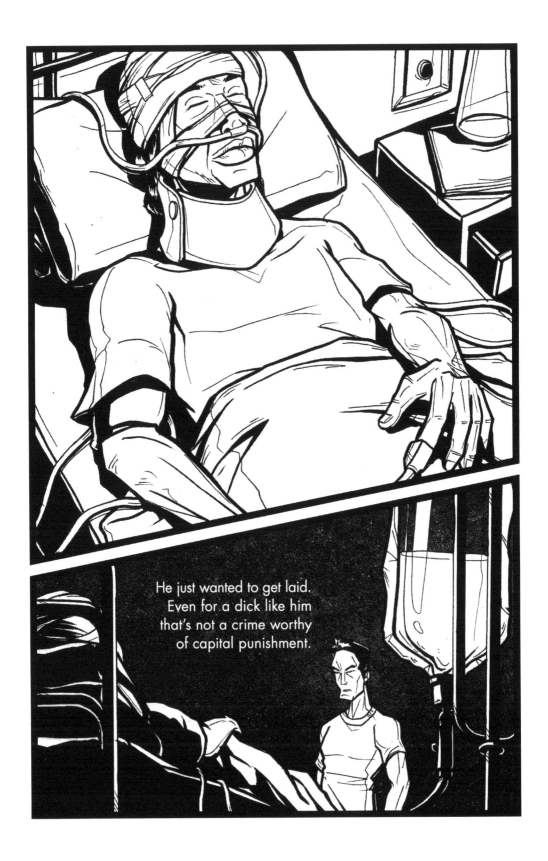

An old friend of mine turned up yesterday, I explain quietly, as if Benny might overhear something he shouldn't. She had someone she wanted looked at.

Oldham raises an eyebrow.

No, I correct him. Not *seen* to. Looked at. She wanted to know what a particular guy was into. Whom he was into. You know what I mean? In a jealousy leads to anger, anger leads to hate, hate leads to the Dark Side of The Force way.

Who's your friend?

That's neither here or there.

Take a look down there, Jack. It's right here. Who was the woman?

You wouldn't know her. And she doesn't need the attention, I say, gallantly defending the privacy of my former lover. She wanted a guy tagged. I told her I wasn't interested. Benny took an interest in her problem. I left them to it. And here we are.

Who's the guy?

Player. Eddie Player. Some miscreant from Macao. Look him up. You've probably got a file on him. He was connected. To all sorts of interesting people.

Who'd you hear that from?

I wince apologetically.

Jack, you're not doing you or your man any favours.

I've told you everything I know.

Except her name. She could be in trouble too.

I'll get her to call you. If I can find her. I haven't seen nor heard nowt since I left her with Benny. Give me an hour.

I take his silent stare as tacit approval. I walk. He follows. You know that guy in Mong Kok? The one that got beaten to death by a mob, with chairs and iron bars, while he was holding onto his two year-old?

Not personally. But, yeah, I heard about it.

We had odds on it being you.

Sorry to disappoint so many.

That's just it. You did. A lot of people were sorry.

I'm all choked up.

They felt sorry, for the kid. You're not popular on Old Bailey, he reminds me. Mess around on this and I won't be either. A lot of the boys think you skated on at least one murder and fuck-knows what else over the years.

Oh yeah, I'm a dangerous assassin. A killer on the loose. The 14K got nothing on me. Do they think it's my fault Sir Edward Youde popped his clogs in Beijing? Tell them I was at Spandau Prison that day. Visiting Rudolph Hess. With John Gotti.

One hour is all you got, he affirms, ignoring the sarcasm.

I collect Mei. She's monopolizing half the healthcare workers in the hospital. We walk to the taxi rank. Before we can make our getaway Oldham calls after me. I turn to face my accuser.

Time's up So. They just pulled your man from the harbour in Quarry Bay. And the son of a bitch is leakier than the Lamma Ferry.

This is no longer a family matter, I think to myself. If it ever was. Benny got fucked all right. Bowel deep. Micki is up to her ass in something and sisterly love has nothing to do with it. I surrender her name and office address. Oldham says he'll drop by. I doubt she'll be sitting at her desk waiting for the mystery to unfold before her.

Mei and I discuss events, over a fried egg sandwich at the *chaan cha teng*. She's too preoccupied with Macaroni In Poor Man's Crab Soup to offer any insight.

7. SISTERS IN ARMS

ANGEL IS TYPING INVOICES. Listening to something on the Toshiba Walky CD I gave her for Christmas. Probably the *Dirty Dancing* soundtrack, if the way she's humming *I've Had The Time Of My Life* is anything to go by. Fuck Jennifer Warnes. And Bill Medley.

I want one of those Olivetti personal computers, she shouts without looking up. I talked to the guy at Gilman. He'll give me a pretty good deal.

What do you have to give him?

She removes the Japanese earrings, drops her voice a couple of decibels. He'll throw in a printer. If I swallow. How's Benny?

Incommunicado. Indefinitely.

His wife is flipping out, she sighs. You'd think she liked him. What happened?

He got beat up. And then someone shot him.

Fuck. Player?

Got more holes in him than the Joint Declaration.

Holy shit Batman.

All kinds of shit. A dredging crew found him taking a long look at the new cross-harbour tunnel in Quarry Bay.

Wow. Bad day at Black Rock. Wonder what your girlfriend knows about that?

I'll ask her when I see her.

Not Micki, she corrects me.

Who?

Whom.

What?

It's *whom*. Not *who*.

Thanks for the grammar lesson, smartarse. Who's zoomin' *whom*?

Turn around.

A comedy of art nouveau is galumphing toward us like a sounder of wild boar. Beardsly and Klimt must wonder how it all went so spectacularly wrong.

Esther Wong.

Jack! she shouts, sporting an ill-advised, big-rimmed black hat atop a Linda Evans perm. There's a face in there somewhere. Her sharp eyes are highlighted by blue and gold shadow. Helena Rubenstein has a lot to answer for.

The puffy, white polka-dot dress disguises two firm handfuls. A thick black belt accentuates her diminutive waist. Hides the twin grips of her hips. Fleshy thighs, clad in printed lace stockings, mask the favourable length of her legs. Thin ankles disappear into a pair of white ankle-boots with seriously attenuated fuck-me heels.

Esther. What are you doing here? Halloween isn't until next week.

Jack! It's so awful! she shrieks and throws herself dramatically at me, telegraphing her emotions as if auditioning for the plum role in a soap opera.

I catch her in my arms. She crushes her cheek against my chest. And throws a gallon of Elizabeth Taylor's Passion in my face. The collision pushes her hat to the floor. It's an awkward moment, to say the least. I peer over her shoulder, eyes stinging. Mei stands in the doorway, bewildered as the rest of us.

Micki said she came to see you, Esther gasps. What's going on, Jack? What happened? Where's Micki? Oh Jack, I'm so confused!

That makes three of us, I say breaking away. I grip her by the elbows, to keep her at arm's length. And introduce her to my daughter.

What's wrong with her? asks Mei.

Oh, dear sweet child! gushes Esther, gazing fondly upon her. Mei-mei! Such a beautiful name for such a beautiful child. My sister is also called-

Esther, I interrupt. It's a coincidence. What are you doing here?

I didn't know what else to do.

Go back to the hotel. I'll come by later.

Oh Jack. The body's not even cold. I couldn't. Not in the same room-

Enough, Esther. Please. Angel, get her a taxi.

It's okay, she says. The hotel gave me a car. They're very worried about me.

Aren't we all? says Angel, to no one in particular.

I ask her to take Mei into my office and watch TV. I won't be long, I tell them. And close the door.

Esther sidles up. Hat in hand, chin in chest, dew in eyes. They're beautiful, she says. Your daughter. And your wife.

She's not my wife. She works for me. With me.

I bet she earns her money.

Esther-

Oh, come on Jack. I'm joking.

Glad you find humour in this. Perhaps you can show it to the rest of us.

I will. When you come see me tonight.

Esther, I plead, growing weary of the sphallolalia.

Jack, I'm worried about Micki.

Funny that. She was worried about you. If only either of you cared.

The police were looking for her. They knew she'd seen you. I didn't tell them anything about that. Don't worry. They won't get anything out of me.

Esther. They know everything except who did it. My art director's in a coma. Your boyfriend just took a dive into the South China Sea. And your sister is missing. All of which appear to be related. If I find Micki I'll take her down to Central Station myself. It's probably the safest place for her. Go back to the hotel, I instruct her. Lie down. If the room makes you uncomfortable, get another. As soon as I find something out, or Micki calls, I'll let you know. Okay?

I'm not going back to the hotel. I need to collect some things from Macao. There's nothing there for me now. The clock is ticking. I have to move on.

Onto what, or who?

Whom, pipes Angel cheekily.

I'll let you know, she says softly. And turns to leave, pausing as she opens the door. She really is a beautiful girl, Jack. Your daughter. Your wife must've been quite a lady. You're lucky to have some real women in your life, you know that? And then, as suddenly as it fell away, her energy returns. Let me know when you're ready for another!

I watch her leave. And wonder how long it will take to get the stink of her perfume out of my clothes. Out of the carpet. Out of my life.

Where do you start with a mess like this?

ACCORDING TO THE CONCIERGE at Mandarin Oriental, Benny was here a couple of nights ago. Asking after Player. He had a few drinks in the Captain's Bar. And took off around eleven. After a call on the house phone. Esther returned just before ten. Killed a cigarette in the lobby and went to the room. Player left shortly after.

Armand knows everything about everyone. And not just within the newly renovated walls of The Mandarin. If it's not on his radar it's 99.9% bullshit. And he knows whom to call to check the other 0.1%. I used to help his special guests with private security matters. We had mutual interests in making sure everyone had a trouble-free stay.

Needless to say Armand is familiar with the recent life and times of Edward Player. When he checked in. And how he checked out. He didn't know who pulled the trigger. The line of people with motivation and means to see it done stretched all the way to Macao. Unlikely it was gambling related. Or rather, debt related. You don't kill someone when they owe you money. It reduces your chances of recovering the cash. There are really only two things that can destroy a healthy man, he says. Love, ambition and financial catastrophe.

That's three things, I correct him.

And there are a whole lot more, he replies. Disrespect and loss of face kills more people than cancer.

The pager nudges my hip. I walk across the lobby and phone Angel. She says my girlfriend called.

Micki? Esther? Oldham, or Lydia Dunne?

She snorts a laugh. Tells me she wouldn't fuck Lydia Dunne with Benny's dick. It was Micki. She's up at her apartment. Says I shouldn't have any trouble finding the place. Every dog remembers where they buried their bones.

Woof.

Micki's bark could be every bit as bad as her bite.

9. A KIND OF HOMECOMING

GRENVILLE HOUSE is a four storey, colonial masterpiece astride the junction of Magazine Gap Road and Peak Road. One side commands huge views of the city and Victoria Harbour, a mile or two beneath. The other observes Aberdeen, Stanley and the open sea. On a clear day you can see Macao.

Mei and I arrive at the gate. History looms large. The proportions are intimidating. Shrouded in the misty clouds of the season and fog of the past, it has a Bates Motel vibe. Spooky, confirms Mei, as she reaches for my hand, staring up at the building. I look to her, summoning the courage to advance the plot.

We take a small lift to the scene of my crimes on the third floor. I ring the bell. Footsteps pad across the wood, behind the large door. It swings open in slow motion, bathing us in light.

Micki wears a fortune-red leotard. It rides high above her creamy hips. The neckline surrenders to her chest. Whatever else is nestled there within the nylon - and it's not easy to imagine there being room for anything else - her breasts are terrified of it. They're frantically trying to escape. Nothing I hadn't seen before. Still, I hadn't seen anything like it in quite a while. Gandhi would have a hard time keeping his thoughts pure.

Wow, offers Mei, impressed as I am. For different reasons, I'm sure. Maybe it's the rainbow striped leg-warmers clinging desperately to Micki's ankles that have caught her eye.

The lady of the house smiles, sinks to her haunches and asks Mei if she goes everywhere with her father. It's a fair question. Por-por is often at me to drop Mei in kindergarten for a few hours a day. Maybe I will, when she's three. It's is only a short walk from our apartment. Be good for her meet people her own age. Get a glimpse of something motherly. Lord knows what kind of impression the current *mater familias* are making on her.

I look through the doorway. Across the room, Jane Fonda urges a group of aerobic women to keep it going. Micki stands and obscures my view of the 36-inch Trinitron. She looks like she just stepped out of it. Hair tousled. Cardio-spectacular. The effect is suitably sudorific. Still, I'm breathing shallower and perspiring more than she is. And there's no sweat on the contours of her chest. To conclude this most unsubtle physical examination, I busy my eyes with the bruises about her thyroid.

Hey, she says, self-consciously raising a hand to smooth over the abrasions. She thanks us for coming and invites us in.

Only if you put some clothes on, I tell her. Mei's still a little young for such graphic lessons in human biology. And you're violating at least three of the new anti-pornography laws.

WELL THERE'S A FIRST.
JACK SO, EMBARRASSED.

YOU SURE YOU
DON'T WANT TO
JOIN ME ON THE
LIVING ROOM
FLOOR?

BET YOU
HAVEN'T HAD
AN INDECENT
WORKOUT
FOR QUITE
SOME TIME.
MIGHT
DO YOU
SOME
GOOD.

Two Filipino maids in crisp, white one-piece uniforms exit the kitchen. They offer well-rehearsed smiles and a choice of beverages. I ask if they'd mind getting Mei a juice box. And some fruit. A banana or some crackers. Whatever. I remove her sandals and pull *The Very Hungry Caterpillar* from the backpack.

Why don't you go show this to the aunties, cream puff?

She takes it and follows The Help into the scullery. I close the door, drop the backpack and kick off my boots. Make my way across the polished floor to a thick, white rug the size of Chater Square. Stopping at the television, I banish Jane Fonda to audio-visual purgatory with a click. Then run my hand across the back of the set. It's not even warm.

I step through the sliding doors to the balcony. Central and Victoria Harbour look protean under dark cumulonimbus clouds and a stiff, shifting sirocco.

Turning to contemplate the interior there's not a lot about the place I recognize. The geography is the same but the landscape has been turned over. The hopes of yesterday ploughed into the ground and engendered lush, luxurious fruit.

Micki stands in the centre of the shagpile. A sheer silk housecoat, tied at the waist, gilds her lithe frame. Vodka tonic. Short glass. Lots of ice and a twist of lime, she says, extending the drink to me. Her other hand nurses dirty brown liquor. The one Faulkner says is not for women, nor boys and children. The one which only hunters drink. Condensation of the wild immortal spirit. Distillation of the fine fierce instants of heart and brain, courage and wiliness and speed.

On the rocks, three fingers. She moves, *dolcissimo*. And sits on the edge of a large white sofa. Like what I've done with it? she asks, gesturing with an arm.

What's not to like? I respond. The apartment looks great too.

A smile acknowledges the flattery. Her eyes move to a nearby spot on the sofa. I accept the invitation. She takes a cigarette from a carved wooden box on the long, low table beside her. Offers one to me. I decline, for now, and take a drink. She exhales a rich lungful of smoke across the back of the sofa.

I wasn't completely honest with you, Jack.

I noticed.

But you helped anyway.

I didn't. Benny tried.

You opened the door. Showed him the way.

I thought there might be something in it for him. So did he. I helped him out. And look where it got him.

Look where it got you, she points out. How's it feel being here, again?

I think about this for a heartbeat or two. Guilty.

Regrets?

Guilty. My partner gets the stuffing knocked out of him. Because of you. And me. So guilty. And curious. I'd like to know why. Is that despite our past, or in spite of it? All I know is it must be something unholy for you to involve Esther. The fact you trust her to play a part tells me you have a big problem.

She's changed, Jack. Really.

Maybe. But we both know she can't lie straight in bed.

How's Benny?

Hanging in there.

I feel so-

M Forget about Benny. He was acting in his own interests. Maybe he'll wake up, find his wife has left him and the nurse giving him a sponge bath. That's win-win for him. Remember, he's an art director. They're simple people. The common clay of advertising. You know, morons.

She stifles a laugh. And fixes me with a stare. Do the police know?

That Benny's a moron? They're professional observers Mick. Based on his current predicament they probably suspect it.

Jack-

No. Not from me. Not yet, I lie. A little fudging of the truth won't hurt. The air is already pretty murky. Besides, when it comes to pointed sentences, I agree with Samuel Johnson. A degree of accuracy must always be sacrificed to conciseness. They'll have to know, at some point, I tell her. If they don't already. They've been to see your sister. What would she have to say to them?

Who knows? Poor kid. She was banking on Player. Really. She's a mess.

Can you do something?

For her?

About this.

I could try. Although that's usually the first step towards failure. Hasn't your problem been dealt with anyway, in a roundabout homicidal fashion? I thought you'd be happy. You've lost a psychopathic rapist and regained a sister. I'm out an art director.

Don't you want to find out who did it?

Not really. I'd like to know why, but I can live without it.

What if they come after you? What if they come after me, or Esther?

Why would they? And when did *he* become *they*?

Micki stubs her cigarette to death. Slips off the couch and throws another healthy splash of Glenn Fidditch into her tumbler.

I reach for a smoke as she makes her way to the table, *scherzando*. She bends and beats me to the lighter. Ignites the flame. The edge of her coat falls open. A dollop of breast flashes before me. She lights my wick. Repostures herself on the sofa. A healthy slip of thigh distinguishes itself. She gives a brief thought to covering up, before deciding it heightens the drama of the scene.

Distance has the same affect on my mind as it does my eyes, I say digging deep into my bag of aphorisms and coming up with a handful of Cary Grant. I've been wary of your type ever since.

My type?

Women. Real, honest to goodness, balls-to-the-wall women.

I suppose I should be flattered.

Go ahead and blush, see if I care.

What's wrong with real, honest to goodness, balls-to-the-wall women?

They put me at a disadvantage. When I meet them I have to pretend I have no desire to fuck them.

You don't have to pretend with me.

I'm not.

Not pretending, or not harbouring the desire?

Both, to be honest.

Why conceal it?

Honest women might find the idea objectionable.

I might not.

We were talking about honest women, remember?

Pans hit the floor in the kitchen. Filipino laughter and childish joy burst from within. I throttle my cigarette and move to investigate. Micki slides closer. Puts her hand just above my knee, to keep me in my place. She looks into my eyes, *con anima*. Asks me to believe her. Takes my hand. Brings it to her face. Holds it against her lips, as if in silent prayer. She tells me she has a good heart. And moves my paw to a dangerous area above her breast.

I look at her. Try to look into her. I get lost. I take my hand back. Rescue my drink. Drain it. You've got some good parts, I say. Your heart might be one of them. Right now, however, the sum of your parts is less than your whole. What happened that night?

We went out to dinner with the Kobayashi's. On the yacht.

I know. I could see Bengal 1 discreetly setting off fireworks in the harbour from my place. Why didn't Player go with Esther?

He wasn't invited. I was. Bring a friend, they said. I thought it would be a good opportunity to talk some sense into her, away from him. Give Benny a chance to talk with him, away from her. She started feeling seasick. We left. I dropped her at the hotel around ten. And went home.

What did Esther do?

Went to bed. Trolled the lobby. I don't know. I haven't seen her since.

Did she know you'd engaged Benny to lean on Player?

Of course not.

Did she meet him in the bar? Did she know Player was leaving the hotel and whom he was going to meet? What was Benny doing in North Point?

I told you, I don't know.

What happened when you went home?

Bed. Alone, in case you're wondering. Although I did get a massage from Mary and Grace. Does that count?

Only if it came with a happy ending. That must've hurt, with your bruises.

A woman knows how to treat a lady, Jack. I went to the office this morning. Heard the news about Player's body in the harbour. No word from Benny, so I called you. Spoke to your secretary. I was worried. I came home. What would you have done?

Your sister's rapist boyfriend is dead. The guy you sent after him is missing. You slot Jane Fonda in the VCR and dance a little jig? Not really textbook symptoms of psychogenic shock. How'd you first meet Player?

She stabs her cigarette into the ashtray. And draws another. He turned up at an event, she says. I saw him at a couple of parties. A dinner. We got to know each other. And, no, not like that.

He might've thought it was leading to that.

Every guy does. But every guy sporting wood doesn't try to take you up the Dragon's Back and fuck you with a 38. Smoke pours from her nostrils. We moved in some of the same circles. He had interests in diamonds, antiques and gambling. So do my clients. I had a project I figured he could help with. And that's when Esther took an interest in him. She made him a little project of her own. His slick veneer turned slimy. And then he screwed me. Metaphorically. He cut me out of my own deal.

That's the price of confidence, Mick. Betrayal. You of all people should've known that. What was the deal?

Doesn't matter.

I don't believe her. The deal is everything to Micki. And certainly more important than her sister's love life. She wanted rid of Player, no doubt. Her motives, however, were a little closer to home. Warriors can be dispatched, but not dishonoured. Gentlemen can be killed, but not humiliated. And a woman can die, but she cannot be defiled.

All this was for Esther's well-being?

For both our health, she reluctantly admits.

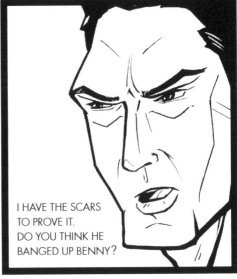

WHO
ELSE?

I DON'T KNOW.
HE'S YOUR PARTNER.

AND BENNY'S YOURS. MAYBE PEOPLE ARE LINING
UP TO PUT A DENT IN HIM TOO. THE WAY YOU WERE
LOOKING AT HIM, IT COULD'VE BEEN YOU.

There's a queue. I might even be first in line. But wanting to take a dip is different to sticking your toe in the water. And a million miles from wading in.

Player had a gun. Maybe the police can match the bullets.

How do you know that? I ask, pretty sure the news made no mention of Benny being shot. Maybe the bullet riddled body and Benny's beating had become entwined during her aerobic freak-out. Maybe Angel spilled the beans.

That's what police do, isn't it? she says, missing the point. Or choosing to ignore it. They get paid to work out who killed who.

Whom.

What?

Who killed *whom*. Not who.

Who killed *whom*. They match bullets to guns. But you wouldn't know that. They never found the heater to match that bullet you put in Lee, did they?

How did you know he had a gun? I ask, moving the conversation on.

What part of rape and getting fucked by a 38 didn't you understand, Jack? He showed it to me. Held it between my tits when he tried to spike me. Put it in my mouth. Told me to suck it. I said put your pee-shooter in there, needle dick. I'll blow both your barrels. He hit me. Tried to shove it between my legs. And that's when it got violent. So forgive me if I'm not as tolerant of your smartarsery as I used to be.

The deadpan delivery tells me this is probably not far from the truth. How do you know he had a gun *here*? I explicate, more recalcitrant than I should be. I know it's pretty much a straight walk through Kai Tak to the cab rank, but it's still high risk to stash a piece in your hand-carry.

They give them away at The Walled City, with buckets of Blue Girl, don't they?

The Walled City is a rogue precinct of Kowloon. Seven acres of buildings packed together like non-modular bricks. There are places in there that never see the light of day. When the Japanese vacated after WWII, squatters commandeered it. There were ten thousand people in there by the seventies. Triple that now. Home to the homeless, entry-level immigrants and base-level triads. Populated by dissidents, outlaws and professionals who lost their licenses, or didn't get them in the first place. Even the police don't go without an invitation. If Hong Kong were Tatooine, The Walled City would be Mos Eisley. A wretched hive of scum and villainy. A hotbed of vice. A country and a law unto itself. Like Vatican City only with a few less tapestries, a lot more hookers and a couple of cheap 'n cheery Chiu Chow restaurants. Good times.

Micki finishes her drink. Asks if I want another. I offer to do the honours. She curls into the sofa, *mancando*. Studies me. Instructs me not to be stingy with the whiskey. I return her glass half-full. Or half-empty, depending on how she views these things. She takes a long drink. A deep breath. Closes her eyes. Presses the glass to the skin above her breasts. Rolls it left to right. Once, twice. Thrice.

How do you know he had a gun here? I repeat.

He pulled it on Esther that night. Told her not to be late. Waived it about. Said he'd come looking for her. He was always doing shit like that. The man had issues.

He must've been great at parties. I'm sorry I didn't get to meet him.

So am I. All this might never have happened.

Or it might've happened to me. What would he want a weapon for?

He probably just liked the idea of carrying one. He was American. Maybe he needed it. And not just to make up for his L'il Abner.

So you did get an eyeful. Or you hear about that in the news too?

Didn't have to. I can tell when a man's compensating for shortcomings.

The secret of your success. Am I compensating for my foibles?

Not from where I'm sitting, she replies. You're compensating for something. Maybe it's guilt, like you said. Or is it lust? Something sinful. She tosses a cushion into my lap. Tells me the twitch in my pants is distracting her. Micki Wong knows men alright. And the effect she has on them.

What kind of shit are you in?

She sits forward. Puts her drink on the table. And gulliver in her hands.

I don't know, she says, staring between her knees.

I've had enough. I stand and walk to the kitchen. Tell Mei to say good-bye. Let's roll Ba-ba! she enthuses, bursting through the swinging door.

Micki rises from the couch and makes her way toward us, *rallentando*. You going to the police?

I won't have to. They're coming to me. My partner's verging on terminal. You think they don't have a few questions?

She wants to know what I'll say to them. I tell her she doesn't have to worry. Even if I tell them everything I know it's still two parts of fuck-all.

Micki straightens her back. Tries to pull up some dignity. Then realizes she's standing in her Marguerite Lee intimates. They suggest quite a few things. Dignity, however, is not at the top of the list. I'm sorry, she says. And steps forward. Puts a hand on my elbow. Leans in. Kisses my cheek. I guess I'm on my own, she whispers.

I tell her she doesn't have to be. We've just hit a wall. And she's the only one who can get us over it.

You think we're at a dead end, she says. I'm past the point of no return.

I open the door and tell Mei to say good-bye. Micki gives her a kiss on the forehead. Bye-bye beautiful, she says. We walk to the elevator. I can still feel her eyes upon me when the lift arrives. I usher Mei in. And turn.

Stay at home, Mick. Don't answer the phone, for anyone. I'll call.

You just said don't answer the phone.

I'll call by. Or I'll call. Twice. Three rings on the first time. Don't answer. I'll dial straight back. Pick it up on the second ring.

Just like the movies, huh? Maybe there is a little Han Solo in you.

He'd take the money and run. Save his own skin.

He came back, Jack. Turned out he was pretty loyal to his friends. Ended up with the princess too.

The elevator doors wipe her from view.

10. LAWYERS, GUNS & MONEY

WE DETOUR VIA THE SHUN TAK CENTRE. Home, amongst other things, to the Macao Ferry Terminal. Darwinian wads of tourists, gamblers, prostitutes and chancers of every kind mill about prior to their early evening sortie across the South China Sea, in search of sordid spoils and cheap thrills. Those who didn't want to leave it all to lady luck could visit the empwhorium on the third floor. Browse binders full of women. Make a selection or two. And have them waiting, upon arrival, in Sin City. We push through the great unwashed, seeking someone engaged in the world's second oldest profession.

Eric Tsoi is Senior partner at Callett, Crambazzle, Dratchell & Feaque. A big, ball-breaking law firm. Years ago I extracted him from a volatile misunderstanding that involved a couple of expensive gas cookers. It prevented a great deal of pain and unnecessary media attention for him. And spared his wife considerable embarrassment. He'd been my unofficial legal council ever since. Over a pot of Iron Buddha, and a *probiotic lactobacillus* Yakult for Mei, we discuss the *casus belli*. He tells me what I'm obliged to inform the police. And what he thinks I can probably keep to myself.

WE'RE IN HAPPY VALLEY BEFORE SEVEN. I take Mei home for washing and feeding. Por-por greets her like it's been months since she left the house. Or wasn't expecting to see her again. She asks where she's been. And whisks her to the bathroom.

Bing emerges from our small, galley kitchen, perma-smile radiating. Hello Sir, she says, presenting a piece of paper for my inspection. Fearing her resignation, I begrudgingly accept it. Por-por give recipe to me, she whispers. But some I cannot understand.

Put cabbage in water. Sit in sink. Add 2 cups of ground flowers. Chop all vegetarians into little puces. Insult soup. Grease pan with Buddha. Put in bowel. Eat with chopsticks.

What we have here, to borrow from *Cool Hand Luke*, is a failure to communicate. I don't recognize the handwriting but suspect a relative of Por-por's has transcribed the recipe for Bing's benefit. I correct the misunderstandings as best I can. Although I have to defer to her judgment on the *put in bowel* thing. Nothing is out of bounds when it comes to Cantonese cuisine. I've had my share of stomach, intestines, trotters, feet and tongues. This could be a long-lost Hainan Haggis recipe for all I know.

I tell Bing I'm going downstairs. I'll be back in a minute.

ANGEL IS ABOUT TO CLOSE THE OFFICE. I thank her for waiting. Standing in the half-light of the door she reminds me there's a lot going on and it's her business too. I'm pretty sure she's not referring to all the briefs she's received. And the rapid turnaround our beloved clients are expecting. At least they're not expecting a rapid reach-around, I say trying to help her find humour in the situation. Can we get a freelancer in tomorrow?

Sure. How is everything on your end?

I didn't look. What's your read on Micki Wong?

Her pitch is as good as her yaw. And I bet she fucks back.

Why don't you tell me what you really think?

A lot of layers to peel, but you know that. You created half of them.

Maybe. But who knew back then?

I know you're going to help her now. And that's all you'll do. Because I also know you're not that stupid, anymore.

The last thing I need in the gynarchy of my life, is another wom-

Angel is distracted by something behind me. Can I help you?

He's slender. Immaculately dressed. Forty going on thirty. I am hoping so, he says quietly. The smoothness of his vowels tells me he isn't local. I am looking for Mr Jack So.

I am he, I reply, imitating his altiloquent tones and extending my hand. The stranger grasps it. Firmly. Although his hands are like a woman's. He's never done a day's work in his life. And is doused in a syrupy aftershave. I can't place it. Probably a cheap imitation of something cheap. *Eau de toilette.* What can I do for you, Mr...?

My apologies, he says with an obsequiously fey smile. Nirawattapattanasserarat, Anurak Nirawattapattanasserarat.

Jeezus, I think to myself. Is there an immigration card in the world with enough boxes to accommodate that name?

It's okay Mr So, he says, reading my smile. I am used to the difficulty Thai names can cause others. You may call me Anurak. Or Rak. Perhaps we can move somewhere more conducive to matters of business?

Perhaps we can. Would relocating to my anterior chamber meet with your approval, Mr Nirawappa- Nirapatta- Anorak?

I direct him to the office with a flourish of my arms, like a medieval second welcoming his liege back from The Crusades. He sails past. Unbuttons the expensive, double-breasted suit. Armani, grey. He surveys the room. And daintily perches on a stool.

What brings you here? I ask from my side of the desk.

I'm sorry to have heard the news regarding your associate.

Hong Kong is the smallest big city in the world. Everyone would know about it by now. Still, it doesn't make this opening gambit any less unusual.

Thank you. I'll be sure to pass on your sympathy to his wife and kids. How do you know Mr Yu?

A short smile flicks across his face, like a wealthy woman acknowledging a compliment. I have never had the pleasure, he says with a tone that suggests he has a different definition of pleasure. I know only what has been reported. And of his association with the death of Mr Edward Player.

I wasn't aware of a relationship between the two.

He gives me that smile again. And shifts in his seat. Like he has something uncomfortable up his ass. He probably does.

Well, we don't normally do classified ads. The South China Morning Post handles that kind of thing directly. Of course, if it's something more bespoke...

We do not wish to make a public appeal, Mr So. We believe finding what we have lost requires no more than a conversation with you. Or Ms Tse.

Ms Tse?

Perhaps you know her as Ms Wong. Micki Wong? Wong Mei-chi?

Not a lot of people outside the Birth Registrar know that. And all of them have been standing here in the last twenty-four hours.

You'll have to hold your conversations with Ms Wong yourself. It is not my practice to speak on behalf of others.

Is that so? My sources gave me the impression you were often charged with precisely those responsibilities.

Perhaps I should have a word with your sources. And correct the impressions they give others. Leave them an impression of my own.

I'm sure that won't be necessary. Misunderstandings happen from time to time. It was, in fact, a misunderstanding that led to the misplacement of the item my employer wishes returned.

Returned? A moment ago it was lost. Why don't you tell me what this item is? Maybe I can help you find it. Perhaps your sources told you that's something else I do.

They may have implied that. It is a vase or, more correctly, an urn. Approximately half the size of your personal computer.

We shift our attention to the Macintosh. I ask if he'd like to see me reboot it. Not at the moment, he declines. I do it anyway. And ask him to tell me more about the jar he's looking for.

It's made from a single piece of white jade. Sealed at the top. With wax and a ribbon. It is decorated with traditional Chinese motifs.

Dragons and shit?

A phoenix, yes. Dragons. And shit. Characters.

The Monkey King?

Calligraphy characters, not personalities. On the ribbon that seals it. Do you read Chinese, Mr So?

Only the funny bits.

As an artifact it appears quite ordinary. To the unknowing eye.

It sounds delightful.

If you have seen it my employer will remunerate you handsomely.

Handsomely? Just for seeing it?

If you had seen it you would know where you had seen it. And that would be valuable information, he says letting loose with that smile again.

Handsome is in the eye of the beholder. Or, in this context, the crock holder. Quite subjective, handsomeness. Subject to considerable differences in opinion.

Would one hundred thousand dollars encourage some objectivity?

Hong Kong Dollars?

US Dollars, Mr So.

Angel enters. If she didn't hear about the one hundred grand, she would've smelled it. I figure that's what flushed her out. She asks if I'm going to make it to that meeting. A meeting that doesn't exist. It's part of a protocol that enables me to exit conversations or situations I have no interest in pursuing. And was developed precisely for unsolicited encounters like this. I remind her that particular meeting has been cancelled. And apologize for not informing her. She can go. I'll close up.

Are you sure? she asks.

Oh, hang on. We might have a ten-thirty meeting here.

Here? A ten-thirty?

Yes. You'll need to come back early. Just in case.

Okay, she says, without her usual confidence. And then addresses our visitor, handing him a business card. Nice to meet you, Mr Nirawattapattanasserarat. Look forward to seeing you again soon.

Anurak stands and half-bows. Presses his palms together, in the traditional Thai manner. And you Ms Fuk, he replies. I'm afraid I have no cards on me at the moment.

Next time then.

Yes. Next time, he dismisses her. Enjoy your evening.

Anurak waits until Angel's heels have diminished into the night before returning his attention to me. Such a nice young lady, he ventures.

Don't let her appearance fool you.

Good help is hard to find, he remarks pithily, reaching inside his suit.

His cigarettes are still on the table. I push the case toward him, as a friendly reminder. He smiles in appreciation. Withdraws his hand. And points a small revolver at me. A Ruger. Or maybe a ladies 357 Magnum, if I was feeling really unlucky.

Well *sa-wat-di*-fucking-*ka* to you too.

Angel slips back into her heels. Ten-thirty?

Not a bad move, eh? I congratulate myself, while massaging my knuckles. In chess it's called the Lucena Position. I knew you'd pick up on it.

I don't care if it's the Missionary Position. What if I hadn't?

I would've had to think of something else. Or...

Or you'd be taking your Lucena up the Khyber-fucking-Pass. It could be you lying down there. Or worse, fucking me.

I would never fuck you on the floor. I'd get us a room. At a cheap hotel.

He had a gun, Jack.

Keep your Alan Whickers on.

I would if I were wearing any.

Then don't get your whiskers in a twist. It's all worked out for the best.

You think so? This is the best thing that could've happened?

It's not the worst possible outcome. Let's get him into the beanbag.

You get him into the fucking beanbag. I'm not touching that oily rag, she decides, tucking her blouse into her skirt.

I roll Anurak over, reach under his arms and drag him to Mei's beanbag. Study him for a moment, to see if he's in danger of waking up. Or dying. It's too early to tell.

I walk across to Angel, put an arm around her and kiss the top of her gulliver. Nice left, I say squeezing her bicep. You been working out?

She elbows me in the ribs. Yes, three times a night. Picking up all the crap you assholes leave lying around. She flexes her hand, inspecting the back of it. And I've broken a nail, she adds.

Don't worry. Between your cuticles and my keyboard, we've got enough to sue him for wilful damage to company property.

How's your hand?

I tell her it's nothing to worry about and close the door.

You'll probably have to masturbate with your left for a while.

You could be my be my right-hand man if you like. Come on, let's see what else he's got in those skyrockets.

Root around for more than thirty seconds and it counts as a fiddle.

Maybe you should do it.

He wouldn't last thirty seconds. These hands can work magic.

I've heard you're not bad with fish balls either.

Any balls, she says matter-of-factly.

The search harvests bountiful fruits. Hong Kong and US Dollars. Macao Patacas. Passport. Keys. An expensive Cartier pen, which I put in my pocket. Notepaper from The Peninsula, with addresses for So Fuk Yu and Carpe Per Diem written in elegant cursive. Comb. Business card. EDWARD PLAYER, GEMSTONE & ANTIQUE APPRAISER. A Mandarin room number scrawled on the back, over Macao and Shanghai addresses. Silk tashtook. Silver pillbox, loaded with a cocktail of heart-starters. I drop the Ruger into the draw beside my desk.

The Rat begins to stir. I stand over him. Angel rests her bum against the studio worktable, between Benny's desk and the bathroom.

Good morning, I say heartily. Enjoying your stay here at the Ritz? Not as salubrious as The Peninsula, but our service comes from the heart.

The Rat shakes his gulliver. Moves his jaw from side to side. It hurts and probably will for a while. He squirms against the uncertain support of the beanbag. Winces as he discovers the beginning of a bruise. Smooths his hands over his hair. And attempts to cross his legs. Have you called the police?

Have you got two hundred thousand dollars?

One hundred thousand was the offer.

That was before you chipped Ms Fuk's nail. And broke my Apple Macintosh. You have a hundred thousand lying around, you can find two. Money loves company.

I don't have it on me. Of course, you would already be aware of that, he remarks, seeing his possessions spread across my desk. But I can get it, if you have two hundred thousand dollars worth of information.

Who would you get it from?

For that information, Mr So, you would have to pay me.

No problem. Let me make a deposit now.

I kick his leg from its position above his knee. And ball my fist as if I'm about to launch an assault. He raises in hands in defence. Please, he appeals to my sense of decency. That will not be necessary. I have the money. Do you have anything worth paying for?

Well, right now, I have your balls in a vice. And you have about five minutes before Angel calls the rozzers. So you'd better find something to put up, apart from those dainty little hands and two imaginary tons of greenbacks.

If you would allow me a moment, he requests. And reaches into his left breast pocket. Then his right. He looks worried. My pen?

You going write me an IOU? I know you don't have a cheque book. You'll have to do better than that.

My pen, please.

What pen?

He searches the floor with his eyes. Angel throws him a plastic Bic from the workstation. This seems to annoy him. I know what it's like to fixate on something. And to be unable to move forward until that something is resolved.

Oh you mean this? I remark pulling the gold Cartier from my pocket. I spin it between my fingers, a habit I find particularly loathsome when clients do it during meetings. I hope he does too.

Yes. Open it. The cartridge end.

I look at him. Then at the pen. Across to Angel. And back to him.

It's okay, Mr So. This is not a James Bond movie, he says sarcastically. Give it to me if you fear for your safety. He moves as if to stand. I push him in the chest with my boot.

Sit down, I command. And unscrew the chamber.

Two diamonds fall out. A couple of carats. I toss them to Angel. One at a time. Like any woman she probably managed to calculate their value mid-flight.

Thank you for banking with us, Mr Nirawattapansi. And here is your special welcome gift. I throw the pen to him, followed by the rest of his possessions. I'm sorry to inform you, however, that Franklin Mint are all out of the ceramic doll you requested. Perhaps you could choose something else from the catalogue?

The urn, Mr So. You know where it is, or who has possession of it?

How do I know your employer is the rightful owner?

You don't, I'm afraid. It's not one of those items that come with a receipt and money-back guarantee. It was stolen from my employer and my employer wants it returned. It is an important piece of history that transcends monetary value. Something those who stole it will never comprehend. You are no stranger to Chinese culture, Mr So. I'm sure you understand these things. My employer's desire to see it returned to its rightful place is strong and unwavering. As you and your acquaintances are discovering.

Yes. I'm trying to find a way for us all to avoid similar lessons.

I'll make it simple for you, he says patronizingly. You give me the information. I pay you. And none of us has anything to do with the other again.

What if I know nothing?

Then I will be on my way. You may keep the diamonds, in good faith. And I shall retreat with tail between my legs, to lick my wounds.

To lick your balls. Or someone else's, suggests Angel

Thank you Ms Fuk. Are all Hong Kong women so charming?

No. Just me.

In my country, a woman would never speak to a man that way.

Neither do women here. But with you we're going to make an exception.

Come on girls, I interject before it turns into a Straw Weight catfight.

I can see how your employees find themselves in peril, The Rat says, glaring at Angel. You should advise them to be more respectful. It is not too late for me to reconsider the generosity of my offer.

Yes it is. What if the information is worth nothing?

Again, my employer and I will be happy to cut our losses and leave. If we are confident you have been respectful and truthful, the diamonds will remain yours.

You're staying at staying at The Peninsula?

The Hilton.

I had you for more of a cucumber sandwiches type of guy. Let me see if I can broker the return of your bowling trophy.

I would ask that you be a little more respectful-

You carp on about respect, Anurak. Yet you're the one barging into my life, waving guns and making threats. It's a curious interpretation of the concept.

Says the man who just extorted a quarter of a million in cash and diamonds from another.

Think of it as opportunity cost. The cost of this opportunity to do business with me. I'm guessing your original offer is a fraction of the item's value. I've just raised the price, to reflect the true market worth.

What guarantee do I have you will honour our agreement?

You know where I work and, no doubt, where I live. A quick look around will tell you we could use the money. Neither do I wish any more of my employees to end up in Queen Mary, or worse. Personally, I'd like to stay out of the news too. I'm betting your employer feels the same.

You are wise in these matters, Mr So.

I'm fucking Obi Wan Kenobi. And here's one you can have for free. You might've noticed the police displaying an interest in what goes on around here. I'm sure it would serve all our interests to keep it off their bulletin board.

It would, he replies, nodding sagely. What's in those cartons?

There's a stack of boxes by the bathroom door. Promotional t-shirts, pens, coffee mugs and post-it notes. A variety of office supplies. Fax paper, erasers, pencils and felt-tipped pens. Typewriter ribbons. Liquid paper. Adhesives. Mounting boards for presentations. Take a look, I say. Knock yourself out. Oh, hang on. We already did that. Help yourself to the t-shirts.

Not sure we have them in girls sizes, remarks Angel.

If you're looking for ancient Chinese artifacts, we keep them in the bathroom. There's one above the sink, between the Oscar and the Grammy.

Behind the dildo, Angel chips in, quite enjoying herself now.

The Rat tries to force a smile, but it hurts too much. He opens the bathroom door. Enters. Looks in the mirror. Washes his hands. Dabs his face with a towel. Retrieves his comb. And slicks his hair into its preferred position.

You look fantabulosa, confirms Angel.

Will you be returning my firearm, Mr So?

Firearm? I don't recall any firearm. Angel, did you find a peashooter?

Check his pants.

That would be nanty, nix, nein and nyet on the firearm.

Bona nochi, omi-palone, says Angel sweetly, remembering some basic Polari. I didn't know Methodists were big on that either.

Come on Romeo, let me show you the door. It's rude to keep a lady waiting. And if I'm not home by bedtime, my daughter will kill me.

MEI IS CLAD IN HER FAVOURITE YODA PYJAMAS. She leaps off the sofa and charges toward me. My arms swallow her. I ask what she's been doing. She says drawing pictures. And scrambles to show me her latest Crayola masterpiece. Two stick figures rejoicing under a bright sun.

Who's that?

You and Aunty Micki!

Where are you?

In the kitchen.

The kitchen? But you should be in… the bedroom!

No! she laughs, as I throw her over my shoulder. And carry her down the short hallway, so our nightly ritual can begin.

A couple of stories. *Green Eggs & Ham. Saggy Baggy Elephant.* A kiss goodnight. Then I lie on a thin mattress, beside her bed. And hold her hand until she falls asleep.

Ba-ba? she asks, as we lie in the dark.

Yes sweetheart?

Was Ma-ma as pretty as Aunty Micki?

No.

No?!?

She was much more beautiful.

Really?

Yes. But not as cute as you. Get some sleep. Okay?

The day has taken something out of me too. The big nowhere descends and smothers me in seconds.

I WAKE THREE HOURS LATER and walk into the living room. Por-por is watching *Enjoy Yourself Tonight.* And clearly enjoying tonight's episode of *Shrimp Crazy Family.* She can hardly breathe. Wheezing as she points blindly to a couple of bowls on the table. I inspect them and wonder how many animals or vegetables suffered for this meal. Clearly Bing lost her battle with the recipe. Green eggs and ham would look positively gourmet by comparison. Por-por can probably hear my stomach turning above the Canto-babble on the television. She apologizes for the efforts of our epicurially challenged helper between seizures. I tell her I've got a little work to do. And will get something to eat from the *dai pai dong* later. She can page me if Mei wakes.

By the time I get to the first floor my hunger will not be denied. I ignore the office. Exit the building. And walk down the hill. A solitary man is smoking on the opposite corner. Leaning against a Mitsubishi Starion. Small in stature, his gulliver barely makes it above the roof. It's Wednesday night. The weekly Happy Valley race meeting brings out all kinds of punters.

I devour a fried pork chop and egg fried rice. Empty two bottles of San Miguel. Across the road I observe the same shadowy figure. And decide to show him the sights. I pay the bill. Hail a cab. And head towards town.

THE LOBBY OF THE HILTON is littered with bookish public servants and bloated, ruddy-faced expatriates. Bad suits, big spectacles and plastered hair rules the night. An event board welcomes The Hong Kong Pest Management Association. It would appear their inauguration ceremony has concluded. I make my way through the delegates to the front desk. And ask a pretty young thing if Mike Midian is working tonight.

Midian and I have done a lot together over the years. Securing gigs. Trading blows with ill-mannered punters. Once, when he was living in Sai Kung, there was a problem with stray dogs. Packs of them would wander into town from a nearby village. Tipping trash cans. Fighting more domesticated breeds of pooch. Killing chickens. Scaring kids. Mike went and told the villagers if their dogs weren't tied up that night he'd kill them all. The dogs, that is, not the village people. He went back at three in the morning. All the mongrels were tethered to stakes in the ground, on short leashes. Just like Mike knew they would be. He doped them with Mickey Finn meat. He watched them lay down. And then he snapped their necks. I didn't always approve of Mike Midian's methods. But I liked Mike.

The receptionist smiles delightfully, as if I've said something cheeky. No, Mr Midian not on tonight.

Mike's probably securing her perimeter. No need for Mickey Finns and tainted meat there. Midian's a class act now. Amazing what a suit, electronic earpiece and having the run of a five-star hotel will do for a man.

I ask if Mr Nirawatteverserarat has returned. And pretend I can't remember his room number.

Room 17-11, she says helpfully, scanning the register. But he's still out for the evening. Would you like to leave a message?

I'll be in the bar, I tell her. Call me there when he arrives. I slip her twenty dollars. Ask her to stall him. Contact me before she turns his key over. I need to talk with him before he goes to his room. She smiles as if privy to a dirty secret. I'm not sure if it's one of mine, or Mike's.

I cut across the lobby. My shadow scopes the crowd, looking for me. I slow down. Alter my course to dissect his field of vision. Then step into the bar.

I tell the attendant I'm expecting a call. I'll have a vodka tonic while I'm waiting. Short glass, lots of ice and a twist of lime. In a tumbler.

A couple of brokers are bemoaning a dip in the market. Fiscal machinations don't affect me directly, but they do affect my cash flow. Ad budgets are the first thing to go when finance departments fart. Some members of the Hong Kong Pest Management Association are making pests of themselves at a table in the corner. The women suffering their advances must be colleagues, or past-it hookers. Or both. None of them seem to have anything better to do. I start to wonder what I'm doing here when the barman informs me the gentleman I'm expecting is at the front desk. I tell him to charge my drink to room 17-11.

The lobby is almost empty. I have no trouble spotting my shortarse shadow by the flamboyant flower arrangement that dominates the foyer.

The Rat makes his way to the elevators. He takes two sideways glances at me before he stops. And waits for me to approach. The god-awful cologne he showered in hasn't dampened his smugness. Mr So, he says superciliously. I wasn't expecting to see you so soon. You have some news for me?

Goodnight, Mr So. It's been a long day and I grow weary. Of it and you. When next we meet I expect it to be worthy of my time. He motions as if to leave, then turns to offer me a parting shot. And kindly take your friend with you when you go.

I don't have to wait long for a cab, but traffic is thick and congested. The racetrack, having fleeced half the population, spews the hapless into Happy Valley. We crawl to the front of my building. If the Starion is still with me it's probably jammed somewhere back at the turn into the home straight.

I ride the elevator home.

Mei is sleeping soundly. Awkwardly. Gulliver in pillow, bum in the air.

Bing is in the kitchen, ironing. Listening to the Filipino hour on the radio. She's been waiting for me to get back and has taken my reappearance as a sign that her shift is over. She unplugs the iron.

I apologize and say I have to go out, again. To make myself feel better about the inconvenience I tell her she can watch TV. A little bit of *Dynasty* glamour goes a long way with her.

I don't care whether your relationship with Dex is personal or professional, Dex is mine, in the boardroom and in the bedroom.

Bought and paid for, Alexis?

I've never had to pay for it, Ashley. Have you?

When Ling was nursing Mei, late at night, I often caught the three of them comparing notes on Linda Evans, Joan Collins, Heather Locklear and Catherine Oxenberg. I was always more partial to Tracy Scoggins myself.

I take the lift to the first floor and slip down the fire exit, to the service entrance. Walk through a back alley to the street behind and jump into a cab.

I've got an itch. And it needs scratching.

13. NIGHTCAP

MICKI HAS ME WAIT THIRTY SECONDS before opening the door. She's wearing grey tracksuit pants, a white cotton singlet and is wound tighter than a junkie in withdrawal. A vein on her neck throbs. Hey, she says flatly, nonplussed by my midnight rambling. Like she's been expecting me.

The room reeks of burnt, stale tobacco, despite wide-open doors to the balcony and the best efforts of the air-conditioner.

I walk by her and shut the balcony door. The dehumidifier is firing on all twelve cylinders. Its collection bucket at maximum capacity, like the Banquiao Dam about to burst the banks of the River Ru. These things were really only designed for the great indoors, I remind her. And sit on the couch. The ashtray in front of me is swimming with dead tributes to Marlboro Country. An empty bottle of Glenn Fidditch watches over them, having flung its highland fling.

Drink? Micki enquires, dropping into the chair opposite, *smorzando*. She tucks one leg up and under the other.

Coffee, thanks. Smoke? I ask with my hand over the pack.

Sure, she says. And calls out for Grace to make a pot of decaf. Or do you want to be up all night?

Decaf's fine, I say, lighting the cigarette. You seem a little strung out.

You forgot the secret knock. Any news?

The stock market is tanking. They're still cracking down on food hawkers. Des O'Connor has announced he'll be touring, which is great news. And they're thinking of building a second airport.

For Des O'Connor?

Yes. They're expecting a large group of fans to meet him upon arrival. Oh, and they're going to ban cigarette advertising on TV. In 1990.

You'll have to find another stream of revenue. What about the police?

The money is almost as bad as advertising.

Anything from them?

Nothing. Yet.

Micki kills the cigarette. Walks across to the CD player, *legato*. She selects a disc. Punches play. *We'll Be Together Tonight.* Sting. She returns to the chair, an exaggerated swing in her hips. Lowers herself into the soft, expensive cotton. And stretches her legs like a cat that's just woken. Thanks, she says.

I haven't done anything. Yet.

Then I'm thanking you for what you haven't done, yet. What's new?

Didn't we just cover that?

Anything happened since then?

My partner's still in a coma. I'm being investigated for a murder. And there's going to be a hike in water rates that I'm not sure is entirely justified.

Mary, or Grace, arrives with a tray. Do you like your coppee cremated, Sir?

No. Decapitated is fine. Spank-you very crutch.

MaryGrace giggles. Collects the empty whiskey bottle. Departs.

Micki stirs sugar into her coffee. Asks if I want some. Do you want some sugar? The way she says it makes it sounds like an invitation. Or segue to something else. I rise. She moves to meet me. I tell her not to get up. And walk to the balcony. It's breathless, bereft of air. The street is bare. Desolate. A stray cab makes its way wearily down the hill. No sign of the Starion.

My host stands at the sideboard. Swirling the remainder of her single malt in a tumbler. You must be exhausted.

What makes you say that?

You've been running through my mind all night.

Your smile is about as tired as that joke, Mick.

You used to like a groaner.

Maybe you and Benny would've hit it off after all.

Who says we didn't? Want to join me in a nightcap?

Why don't you offer me something useful instead?

She savours the liquor, *adagio*. I don't respond. Not in a way the naked eye can detect. I told you, she affirms. I'm in trouble.

I move into the room. Does this get better every time you practice it, Mick? Or do you change it around, depending on the audience? To be honest, it did sound a little more convincing the first time. Tell me what you're into.

Micki drains the glass. Drugs, she says. Porn. Fur seals. Human trafficking. Disposal of toxic waste. All the high margin stuff, Jack. Cigarette smuggling. I'll cut you in, if you like. Vital organs.

Really? I met a friend of yours. He gave me the impression it was something else. That catches her dead in the headlights. I accelerate toward her. So why don't you tell me what you know about Mr Anurak Nirawattapattanasserwhatever?

A bolt shoots up her spine, like it's going to burst from the vein in her neck. She wants to know where I met him. And steps around me, *agitati*. She sits on the sofa and lights another smoke. What did he want?

I stand at the back of the couch. Look down on her taught shoulders. He wanted to give me some money, I inform her.

You wouldn't like how he'd make you earn it.

I got the impression it's you that would feel the pain. The amount of pretty polly he's throwing around, sounds like you're the one he wants to fuck in the ass.

You wouldn't, she says confidently. Then turns to look at me, just to be sure. She winces, like her bruises have just reminded her of their existence. Or something else, just as painful, has returned.

I sit beside her. I need a new stream of revenue, remember? I've got mouths to feed. Water rates to pay. Des O'Connor tickets to buy.

You wouldn't. You said-

You said, I said. He said, she said. When all is said and done, Mick, you're not really saying anything. Or nothing I haven't heard before. He, on the other hand, is offering more than just a ride down memory lane.

Micki faces me. Shifts her body to confront me, *teneramente*. Sweeps a thigh across the space between us. Opens her pelvis. Lowers her voice. We have a decent history, she reminds me. That should be worth something.

Indecent, at the best of times. That's our history. The way things didn't have to be. The story of what might have been. It's getting rewritten every day.

You change it with every tack you make. If I was after the highest bidder, I wouldn't come here.

What are you after? Why did you come here?

I'm trying to help you.

At midnight?

You're not helping yourself.

I want to. I just...

She crushes her cigarette into the ashtray. Pushes up from the couch. Draws her shoulders back. I just want to sleep on it, she says, moving to the corridor, *largo*. Why don't we both sleep on it? she calls, disappearing into the darkness.

I take the coffee cups to the kitchen.

Mary and Grace sit at a small table, eating segments of an orange. They smile. I could have an axe in one hand and Micki's gulliver on a stick in the other, and their expressions wouldn't change.

I've changed my mind. I won't be staying the night.

They laugh. And move out to clear the living room. I help myself to a glass of water. MaryGrace asks if there is anything I want. I say no thanks. She ties a knot in the garbage bag. And takes out the trash.

I step into the hallway. The apartment is dark. A shower runs behind Micki's door. Music whispers. U2. *With Or Without You.*

Fuck Bono. Cankers and root rot upon his Joshua Tree.

THE TAXI DOES A FLY-BY of my building. There doesn't seem to be any small shadows lurking. Still, I have the driver take me around the back anyway.

Bing is asleep on the couch. I make a few unnecessarily loud noises to wake her. Apologize for being late. Give her the rest of the night off, magnanimously.

I brush my teeth. Twice. Kiss Mei on the forehead. Tell her I love her. Lay on the floor beside her. She stirs and rolls toward me. Extends her hand.

I reach up and clasp it in mine.

14. BLACK THURSDAY

MY PAGER SHIMMIES INTO LIFE. Nine-thirty. Angel wants to know if anyone is coming to work today. Nine-thirty. I haven't slept this late in over a year. Of course I haven't been up as late as I was last night in a while either.

It takes a little more tickling than usual to get Mei moving. She's like her mother. Happy to stay asleep until someone demands otherwise.

We brush our teeth. Twice. Have breakfast. Milk and bread for Mei. Coffee for me. Bing has finally mastered the espresso maker that sits atop the gas burner. A double shot of caffeine blows away the cobwebs.

The *South China Morning Post* has shuffled Eddie Player and Benny Yu deep inside its pages, thanks to a triad-related bomb blast in Tsim Sha Tsui. And the amazing story of a newborn that survived being thrown from a fourteenth floor window. Police have shot a sailor on a Kowloon stairwell. And tons of cement rained down from a construction site in Financial Square. An apt metaphor for the latest tragedy to befall the city.

Black Thursday.

The stock market has crashed. Globally. Tuesday and Wednesday were a little dark too. Just ask Benny and Player. Today, however, the full weight of a financial fiasco is upon us. The bear market has awoken like a Wampa in a vendetta mood. And pulled the arms off a Gundark. Deng Xiaoping is no doubt heralding this as a reason for the fight against bourgeois liberalism to continue.

I'm imagining the streets of Central littered with the limbs of bourgeois brokers when the telephone rings. Por-por has to walk from the kitchen to pick it up. She mutters something about how useless a phone is if no one answers it. It's for you, she says grumpily. And passes the receiver.

It can't be my telephonophobia that's darkened her mood. She's been dealing with that for years. She dabbles in the market. Maybe she lost her shirt as well. I hope not. We're counting on her to care for us in our autumn years.

I take the handset. It's Angel. She apologises for interrupting. I tell her not to worry. I had to get up and answer the phone anyway. Destiny was calling.

Really? Because it's down here in the office now.

Great. What's it wearing?

Versace. And about half a million dollars of fuck-you.

ANGEL ALSO APPEARS TO BE MOURNING the market, in her own inimitable style. Sixties baby-doll dress, with groovy floral print. Knee-high black suede boots. Hair in an off-centre *I Dream Of Jeannie* ponytail. She takes one look at me and asks Mei what Daddy was doing last night.

Ba-ba was snoring!

Like a pig? she asks. And makes a porcine rutting sound. Mei thinks it's hilarious and runs in to the studio grunting. Angel turns to me and quietly suggests someone must have worn me out.

No. But it was exhausting all the same.

She raises her brow and gestures in to the office. Well, I hope you had your Weetabix. Destiny wants another dance.

Micki swivels on the chair at my desk. Legs crossed, cigarette perched in extended fingers. The sleeves of a black and white striped blazer are pushed up to her elbows. Shirtless, the space between the lapels presents a familiar swathe of flesh and hints at the curves that lurk in the shadows. Where the horizontal lines of the jacket stop a tight pair of black shorts begin. Thin nylons stroke her thighs and slip into black champagne-flute heels. What was it Rilke said? *Destiny is an exquisite tapestry in which every thread is guided by a tender hand, placed beside another thread, held and carried by a hundred others.* The relative simplicity of her fashion statement is offset by a strategic display of jewels. Platinum and gold, diamond-encrusted rings. Cartier Pasha timepiece on her left wrist. Chunky gold Wonder Woman bracelet on her right. I want to see Nirawattapattanasserarat, she says.

I'd settle for being able to pronounce it.

She steps off the stool, pokes her dart into the ashtray. Slips a weighty, wood-handled Gucci handbag onto her elbow and collects her portable phone. It's hard to say which accessory is the greater burden as she strides towards the door. She stops at the elevator and turns her head my way.

Are you coming?

Almost, I reply, collecting Mei and her backpack.

You can't leave her here?

Does this look like day-care?

I just thought...

You thought I'd leave the moral guidance of my daughter to Mary Quant? I say. Then offer a quiet apology to Angel. No offence, sweetheart.

None taken, dribble dick.

Dribble dick! shouts Mei.

I remind Angel how we agreed not to leak inside information in front of clients. She apologises. Sorry about that Chief.

Thank-you 99. We'll see you later.

See you later alligator! laughs Mei.

In a while crocodile! rejoins Angel.

I turn left at the elevator and suggest we take the stairs. Micki says she'll ride the lift. She had enough trouble getting down from that chair. I give her the benefit of the doubt. And the three of us descend to the street. I hail a cab. It swerves at us and jerks to a halt. As I open the door for the girls, the wail of a wounded mammal trills in my ears.

Esther seems to be channelling Cyndi Lauper. Or she's just finished reading *Love Is A Battlefield: The Pat Benatar Book Of Bereavement Fashion*. Like a post-modern Salomé colliding with Picasso's *Dora Maar au Chat*, she teeters on glam-rock heels, cubism brawling with fauvism, threatening to spill onto the pavement with every step.

What's she doing here? Micki wants to know.

You tell me, Mick, I say, feeling some Bard coming on. It's your show. The world's your stage. The rest of us are merely players. We make our entrances and our exits, while some play many parts. Some more than others, in her case.

I haven't spoken to her since opening night, Jaques. You've seen more of her than I have lately. And you know what she's like. Her curiosity gets the better of her. She sees everything as an adventure.

An adventure to be mounted. Her curiosity could be the death of us all.

You don't have to worry about that.

I wonder what she means by that as I move to confront her sibling. What are you doing here, Es?

What's Micki doing here?

I don't know, I sigh. Waiting for an end to this strange eventful history. What are any of us doing here? I thought you were leaving.

The police say I can't. And I needed to see you. There's things you-

I have to go. I'll call you. When I get back.

She looks into the rear of the cab. Micki going to play mommy now?

Esther, if I had time I'd slap some sense into you.

Make time. I like a spanking.

Later, I say walking away.

Offer might not be available later, she calls after me. This is a clearance sale Jack! For a limited time only! While stock lasts! Everything must go!

I climb into the taxi. Micki wants to know what Esther wanted. I tell her I have no idea and instruct the driver to make for the Hilton.

No one says anything for a while. I don't know what's worse, the silence or Richard Marx's *Should've Known Better* seeping from the radio. I reach over the front seat and change the station. *I Think We're Alone Now*, sings Tiffany. Mei voices her approval and we're stuck with it as we dawdle up Queen's Road East. Tommy James & The Shondells would find the whole scenario hilarious.

Micki tells me what a good job I'm doing with Mei. It can't be easy.

Kids are not that difficult. Grown-ups are the problem. Mei pretty much came out this way. The hard work was done long before Ling's funeral. Have you been to one recently?

A funeral? Not really. A friend of mine died. I didn't make it to the send-off.

You should've gone. They're for the living, you know. The dead don't care for them. People live for them. You'd be amazed. When my mother went, women I'd never met were offering themselves. Cooking. Cleaning. Succour came in all forms and functions. I had half a dozen surrogates lining up.

And yet you chose to go it alone?

Mothers are not really an impulse item.

I don't know. They're created on a passionate whim, more often than not. Mine was certainly a flash in the pan. How about yours?

I had more time with her hard-working, all-dancing, all-fellating friends.

That explains your natural rapport with women. And why you esteem them so highly.

It was the same at Ling's funeral, I continue. They all offered to help me through it. Nightly. Why do people think sex is the answer to your troubles?

Sometimes it is.

Have you known it to be anything other than the start of your problems?

It would probably be prudent of me to take the Fifth Amendment.

All I could think of was the shitty things I'd done to women. And how, one day, a guy like me was going to do those same shitty things to Mei.

Everyone does things they regret, Micki offers. Women too.

Running just fast as we can! sings Mei, until the news dampens her mood with a woofer-load of worldly woe.

Reagan can't remember anything about US weapons used to attack Iraq. Communist hit squads are terrorizing Manila as Filipinos celebrate Aquino's first year of People Power. Closer to home, Sir Murray Wells has stood down as Chairman of Hong Kong Bank, believing others are better equipped to steer stakeholders through these uncertain times. Others believe it is because he is better equipped to adopt a classic take-the-money-and-run strategy. In a similar vein, businessman, raconteur, philanthropist and patron of the arts, Liu Pang, is celebrating his first year of marriage to wife number six by divorcing her. And a diplomat from Zaire is the fourth person in Hong Kong to die from AIDS. To compound our misery, Bruce Hornsby launches into *The Way It Is*. Like he'd fucking know.

We arrive at the hotel. You're not calling up, to tell him we're coming? Micki asks, as we storm the building.

Mei and I like surprises.

Mei agrees. Surprise! she shouts.

Who are you doing this for? Micki wants to know. Him, you or me?

That's part of the surprise. Go about your business. We're just enjoying the ride, hoping to learn some valuable life-lessons along the way.

The lift doors open. Lay on McDuff, I enthuse with a gallant wave of my arm. And wonder which of the seven stages of life we're about to enter.

THE DOOR SWINGS WIDE before the bell rings out. Anurak is dishevelled. His suit crushed, like he slept in it. Even his aftershave has worn off. And he's so wired he could give the windows a treatment in the time it takes to cross the threshold. Surprise! Shouts Mei, in case The Rat has failed to notice her.

Like a confused spaniel he tilts his gulliver, trying to comprehend the humanity before him. It's all too difficult. He pulls Micki through the door.

Dilated to see you too Mr Nirawattapattanasserarat. Have we caught you in the middle of someone?

Mei giggles, figuring I've made the name up for her benefit. She tries to pronounce it herself. Over and over again.

It's a small suite. Bathroom on the left. Double doors on the right offer glimpses of a king-size bed. Either housekeeping has been early, or it spent the night unmolested. Standard issue couch, lounge chair, TV, desk and coffee table appoint the space between. Cigarette butts fill an ashtray.

Shall I make introductions, or do you girls already know each other?

We are acquainted, The Rat replies dryly.

Micki takes a place on the sofa, *fugato*. Lights a cigarette. I steer Mei to the bedroom and switch on the television. CNN's special report on the tenth anniversary of Mao's death is unlikely to keep her amused for long. I take a pair of plastic scissors from the backpack and give her a stack of magazines from the nightstand to dismember. Then return to the party.

A carcinogenic cloud envelopes the population. Something is being discussed in hushed tones. Did your boyfriend stop by last night? I ask, dialing Room Service.

I'm not sure I know to whom you refer, Anurak replies curtly.

I order French fries and a ham sandwich.

Who's he talking about? Micki asks, as I put the phone in its cradle.

Some chancer in an ill-fitting suit. Not much bigger than Mei. He's been flirting with me for a while. I introduced him to our Siamese cat here. Thought they might have something in common. I don't know if he's a millicent, one of your droogs or an addition to the burgeoning list of your admirers.

Micki looks to The Rat, like she's expecting an answer or clarification. Then returns her attention to me. Did he follow you to my place?

Don't think so. He may still know where you live though.

This doesn't seem to worry her. Maybe she has a list of things to be anxious about. You offered Jack a lot of money, she says to her nemesis.

The Rat looks at me, raises an eyebrow and gives The Smile.

When can we see it? asks Micki.

We? Ms Wong, my offer was to Mr So. If you have the urn then it is in your best interests to simply return it. There are no package deals, he says and turns his attention to me. I engaged you in good faith, Mr So.

And here I am. In your faith. She's my client.

And what am I?

I have my suspicions. But let's leave sexual preferences out of it. When a man begins with certainties, he ends with doubts. If I keep my doubts to myself, I'll end up with a dead certainty. Do you follow me? Of course you don't. That's what your little friend was doing. For now, let's just say you, Sir, are an enigma wrapped in a riddle. And a potential business partner.

I see, he says truculently.

And now the lines of demarcation are clear, when do we see the money?

When I'm satisfied you have the object of our mutual affection. And intend to make it available for collection.

Micki is agitated. Fidgeting. You'll give us two hundred thousand dollars, cash, now? If I give you the urn?

The money is not here but it is in the hotel. The urn?

Do I look like I'm carrying an urn? It's a big handbag, I know, but it was a choice between that and a box of tampons. What can I say? Hygiene won.

Charming, he says disapprovingly. You and Mr So's assistant must have graduated from the same deportment school. Perhaps your boyfriend is in possession of the antique?

Mei enters the room dragging her backpack. She wants to leave. She's bored. And the room is stinky. I tell her the room service is lousy too. Lunch will be here soon.

The Rat asks if I conduct all my business in the presence of children.

Not if I can help it. Although most of my clients are nothing but. She helps level the playground. Gives me insights into developing minds like yours. With regard to your lost property, however, I'll have to defer to my client.

You'll get it within a couple of days, divulges Micki.

My employer is expecting a more expedient resolution.

Then you'll have to manage those expectations a little better. Eddie Player was responsible for shipping it here.

Anurak looks at me, sneers and tells Micki she really scrapes the bottom of the barrel when it comes to acquaintances. I let the comment slide. I can always stab him in the neck with a blunt pencil later.

There weren't a lot of options, Micki replies. Player has moved on. The rest of us will just have to get over it. She rotates the bejewelled platinum and gold combinations on her fingers, like she's about to confess some almighty sins.

The Rat wants to know why he must wait to collect the urn. Micki turns to confront him. Whose barrel are you scraping?

You know the answer to that question.

You could be pursuing this purely for personal gain.

It serves my interests to see the artifact returned to its rightful owner.

It was a gift, Micki affirms, ignoring the peanut gallery.

It must be returned, insists Anurak. You will be compensated. Money for nothing. It holds no sentimental or historical value for you.

Its value seems to be appreciating daily.

Look at the price Player paid for it, I remind them both. And start to wonder what it's going to cost me.

Micki's attention remains on The Rat. She suggests that had his employer asked nicely in the first place she may have just handed it over.

I believe she said the same thing to you regarding her husband, Anurak snipes. The urn, however, is another matter.

Yes it is. And you can tell her it's a matter of principle now.

It belongs with those who respect its heritage and value its legacy, not a gambler and a whore.

My sister is not a whore, says Micki. I'm sure she finds it as hard as the rest of us to keep a straight face in the light of that statement.

I wasn't referring to the gambler's mistress, smirks The Rat.

Micki fires her right hand with admirable speed. It strikes Anurak, hard. Across the face. Full *brio*.

Surprise! shouts Mei.

I stand and step toward them. That's what happens when you don't respect The Code, I inform The Rat.

What code? he asks, nursing his zygomatic bone.

Any insult to a lady under a gentlemen's care is considered a greater offence than if given to the gentleman personally, and must be regulated accordingly, I inform him, reciting the tenth commandment of *Code Duello*. Traditionally, of course, it should've been me who did the regulating. I guess you can be thankful we live in more liberated times. I might not have been so lenient.

The Rat reaches into his jacket, retrieves his silk tashtook and dabs his cheek. The carats from Micki's rings have already left their mark and will do for days to come.

As quickly as she erupted Micki returns to her former grace. Hands in lap, caressing the palm of one with the thumb of the other. She looks at me. Blank.

If you kids can't get along, this will be our last playdate.

She smiles briefly then turns to a shell-shocked Nirawattapattanasserarat. Fuck you, she says. And fuck Wu. Her husband gave it to me. It was a token of appreciation. Reward for a year's work and his company's success in China.

The Rat appears to be choosing his words a little more carefully before he replies, not wanting to breach The Code again. Madam Wu has seen the books. She believes you were remunerated for your services. She suspects, however, the urn was recompense for physical labours.

The thrill would have killed him.

Some think it did.

They are misguided.

So are you if you think I care who was fucking who.

Whom, I interrupt.

What?

Who is fucking *whom*. Not who is fucking who.

If you think anyone cares who was fucking *whom*, he continues. And so was Player if he thought he could profit from your immoral affairs.

Or who was fucking Wu? as the case seems to be. Or is it Wu was fucking who? I ask blithely. This is getting confusing.

Wu was fucking whom, snaps Micki. Although it's probably more of a reflex quip. She doesn't seem to be having as much fun as I am.

Who cares? inquires The Rat.

Wu cares? I'm sure he did. Before someone went and fucked him to death. After that he became kind of apathetic.

Woo hoo! cheers Mei.

Enough! shouts our confounded host. Quite rightly. Mei is just being silly.

I had no part in Player's game, says Micki, rescuing the dialectic.

You seek to profit from it now.

Consider it compensation for the inconvenience my sister and I have endured. Reparations in lieu of Madam Wu's slanderous musing regarding my morality. Restitution for the *principle* of the matter. She owes me some face.

Two hundred thousand buys a lot of face.

She should know. That's probably what is cost to reconstruct hers.

The doorbell rings, startling all except Mei. She rushes to answer it. I tell Micki and The Rat to behave while daddy goes to see who it is. If they're really good while I'm away, they can have a French fry. I scoop Mei into my arms and open the door.

Oldham is flanked by a couple of local detectives. One is tall and apparently a big fan of Miami Vice, judging by the blue pastel suit. Even David Byrne would've found the shoulder pads comical. I can't remember where I've seen the other guy. Short and sporting a buzzcut atop his brachycephalic gulliver, he favours one of those sleeveless vests with lots of little pockets. Like the ones photojournalists wear when living crowded hours or traipsing across killing fields. Oldham still looks like Bobby Kennedy. Only angrier.

Surprise! cries Mei, welcoming them.

Can you ladies come back and turn the bed down later?

Buzzcut attempts to enter. I block him with a two year-old. Sorry, members only. Leave your name with reception. We'll call when we have a vacancy.

Miami Vice smirks. Buzzcut seethes. Oldham sighs. I tell him his court jesters are short on manners. Or at least Yorick here is. A bit short. On manners.

Jack So, this is Sergeant Chau. And Sergeant Chau.

No relation, adds Vertical Chau with a flat grin.

Chau and Chau, meet Jack So. And his daughter Mei.

Chau-chau! squeals Mei, delighting in the phonetic similarity their names have to the Cantonese words for *smelly*.

Now now, Mei-mei, I say. Show some respect for the law. Say hello to Chau Yun-fat. And Chau Yun-fatter.

Where's my French fries? she asks, mistaking them for room service.

Can we take this inside? asks Oldham.

No, I stonewall, stepping back in an effort to bid them farewell.

A lot of people are looking at you Jack, presses Oldham. They figure you had a hand in Player's demise. And we know you have a history with Esther Wong.

And her sister, remarks Buzzcut, as if I don't already know.

She tell you that? I ask Oldham.

She's not the only one you have to worry about, Jack. You haven't made a lot of compeers over the years. On any side of the fence.

We're still friends, aren't we? I ask sweetly.

I've got a corpse and an attempted murder. Both collected bullets from the same chamber. The only link is you and two women. And they've all been in your company since the bodies started piling up. So give me a break, okay?

Give me one. You'd be amazed at the shit that's nowt to do with me.

Let us in. And you can explain how nowt you're involved.

I've bupkis to do with Esther Wong too. Biblically or metaphorically.

And her sister? asks Vertical Chau. We won't find her in there with you?

Buzzcut smiles lasciviously, exposing the crooked, stained teeth of a chain smoker that has little regard for dental hygiene. If I didn't have one hand on the door and one on Mei, I'd clock the jeeter. In fact, even if I just met him on the street I'd punch him. He's got that kind of face.

We're done here, I say. And swing the door on them.

Before the lock can snap shut there's a high-pitched yelp. I can't tell if it's female, or Micki. Something lands on the carpet.

Mei grips me tightly around the neck.

Maybe we're not done, says Oldham. Maybe we're just getting started.

16. BOLLOCKS

THE SUITE APPEARS VACANT. The sofa is empty. And the coffee table is on its back. Cigarette butts are strewn across the floor. The Rat amongst them, curled into a fetal ball. His expression suggests he's just been struck by an idea for a poem. The small pool of vomit congealing beside him says otherwise. Micki has relocated to the bedroom. She sits on the edge of the mattress. One leg tightly crossed over the other. Rolling her ankle around its joint, *adagio*. And staring at the incapacitated Thai. A Beretta lies on the carpet between them.

Surprise! says Mei, in an attempt to break the tension of the room.

Oldham goes for the Beretta. Picks it up by the finger guard. Tweedledee and Tweedledumber survey the scene with detached bewilderment. I sit beside Micki on the bed. Ask if she's okay. Better than him, she says.

Oldham helps The Rat to the sofa. Tall Chau rights the table. Little Chau looks around. He wants to know what happened. Micki snaps her gulliver in his direction, as if suddenly aware of others in her presence. She asks Little Chau if he'd like to participate in a re-enactment. He bristles. That prick threatened me, she volunteers. With that gun. When you went out. He was standing over me. Pointing it at me.

I look at The Rat doubled on the couch trying to regain the power of speech, hands clasped around his groin. Don't rub them, I say helpfully. Count them.

Anurak hyperventilates. She had the gun. In her purse.

Before anyone can question the veracity of this statement, there's a knock on the open door. A sheepish hotel employee stands at the threshold, wondering if he should push a trolley into the room.

Don't worry, I assure him. Family reunion. Wait 'til they start drinking.

He takes the food through to the bedroom. I warn Mei not to touch the ice-cream until the sandwich is history. Crusts and all. I sign the docket. Dismiss the waiter. Tell him to put housekeeping on high alert. It could get karaoke ka-razy any minute.

RICHARD TONG

174

Fantastic, he sighs wearily, wishing he'd never mentioned it. Make sure you spell that correctly when you take his statement, Chau. Both officers look to each other and smile, assuming the other has been deemed responsible for authoring that report. Oldham looks to me. Jack?

I can't spell it either.

Jack, he repeats, in a tone that suggests I am testing his patience.

She's a client. She asked me to attend a briefing. I couldn't get a sitter on short notice so Mei came along. They were just wrapping-up when you arrived. As for this mess, I say gesticulating around the room, I was out there with you, remember?

Miami Vice asks why Micki called for help if she was on the offensive.

She wasn't the one trying to get your attention, says The Rat. I was.

It's difficult to suppress a laugh. I suggest the next pair of testicles he'll find is when someone rests them on his chin.

I knocked the gun from her. She assaulted me!

Bullshit, declares Micki.

Bullshit! shouts Mei, with a mouthful of sandwich.

They came here to extort money from me, proclaims The Rat.

You know what? says Oldham, exasperated. Save it. All of you. I don't care. Call it in, he instructs Vertical Chau.

I stand. Tell him to wait. Enough of this bollocks, I say. And quickly apologize to The Rat. Sorry, I know that's probably an insensitive choice of words at the moment. Take some notes Colquhoun. I'm not going to repeat this. And there'll be a test on Monday.

I pause to see how this rankles him. And draw breath before continuing.

This is my client, Micki Wong. Who used to be Micki Tse. Who used to be Micki Wong, my ex-flatmate and ex-girlfriend. She's the sister of Esther Wong. Another ex-flatmate and, well, ex-girlfriend. She is also an ex-associate of the ex-Mr Edward Player. My client was worried about her sister's involvement with Player, which is why she came to see me. In the course of that ex-change my business partner, the almost expired Benny Yu, attempted to ingratiate himself with Ms Wong. He went to advise Mr Player against continuing his relationship with my client's sister. It would seem Ms Wong's concerns have been validated, given the current state of the aforementioned gentlemen.

I survey their reactions. No one seems to have any objections so far. Most are probably wondering how and when it's going finish. So I continue.

Anurak Nirawattapattanasserarat - he'll spell it for you later - is also an acquaintance of Ms Wong and Mr Player. Knowing my proximity to this sordid vortex of intrigue he asked if I could help recover a certain decorative item. An antique vase. Player was supposed to be in possession of said antique at the time of his disappearance. He was charged with delivering it to Nirawattapattetcetera on behalf of Ms Wong.

Which Wong?

This one. Either. Both. Don't interrupt. Question time is at the end. I was of the opinion matters might be expedited if all parties met. This was poor judgment on my behalf. The conversation became heated as both our ladies here blamed each other for the object's disappearance. I don't think any of us were expecting things to get physical, particularly between these two. For obvious reasons.

And the weapon?

Maybe the Gideons are distributing them with their Bibles. Call housekeeping and check on that will you, Muttley? Maybe they can help dust it for prints too.

Micki and The Rat eye the fuzz, to see how they're taking it. Quiet consideration best sums up their reaction. I decide to capitalize on it. And put a hastily erected exit strategy into play.

So unless anyone here wants to charge me, it's time I got my daughter home. Let's roll Mei-mei.

She leaps from the bed and darts across the room. I collect her backpack and, pushing past Little Chau, quickly learn a couple of things.

One. His seborrheic dermatitis is so bad even his eyebrows have dandruff.

Two. The flaky little oik has quite an arm on him.

Ba-ba! shouts Mei, running to my rescue.

Chau! warns Oldham, to stop him issuing a follow-up blow.

Engulfed in a short, sharp flurry of furious flakes, I'm down on one knee and sucking wind. From certain angles it probably looks like I'm summoning the courage to propose. Or waiting for His Royal Psoriasis to knight me.

Mei, on the verge of tears, asks if I'm okay.

I take a deep breath. And then a few more, to stop me from doing something we'll all regret. The Rat gives a shallow snort of laughter. Or maybe he just coughed up his sole remaining yarble. Assuming he had two to start with. Standing slowly, I eye Deathwish Chau and his idiot grin. The first one's free, Da'Gonet. The second one will cost you.

I pick Mei up. Place her on my hip. I'd be lying if I said it tickled. Everything's doobie-doob, I tell her. Some boys play a little rough. But we're okay. See? We're all smiling. It's just a little harmless police brutality. Can you say *police brutality*?

Police brutality!

That's right. Police brutality. Let's go see if anyone else can say it.

Pushing my luck, I ask Micki if she wants a ride home with the rozzers. Or would like to share a cab with us? She collects her handbag.

I tell The Rat I'll have Room Service come by for the food trolley. He can help himself to the leftovers. Maybe he'd like to put those crushed nuts on the ice cream. It might soothe them.

I don't want nuts on my ice cream, complains Mei.

You're not getting any ice cream, I inform her. And we exit room 17-11.

We'll be in touch, calls Oldham down the corridor. I can hear him glaring at Hobbit Chau as he says it.

Micki slides across the rear seat of the cab. I give the driver her address and stick the BABY IS ABOARD! sign to the window. She stares out the window at the rain-soaked grey of the city while Leslie Chung croons *Enduring Together*. Thanks, she says. For up there. You could've walked out.

I did. It turned into quite an event. I'm surprised you missed it.

You know what I'm talking about.

Actually I don't. What are we talking about?

What happened, there.

When you bibbled him with your pitching mashie? What did happen there?

He pulled a gun.

So you stabbed his scrotum with a stiletto?

He killed Player you know, she deadpans, sidestepping the point.

I thought that would've earned him a gratuity. He told you?

Yes.

He was probably bluffing. Trying to scare information out of you. I don't think The Rat has it in him. I bet it wasn't even a real gun.

Her expression says she wants to believe me, but has doubts. Leslie Cheung concedes the airwaves to Danny Chan, who bemoans that his hopes for something have been dashed. And the low-lying city gives way to the heights of Magazine Gap. We pull up at the entrance of Grenville House. Micki says she'd ask me to come up but, well, you know...

I pay the driver. Peel the sign from the window and tell Mei we're getting out too. Micki's eyes question mine across the roof of the cab. Chivalry is alive and well, I tell her. She gives half a smile. I wipe it off by suggesting that it could be her day for unexpected visitors.

Nervous tension fills the elevator. It heightens as we ascend.

In the foyer, I'm almost relieved to hear the laughter of Filipino maids behind the door. And wish I could see the humour in whatever it is.

Mei kicks off her shoes and charges into the kitchen. Grace and Mary greet her with cheers of welcome. Micki flicks her heels to a corner, dumps her bag on the table and lights a Marlboro. What the fuck, I figure. I join her. And lean against the back of a chair to savour the smoke for a moment. Then ask about her chat with The Rat.

I didn't get to finish speaking with him.

I got a sense you were the one who shit-canned the conversation. Hard for a guy to talk when he's choking on his epididymis. I can call the hotel if you like. Have a car bring him over. You can pick up where you left off.

She draws on her cigarette with a bionic lung. The last half of the stick glows red and fades to grey. Why don't you get Mei-mei home? Come back later. She's had quite a day. And it's a long story.

I'm waiting.

So am I.

Mei runs in. Tells me she has to go to the toilet. Now. Mary Grace offers to take her. I say I'll take care of it.

Like everything, since I backdoored Micki and made a Mersey trout of our living arrangements, the khazi has been thoroughly renovated. This is a woman's washroom now. There are full-length mirrors on the walls and behind the vanity basin. Heatlamps in the ceiling. Fresh, thick towels on stainless steel racks. An indulgent white bath alongside a large glass-walled shower.

Mei sits on the Royal Doulton. Hums *Twinkle Twinkle Little Star.* I gently push on the mirror over the basin. It springs back to reveal a deep cabinet. Amongst the potions, lotions, perfumes and sanitary products are birth control pills and a half-empty box of ribbed condoms. *For her pleasure.* Sexual congress is, obviously, still a healthy part of her diet. Although I'd never known her to employ prophylactics. Maybe all the talk of AIDS has spooked her. That would go part of the way to explaining the tube of lubricant and painfully large vibrator standing proudly in the corner. As if in response to this observation the top shelf is stacked with Tylenol, Aspirin, Valium, Xanax, Halcion, Librium, Somnol, Dilithium Crystals and a host of prescription drugs that are available over the counter, in Thailand.

I give a quiet whistle of exclamation. It slides into the opening bars of *Mother's Little Helper*. Mei would like to join in but hasn't heard of The Rolling Stones. Or Wilson Picket and Steve Cropper for that matter. Neither has she learned to whistle. So she hums along as best she can.

Things are different today, I hear every mother say...

I flush the toilet and we go back to the living room. Micki is standing by the balcony doors, smoking. Drink in hand.

Dark, threatening clouds roll toward the harbour. Lightning flashes across the distant New Territories horizon. It's going to be a bumpy night. Micki is right. I should get Mei home and strap her in for the evening.

Today is gone. Today was fun. Tomorrow is another one.

I'll be back later,I tell her. Around seven. You want me to bring anything?

Just an appetite. I'll fix you something special.

Her tone suggests I could end up with more than food on my plate. Then again, she is Chinese. And a woman. The hospitality gene has a dominant position. Ensuring people have enough to eat is inherent.

Nothing too spicy, I caution her. My appetite's not what it used to be.

Maybe you just need something to stimulate it.

I'll get a bottle of wine.

Bring an open mind too.

18. OFFICE POLITICS

I PUT MEI DOWN FOR AN AFTERNOON NAP and return to the office. Angel is only partially interested in the Reader's Digest version of events. She'd offer more editorial comments if she wasn't in the middle of making a dozen executive decisions. A freelance art director and copywriter are also attending to the demands of our business. One looks about twelve and has managed to reboot my Macintosh on her own. She apologizes a hundred times while attempting to climb down from the chair. I tell her not to worry. She's clearly discovered a higher purpose for the computer, beyond assaulting people, and is optimising my investment in technology. Even with half the keys missing she seems to be making a better fist of it than me. I'm surprised Angel hasn't had the guy from Gilman over to fix it.

Changing my opinion on typefaces consumes an hour. Trying to get the art director to use something other than Helvetica. I know there are at least seven more. Palantino or Bookman? It would be easier to change governments.

The Siberian Fur layout vexes me as much as the Mild Seven tagline.

Angel is of the opinion that Siberian Fur is a good euphemism for Macao's growing population of Russian prostitutes. Maybe we could sell the line to them if the client doesn't like it? I tell her that would be a little off-brief and contrary to brand character. Soviet hookers aren't really known for tenderness. Unless they're repositioning their product, as part Glasnost.

Fuck Glasnost, she says. And the fallout from Chernobyl. Perestroika will spread her legs across the map, you watch. First Macao, then Hong Kong.

Tomorrow the world, I add. Conquered by a militia of molls. And no one saw them coming, so to speak. You don't think what Gorbachev is doing is a good thing? It could mean the end of the Cold War. No more Iron Curtain. *Tear down this wall*, I say, giving her my best Ronald Reagan impression.

Tear down that Iron Lady, she ripostes. Everyone's abandoning all that communism jism and Thatcher sells us back into it.

I remind her of Deng Xiaoping's edicts. *No Change for 50 Years. One Country Two Systems.* She reminds me that the man who killed more people than Hitler and Stalin, combined, still happily watches over Tiananmen Square. Inch by inch they will take a mile. You watch.

I will, I say. I like to watch. Especially if it's a battle for global domination between the Chinese and a horde of Russian whores.

Truth be known, I'm not as pessimistic or passionate on this particular matter. My apathy usurps my ignorance. Besides, I've got to make it through the next

24-hours before I can worry about the future of mankind. I move toward the door. Angel repeats her warning. Watch out, she says brandishing an accusing pen. The exhortation echoes off the walls of my gulliver as I make my way down the stairs.

Watch out.

Was she referring to the red menace waiting across the border, or the more immediate peril on my horizon?

A CAB TRANSPORTS ME TO MY FATE. Through the rear window I can see my undersized shadow has traded his Mitsubishi for a less conspicuous Mercedes 190E. Silver. I'll probably have to confront its driver at some point. See if he's as slow to respond as his vehicle. Push some buttons. Test his brakes. Find out how he handles himself. What safety features come standard. His tailing is as subtle as a deploying airbag. He almost rams the taxi, twice. And even flashes his high beam. Although it had started to rain. He was probably looking for the wipers. This guy would crash out of the pedal-kart race in Victoria Park.

Micki's ectomorphic silhouette and the red pulse of a cigarette command the third floor balcony.

I should tell the driver to stop further up the hill and discreetly work my way back. Avoid signposting Micki's residence for my pursuer. That information, however, is hardly a state secret. He might even be working for her. Or the state. Besides, it's dark, it's raining and he's so far up my tailpipe I'll need surgical procedure to extract him.

The radio fades from *Love Is A Stranger* to a Canto-facsimile of *Should I Stay Or Should I Go?* I run from the taxi, through the rain.

Where is Joe Strummer when you need him?

19. DINNER FOR TWO

THE ONLY ILLUMINATION comes from a lamp in the far corner of the room. And a few strategic candles. There is, however, no dimming the lucelence of my host. An igneous, incandescent pneuma, kindling long dead embers. Pink Floyd's *Momentary Lapse Of Reason* provides a throbbing score to the first act of an otherworldly production.

Micki wears an oversized silk shirt. And that's pretty much it. Unbuttoned to a point just above her navel, girded by a thick leather belt. The sheer material tapers over butyraceous thighs. She smiles and slinks across the amber glow of the room, *scherzando*. Backlit to optimum effect. Warp Factor 9. Phasers set to stun. Jimmy Choo heels keep her on her toes, on-song and the eloquent curves of her legs in fine voice. The Hakka shoemaker from Hackney had stepped into vogue this year. With advertisements like this I can see why.

I push off my boots and follow her in. She stops at the cabinet. Collects two long-stemmed bowls of red. Offers me one, hovering tipsily on one leg. Smirking in a brief acknowledgement of her clumsiness.

Bitch-heels, she says lifting a leg. I'll be flat on my back before the night's out.

She's capernoited. And has probably been snacking on her *en suite* stash of mother's little helpers too.

What if I brought company? I ask, raising my glass.

That would be rude, she replies, lighting a cigarette.

Come here, I say, leading her to the balcony. Stopping just the other side of the threshold. Look down there, I instruct her, with a swirl of merlot.

My conspicuous minion leans against his vehicle, like a damp noxious weed. Searching the sky for the break in the rain, or the building. He lights a cigarette.

Who's that? Micki asks.

You want to meet him?

I want to eat, she says and necks her glass of wine. Three strides see her across the lounge, *bravura*. She refills at the drinks cabinet. Then disappears into the kitchen. I make my way to the table and deliberate over seating arrangements.

There's clatter in the cookhouse. I listen for voices, someone telling others what to do. Not a peep. Just a gritted oh-fuck, as a hand brushes against something hot.

The maids, it seems, have been banished for the evening.

U2 launch the opening bars of *Where The Streets Have No Name*. The Edge's haunting guitar hangs in the air like resounding chords of kismet.

Micki emerges, balancing two plates. Steaks and what is known in epicurean circles as a medley of vegetables. It all looks lovingly prepared, replete with knob of butter and sprig of garnish. The disinterested way she dispatches the dishes to the table, by contrast, gives the meal a metutial character. I ask if she's okay.

She says she's fine and holds up her hand. Second-degree burn. Nothing to worry about. You rub a little alcohol into these type of things and they disappear.

Doesn't the alcohol sting a bit?

That's why I take it intravenously. Or orally, she replies. And lifts the decanter from the middle of the table, to slosh wine into clean glasses.

Where are the Sisters Of Mercy?

Prayer meeting, she says, sharing the blood of Christ. Then motions to the tenderloin in front of me. Medium, right? I'll play mum, she says taking the head of the table. Sit down.

I love it when you take charge, I remark cheerfully, spreading a napkin.

Can't make love on an empty stomach.

Is that why you were always on top? I told myself it was a control thing.

It was.

A brief, awkward silence ensues. Generous portions, I eventually remark, trying to keep the conversation out of the bedroom.

I've got a big appetite, she says, keeping it locked in there.

I raise my glass. Touché. To our ships at sea, I toast.

To a bloody war or a sickly season.

A willing foe and sea room.

Here's to swimmin' with bow-legged women, she growls, in pirate mode. And makes a precise incision on her steak. The seared flesh peels away. Crimson runs across the bone china. Micki always had taste for life in the raw. And the fillet before her is bloody as hell. She delicately massages the juices from the morsel in her mouth. There's something feline in the pleasure she extracts from it. I wait for her to purr. She dabs at her lips with a serviette, leaving a thin smear of rouge on the fine cotton. This would be the part where you compliment me on my culinary skills, she says.

I take the hint and carve a portion. Great, I say. It is. Fantastic.

Been a while, she muses, stroking the stem of her glass.

Just like old times.

After dinner we can waltz down memory lane. I've got my fuck-me boots on and everything.

I'm not some chambermaid looking for a tumble in the bedroom closet.

You're no schoolgirl either.

Sex is a killer now, Mick. Haven't you heard?

At least we'd die happy.

These days, I usually find myself reading women, and embracing books, I admit. She raises a disbelieving brow. I came for the story, I remind her.

Micki devours another thin slice of dead animal. Runs her tongue across her lips. Doesn't mean you have to leave empty handed, Tucholsky, she says acknowledging the source of my purloined epigram. You can pore over me. Cover to cover. Read deep between the lines.

I know that story. Inside out.

I could change the ending.

You going to keep the plot of this one to yourself as well?

No. Maybe. What if I did?

What have you got left to hide? It's all pretty much on display and out in the open now. What isn't, I can probably guess. At this astonishing rate of self-discovery, I'll know more about it than you come daybreak.

She drains her glass. Enough of this tap dancing, she says. Let's get drunk and fuck around.

You know The Code, Mick. Challenges are never to be delivered at night.

Unless the party being challenged intends to leave before morning...

We could be up to our necks in all manner of crap by then.

Not if we hide in bed.

I take a drink and push my plate aside. Out of frustration I grab a cigarette from the pack beside the decanter. And return it to a position just out of her reach. Tempting. Bargaining. Bartering for information.

It's about yay-big, she eventually volunteers, raising her hands from the table. One is a foot and a half over the other. I slide the pack across to her, withholding the lighter. It's old. Really old, she continues. Heavy too. Decorated with dragons or a phoenix or something. It's got someone's ashes in it.

Like a dead body?

No, like a packet of Marlboro and a coil of incense, she retorts sarcastically. Yes, like a dead body.

That might make it expensive. What makes it so important?

I don't know, she says after a while. I guess Player did. He took an interest in it. Asked a lot of questions. Used it as an excuse to come around. I wanted nothing to do with him. He gave off a bad vibe. It was more than just cheap cologne. I tried to tell Esther, but you know how that went. And what he did to me when I confronted him that night. In the end I just gave it to him.

I raise an eyebrow, implying she had given something of herself.

I didn't give *it* to him, Jack. I gave him the urn. Told him he could look at it all he wanted, just to get rid of him. It's probably what he was really after anyway. I figured I'd send someone over if I needed it back. Or have Esther grab it for me. And then he disappeared. I never saw him again.

How'd you end up here, chasing it?

She ploughs her cigarette into the ashtray. And lights another. A few things happened around the same time, she says. I wanted to know why he was so interested in this particular piece. I made a few independent enquiries. Got an indication of its potential value.

Which was?

Significant.

And you wanted it back?

I still figured I would get it back. That he'd return it.

So what happened?

The old man croaked. It's Li by the way.

What?

Old man Wu is old man Li. His name, it was Li Longji. Or at least he was until someone, as you say, fucked him to death. I was going to correct you at the hotel but you seemed to be enjoying your version of *Who's On First*.

You mean Wu's on first.

Don't start that again. His wife is Wu. You know how it goes.

I do. It confirms my belief that nothing is what it seems. How'd he die?

Trampled to death by an elephant. Gored by a buffalo. Or maybe it was a bizarre gardening accident. No. Wait. He laughed to death when informed by a visiting merchant that Venice was a free state without a king.

NOT IN ANY SENSE. HE WAS OLD.
THEY POP THEIR CLOGS ALL THE TIME.
WHY CAN'T HE JUST HAVE DIED?

YOU ENJOYING THESE QUESTIONS, JACK?

IF IT'S A NEAR-DEATH EXPERIENCE
YOU'RE LOOKING FOR...

So he died, I say, moving the story along.

So he died. And I got a visit from people who claimed to represent his estate. They wanted to know if I was in possession of the urn.

And what did you tell them?

Why would I have it? It used to be in his office. I guess his wife was stocktaking and asked his secretary where it was. She pretty much ran his life, the PA. If you want to find out who he was boning, check with her.

Whom.

What?

If you want to find out *whom* he was boning. Not *who* he was boning.

If you want to find out *whom* he was boning, Jack, go fuck yourself.

I laugh and ask what happened next. She says she told them to return in a couple of days. She was going to get it back and turn it over. Figured it was some kind of heirloom. The crone probably had more right to it than her.

Why didn't you give it back?

I couldn't find Player. Or Esther.

What happened when the estate agents returned?

I told them I still didn't have it. They offered me money. A lot of money. More than I figured the thing would ever be worth. I mean, why not just demand it back? Or threaten legal action? They came on like I was holding out on them. Like I knew how much it might really be worth. Like I was trying to up the ante.

Which you couldn't resist.

I figured if that's what they think then, okay, let's make it so.

You played along.

I had to. It was like a Scooby-Doo mystery, with a ton of money at the end. This thing comes into my life and all sorts of shinola starts happening. It vanishes. People die and disappear. It turns into an under-the-table deal. You'd play it out too, just to see what happens when the mask is ripped off. It's part of the reason you're here now, she says with a curl of her lip. We'll get to the other part soon enough too, even if you won't admit it.

I empty my glass and walk to the sideboard. Pour myself some bourbon, offer her a scotch. She accepts but she stays at the table. I hold my ground. The CD player rotates George Michael's *Faith* into the mix. Fuck Wham! And their exclamation mark.

How did we get from there to here?

I said I'd return their Thanksgiving centrepiece when they brought me the money. I thought that would buy enough time to track it down. To find Player, or Esther. I finally got through to her in Macao. And here we are.

She extinguishes her smoke. Stands. Steadies. And walks the room.

That's it? You don't kill for the sake of a trinket. And a little face.

WHY IS IT WORTH
SO MUCH?

IF THEY'RE
WILLING TO
COUGH UP
TWO HUNDRED
THOUSAND
IT HAS TO
BE WORTH
TEN TIMES
THAT.

MAYBE
MORE.

There you go with the romanticism, Mick. Not that story. This one. It's 1987, I remind her as she slips in and out of time. She looks childlike, gulliver hanging low. What did you leave out? I ask, lifting her chin and looking into her eyes. The pupils are enlarged to the point they usurp the iris. I can see candlelight causing confusion behind them. Her mind is probably somewhere near the Appleton Layer by now, about to enter the thermosphere.

Micki parts her lips as if to answer, then pushes them against mine. Gently at first, *piano-forte*. Firmer, as she sweeps my hand from her face and buttresses me with her body, raising prurient awareness of pleasures past.

She breaks away. Takes a step back. And slaps me.

There she goes again, I think. Flouting The Code. *Blows are prohibited, under any circumstances.* She knows that. Like she knows no verbal apology can be received for such an insult. I consider my choice of weapons. Cock my pistol and prepare to stake my ground. That's twice today, I say without daring to flinch.

I owe you, she asserts.

That's still once too often. Happens again and I'll have a hard time curbing my Confucian instincts.

Evil flashes across her eyes. Maybe you're seeing my true face. Maybe it's time to retaliate. Am I cute enough for you yet, or do you need another drink?

I try to think of something to say. She hits me again. I grab her shoulders, forcefully. Her smile is all the permission we need.

I pull the provocateur onto me. Our mouths crash. My body twitches in anticipation. Or conflict. Five years of anger, betrayal, grief, longing, guilt and denial are colliding in this moment.

The Furies writhe in my arms. *Appassionato. Rigoroso.* And like Alecto, Tisiphone and Megaera, Micki Wong can be intensely unforgiving.

20. FORCED ENTRY

I NAILED HER TO THE LIVING ROOM WALL. I didn't have much choice. And the exhibition that followed was more or less a primal courtesy. The last time I'd seen a woman naked was from the boundary of the Rugby Sevens. A glimpse of a streaker. Now I'd been complicit in a lethal *pas de deux*, executed with fluidity, precision and extreme prejudice.

Micki Wong's art is fornication. And her lissome figure created a masterpiece upon the canvas of the apartment. A beguiling enchaínement of fouretté, relevé, jetté, camber and plie. With a savage terre á terre to the bedroom, for a standing ovation and encore performance. Pounding each other, *martellato*, into the mattress. We smote each other hip and thigh. Sailed Dante's River Phlegethon, with Latini and Capaneus running the hot sands of its riverbed. By the time we got to the Lake Of Cocytus, Archbishop Ruggieri, Branca D'Oria and Napoleone Alberti were cheering as we rode bareback into the dawn.

When the curtain came down on Act Three, it occurred to me there might be more than just carnal pleasure to be extracted from the encounter. A combination of physical exertion, chemical inebriation and interstellar travel eventually laid waste to Micki's consciousness. I slipped from the bed. Found my clothes and her keys. Then made my way downstairs. The Weed, presumably deciding I was in for the night, had gone. I flagged a wandering taxi and gave the driver directions to Carpe Per Diem.

The security guard was asleep in the lobby of the Wyndham Street building. I moved by him quietly. Climbed three flights to Micki's office. And tossed the joint. Made it look like a botched burglary. Took some petty cash. Found a small handgun. Norinco 19mm. Does everyone have one of these now? The clip was half full, or half empty, depending on how positive you are about these things. It was in the cabinet behind her desk. Along with more pills, toothpaste, toothbrush, make-up, a small vanity mirror, sanitary napkins and a couple of changes of underwear.

I wasn't expecting to find the urn. But revealing photos or incriminating documents would've been nice.

Returning to Grenville House, 45 minutes later, Micki didn't appear to have moved. So I took the opportunity to poke around the old homestead. The exploration ending prematurely, with keys rattling in the front door and the hushed babble of Tagalog. Mary and Grace, back from Vespers. I retreated to the master bedroom. Disrobed. And the Norinco fell onto the floorboards with a thud. Micki stirred. I gathered the weapon into my clothes and bolted to the *en suite*. To wash away my sins.

Micki's naked silhouette was soon leaning against the door. Had enough, or do you want some more? The smile as drowsy as her eyes. Disinterested. Losing the battle with hypnerotomachia, she disappeared into the darkness.

I walked through the bedroom, post ablution. She was either asleep or feigning it masterfully. I pulled a sheet over her shoulders. She rolled and extended an arm, as if reaching for someone beside her. Halfway through the movement she gave up. And surrendered to her slumber.

The maids were clearing the table in the living room. Hello Sir, they said with knowing giggles, as only un-practicing Catholics can.

I walked homeward, to Happy Valley, in the early morning miasma. Down Wan Chai Gap to Bowen Road. Past Lovers Rock. Young couples and hopeful women were lighting joss sticks at the base of the phallic monolith. For a lot of marriages this was probably their best shot.

Bing was snoring on the couch, wrapped in the warm glow of the television. I didn't wake her, even though she would've got a kick out of the Benny Hill rerun. Ribald slapstick and crude innuendo is another of the universal languages. Filipinos get a bigger bang than most out of the sexploits of others. And that's probably the real reason I didn't wake her. She'd see Micki all over me. And be happy that I'd finally moved on. Which would leave me with embarrassment and shame. I'd have to borrow some of that industrial-sized religious guilt of hers.

Amazing how shitty someone can make you feel, when they're asleep.

That emotion turned in upon itself like a mutating virus when I looked at Mei in her bed. Oblivious to her father's weakness. Motionless, save for the rhythm of her breathing beneath the covers. Pure. Innocent. Diametric contrast and contradiction to the woman I'd just left on The Peak. Such a delicate frame. What was it Kafka said?

How short must life be if something so fragile can last a lifetime.

Had Micki's father looked upon his daughter in such a light? How did she get from there to where she was now? How does a girl like her get to be a girl like her? Would men like me happen to Mei? How would they leave her?

I sat on the floor, waiting. Back against the wall. I watched her until she woke. Waiting. Hoping for the smile of recognition that would bless me. And validate my life. Waiting for even a hint of unwitting forgiveness.

Waiting.

SHE STIRS. Asks where I've been. I tell her I couldn't sleep. I walked around.

In a circle, Ba-ba?

Yes noodle, in a circle. Around and around. Come on. Let's get some breakfast.

We brush our teeth. Twice. Wash our faces. Change into clean clothes. I mix milk formula into a glass. Mei drinks it through a straw.

Por-por asks if I'm going to be home late again. I say probably not.

Probably not home? Or probably not late?

Probably not late.

Probably you tell me something different later, she says dismissing me with a click of her tongue and wave of her hand.

It's too early for Angel to be in the office. This is a good thing. I need to work on my defence before submitting to her third degree. Like some kind of copulation coroner she can discern the exact time of an indiscretion just by looking at you. If they gave out doctorates for coitus she'd graduate *cum laude*.

I leave a note. I'll be back before lunch. Page me if there's any drama.

It has guilt written all over it.

21. ARRANGEMENTS

MIKE MIDIAN IS IN THE HILTON LOBBY. Propositioning the woman arranging that large vase of flowers at the concierge desk. The shadowy figure that has been dogging my heels is exiting the lift. The Weed tries in vain to make it look like he hasn't seen me. I pull him aside. Where is he? I ask quietly.

Who?

Anurak. Where is he?

I don't know who-

You know exactly who, I say sharpening my tone. And if I have to attempt his last name, it's going to make things worse for you. So, again, is he in his room?

He reeks of aftershave, even though he's barely old enough to use a razor. It's the same toilet water The Rat bathes in. I grab his arm. Spin him to me. Notice the Armani label is still sewn into the cuff of his suit. Mainlanders do things like this. Take every inappropriate opportunity to display their affinity for luxury brands. I tell him he's not impressing anyone and tear it loose. Judging by the expression on his face you'd think I'd just raped his childhood. I toss the tag in the air. Mei chases after it.

Got your attention have I? You couldn't take your eyes off me before. I was starting to think you'd found someone else.

Beware, he says earnestly. Or I will disconnect your skeleton and make a present of your intestines.

Great. Not only has he seen too many movies he's now casting himself in them. And speaking in subtitles. I look at Mei chasing the tag across the floor. It's all I can do to stifle my laughter. That and grip his arm a little tighter.

Take my advice, he warns. Or, like a child, I will spank you without pants.

I tell him he should be a little more respectful when in someone else's home. Not everyone is as nice as me. Others might take offence.

He says he has no need for a baby-sitter and that I should go and change my diapers before I am beaten out of unrecognizable shape, like my partner.

I flag Midian. Bring him out from behind the flora. His six-foot-five frame has an immediate impact on The Weed. His forehead creases with concern. Mike is also unimpressed. I've taken a cold spoon to his floral sex. I ask him how he's doing.

I was doing okay, he says, giving The Weed the once-over. Until you interrupted. Is there a problem here?

I caught this kibitzer eyeballing my girl. And offering her candy.

Is that so?

No! This man is grabbing my short hairs!

Midian signals a colleague, who makes his way across the lobby. The Weed continues his objection, although it's rendered somewhat mute. He's neither a registered guest, nor visiting one. He's a dustball that must be swept from the room. Midian and his flunky brace the limp lint between them. Escort him to the entrance and purge him from the building.

Now I feel flatulent, he mimps.

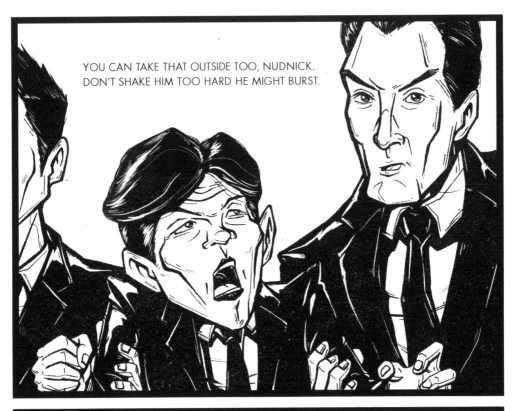

Mei joins in the send-off, waving bye-bye cheerily, the Armani tag between her thumb and forefinger. I point her in the direction of the florist. Midian returns and I ask if he knows anything about the Son Of Siam on the seventeenth floor. He says no. And runs it by the front desk. Checks with housekeeping. They all seem to be of the same opinion. The Rat hasn't been in all night. He offers to page me when Anurak eventually shows. I say I'll wait, if that's all right. Mei's enjoying her introduction to the fine art of ikebana.

Mike has no problem with that. I'd be surprised if he did. He only has a problem with people who make his job difficult. Not those who make it different.

I take a seat. Observe the ebb and flow of lobby activity.

Two call girls discreetly make their way to the elevators. Attempting to walk with purpose, like returning guests. Mike zeroes in. Pretends to give them an official hard time. Angling for a cut of their stipend or a freebie in a vacant room. Or both.

A fat German is shouting at the girl behind reception. I want to go over. Tell Hans that she's Chinese, not deaf. And smash his face into the counter.

I look at Mei, passing flowers to her new friend.

The Rat limps into view, worse for wear. Hair all over the place, the mousse effect has come unstuck in thick strands. Life isn't thrilling him. We make eye contact. His expression doesn't change, neither does his pace nor direction. He's making a beeline for the lift. Hopefully housekeeping is still making up his room, to further add to this malchick's misery. Morning squire, I say way too cheerily. How was the party?

He doesn't reply. I change tack and tell him we need to talk.

Our dialogue has never resulted in anything but pain. You can probably understand why I might decline your request.

Midian glances sideways as we walk by. The harlots smile. I know one of them. She drummed up a fair bit of trade in Disco Disco when I was on the door. I'd even let her blow me once or twice, in lieu of the cover charge. I might've thrown in a couple of drink vouchers. That's the big-hearted kind of guy I was. She kept a tube of Darkie toothpaste in her handbag. Applied it like lipstick. Rinsed it around her mouth just before she smoked your bat. It brought a little extra zing to the experience. Gave you a fresh ring of confidence. Midian was in for a treat. But he knew that. Candy. That's her name. Candy Wang. She licks her lips and winks, in case I need help remembering. I blush. She laughs. And Mike escorts the girls upstairs. I return my attention to The Rat.

Come on Rak. Tell me who you've been up to. You know you want to.

Your police friends kept me in the station all night.

You didn't enjoy that? I figured you had a thing for men in uniform. You're lucky they didn't repatriate you with all the other Vietnamese refugees.

I am not Vietnamese, Mr So.

Then you're really lucky they didn't send you packing with Charlie, aren't you? They give you back your pistol?

It wasn't mine. She had it in her purse. Said she'd shoot me and say it was self-defence. Watch that woman. She will not be as straight with you.

Yes, you're as straight as they come. I'm sure a man can put his trust in you, amongst other things.

Mark my words. You are, as they say, sleeping with the enemy, he cautions. I do my best to ignore his metaphor and move the conversation on. This, of course, is an admission of guilt. You are, aren't you? he says with an unsavoury smile. Oh dear. Did you go behind the sibling's velvet curtain as well? It's a wonder you're still alive.

The German arrives as the lift door opens. After you, Fritz, I say politely. We'll take the next one. We'd like a moment alone.

The Rat sighs. I ask if the police believed what he had to say.

No one would. She could have her name engraved on the pistol's handle, admit it was hers and they still wouldn't suspect her.

What else did you tell them?

As much of your story as I could remember, or fathom.

How was it received?

They liked it even less the second time. Although Detective Chau was not quite so physical in his rebuking of me.

He's low but I don't think he'd stoop to hit a lady. Why don't you go and wash that man right out of your hair. Will your employer be ready to trade this afternoon?

Will yours?

I collect Mei. The florist has given her a couple of orchids. She's going to give one to Por-por. And one to Angel.

What about me?

You don't need a flower, Ba-ba. You have me.

22. INVITATION

ANGEL LOOKS UP FROM THE PHONE. Crosses her eyes comically. And tells whoever's on the other end that I'm not in. She doesn't know when I'll be back but she promises I'll call when I am. Okay?

Some people just can't get enough of me, I remark as she cradles the receiver. Perhaps a little too cocksure, for someone hoping to conceal transgressions. Post-coital swagger can be a bitch.

I'd settle for a small portion. That's the fifth time she's rung.

Micki?

She doesn't strike me as the neurotic type.

Esther?

Bingo, she says. Mei presents her with an orchid. Oh Mei-mei, she gushes. That's lovely. It's been such a long time since anyone gave me flowers. Not even on my birthday. Everyone should get flowers on their birthday, don't you think? She says this looking at me, as if to suggest a floral tribute would have been appreciated. If I knew when her birthday was I'd be in more of a position to help her out.

She stands and walks to the fax machine, ponytail swinging between her shoulders over a white cotton singlet tucked into impossibly tight, high-waist denim jeans. Aggressive heels echo across the polished wooden floor.

How's the rest of my flock?

Inspector Chau phoned. Had some questions but said he'd call back. Nothing urgent. And a woman called Wu rang.

A Wu-man?

Very good Jack. You made a pun on a Chinese name. How fantastically *gweilo* and clever of you. Wu, she repeats. Whiskey. Uniform.

W for quits? U for mizzam?

Yes. X for breakfast. And Y don't you shut the fuck up? Wu Zetian. She said she received your message and was looking forward to meeting. Who's she? Sounded a bit old for you.

Experience, Angel. No substitute for it. Especially in the sack.

I mean really old. There was an emperor with the same name.

She used to be a man?

Wu Zetian. China's only female emperor.

So you did learn something in high school. I thought you skipped history class that day and grouted the football team instead.

Only one female emperor to remember, Jack. Pretty easy, even for you. Not a nice lady. Tang Dynasty, I think. Twelve or thirteen-hundred years ago.

Thanks professor. She'll have lots of experience then. Might even know some of those imperial bedroom secrets.

I'll bet she can take her teeth out. And her tweeter is probably tighter than her woofer. You might have to spray for cockroaches too.

Steady on. You're talking about the emperor I love.

Well you're going to love this. She wants to see you. At The Pen. Marco

Polo Suite. Looks like you're finally attracting a higher class of Wu-man, Jack.

Angel knows I hate going to Tsim Sha Tsui. The harbour is a psychological barrier I rarely overcome. What time does she expect me?

Tout suite. Two, sharp. Oh. And the hospital rang. Benny came out of his coma this morning.

Send flowers. For his rebirth-day. It's a new company policy. Actually, we should go down there. Maybe he can tell us who plugged him.

It was only for ten minutes. And then he went under again.

We should go down there anyway. Take photos for this year's Christmas card. We could all dress up like apes. In hospital scrubs. When he comes around we can tell him it's 3928AD. And The Handover didn't go quite as expected.

Angel fixes me with a stare. She stays with the Christmas theme and wants to know if the good shepherd was amongst his flock last night. Or has been out stuffing stockings?

Micki, right on cue.

The prospect of being pinned between her and Angel would appeal to 99.9 percent of the male population. My balls, however, have retreated to the relative safety of my abdominal cage. I pivot, slowly, knowing Angel will pore over every detail of the next few minutes.

Micki is dressed conservatively, for her. Loose silk blouse, buttoned to the chin. Sensible skirt, halfway to her knees. Large Chanel clutch bag. Black patent leather shoes. Modest heels. No make-up, except for a tactical use of mascara and lipstick. Just three or four rings displayed across her fingers.

Angel was just asking about last night, I divulge.

Is that right? Well, I can tell you he was a perfect gentleman, she smiles, *parlante*. Opportunities like that don't come every day. And he missed them all.

I have no idea whether she's aware of my clandestine activities. Maybe she's just keeping quiet out of respect. Denial. Professionalism. Whatever. Maybe she has no recollection of our attempts to copulate each other to death. She was pretty far-gone. Dilithium Crystals can do that to you. Or is it her way of telling me she knows exactly what went on and I'm the one who missed something?

Lost opportunities. The story of my life.

A little rude of you to eat and run, she chastises haughtily.

I have a curfew. If I'm not in before sunrise the little lady goes ballistic.

My office was broken into, she announces coldly.

This catches us all a little off-guard. Angel more than me, obviously. What's the damage? Anything taken?

Not that we can work out. For now anyway. Some petty cash.

So they didn't find what they were looking for?

How do you know they were looking for something?

It's why people break into places isn't it? They want something. Maybe it was that be-bop little weed who's been following you around.

Following you, she corrects.

I'm not the one at the middle of this.

Really? I could've sworn that's where you put yourself last night. Right in the middle of it. If not, well, you're getting closer to it every day.

Maybe it was Anurak. I saw him this morning. He looked like he'd been out all night.

She wants to know what I spoke to him about. I ask her to come through to the office. She declines. She wants to go home but doesn't feel safe or like the idea of being alone. I agree. You're in bad company when you're alone.

Player's dead, she says looking wounded. Your partner's in hospital. Esther's a mess. Anurak's creeping about. And after that thing with the gun-

Gun! interjects Angel. What gun? Jack?

I'll tell you about it later. No big deal.

No big deal?

It was a small gun. All taken care of.

Now there's a guy stalking me and the office has been rifled, Micki continues quietly, content to have bred a little dissention in my ranks. I tell her to take a seat inside. Show her through to my desk. Introduce her to the freelancer. Pull the partition, in case they want to smoke.

Mei is at Benny's desk. Telling the art director how much nicer everything would look with flowers and a rainbow. She's probably right but I'm not sure it's the look Phillip Wain has in mind for the Save 'n Slim promotion.

Back in reception Angel leans against her desk. Arms folded across her chest. It's not a confrontational look, in the classic sense. Although I'm not sure Micki and I convinced her with our plutonic disinformation. I try to diffuse the situation. Would you like a flatmate for a while? You can paint each other's toenails. Tell ghost stories. It'll be like a high school sleepover.

We can play truth or dare. Imagine some of the things I might learn... about last night.

If you could get her to admit the truth about anything I'd be impressed. Give her the corporate rate. And no visitors after midnight. Especially boys.

Is she really in trouble?

She is trouble. But I don't know if she's in any real danger. She's scared. And it won't hurt to know where she is until this gets sorted out. Keep an eye on her for me. Flora and Wing can lock up when they leave. Best you take off now. Micki will follow in half an hour. You're still on Ladder Street?

Why don't I just take her with me?

The Weed might be lurking in the shadows.

I thought you said-

Better safe than sorry. Besides, you two probably shouldn't be seen leaving together. People will talk.

I wouldn't mind. If you're not interested maybe I should jump her myself. It'll give me bragging rights over Benny, next time he comes around.

I'll stop by her place later and bring a few things over. Any requests?

Crotchless panties. Nitrous oxide. And don't forget the nipple clamps.

Two nuns. And a donkey, I add. Just like high school.

23. THE PEN

THE NEW SLEEPING ARRANGEMENTS are explained to Micki. She seems appreciative. Of course she also expressed a great deal of gratitude during our *in flagrante* epic the night before. Yet here she is now as if it never happened. I'd like to think it doesn't worry me. That it doesn't make me feel used and discarded, like that twelve-inch tickler in her toolbox. That it isn't the reason I forget to tell her about my upcoming appointment with Madam Wu. I'd like to think the reason I keep that from her is because I've seen the effect one of the widow's minions has on her. And I have no wish to see how that discontent manifests itself when she encounters the matriarch.

I'd like to think all that.

Maybe she's as insecure, guarded and childish as I am. Maybe she has more to lose. More than I'd like to think, or know. More than I'll ever know.

I give her Angel's address. Take her down to a taxi, via the tradesman's entrance. And return to the office. Tell the freelancers I'll be back around six. If artwork needs to go out before then, to meet a deadline, dispatch it.

Mei and I are making our escape, when Esther steps out of the lift.

If I need conclusive proof that my life is descending into a Sino-British farce, this is it. Women and doors, entrances and exits. Slapstick gags. Hilarity ensues. Esther's outfit is a grand comedy of errors too. Bright red Issey Miyake, heavy on pleats. Baggy. Sharp angles. She looks like a Chinese lantern on legs. You really have to be Grace Jones to get away with this type of thing.

Look Mei. They've raised the red lantern. It's the little steam engine that could. Woo-woo! I say pulling on an imaginary whistle.

Ding a-ling! shouts Mei.

Esther is worried, or doing a good job of faking it. Her voice is infused with regret. Oh Jack! Can you forgive me?

I did, years ago. Or do you mean for that outfit? That might be a little more difficult. It's burning my retinas and scarring my occipital lobe.

For yesterday. I told the police where to find you, she confesses.

How did you know?

I told them you were with the people who killed Eddie.

You know who shot him?

Yes. No. I told them I knew. I wanted to make things difficult for you.

Mission accomplished.

Seeing you with Micki made me crazy.

Just wait until she finds out we bounced each other six ways 'til Sunday, I think. It'll make her eyes pop. Then she can really number herself amongst the almonds. Or did she already know? I'm not *with* anyone, I inform her. I'm trying to make sense of all this fetor.

We're... I'm sorry, Jack.

We all are, Es. And we have to go. Where are you staying? Don't tell me. I don't want to know. Tell this guy. I take a pink colouring pen from Mei's backpack and write Eric Tsoi's number on her arm. Get down to Callett, Crambazzle, Dratchell & Feaque, I instruct her. You're going to need a lawyer, sooner than later. His chambers are at the Shun Tak Centre. You might even find your next conquest there. At the very least you'll get a free meal. Tell him everything. And by that I mean tell him more than you haven't told me.

Esther grabs my arm, tenderly. Assures me she only came because Micki said she was in trouble and needed help. I brush her off. Remind her where that simple act of kindness has got us all. And suggest she really should tell Eric what she knows. Come with me, she implores.

Later, I promise. And kiss her on the lips, gently. An incentive. Let her think she has me halfway hooked. I'm not sure what Confucius or Laozi would think of this tactic. Mei isn't sure what to make of it either. Surprise! is about all she can muster.

We throw Esther into a cab then head around the corner for fried egg sandwiches, with luncheon meat, and a glass of soy milk. This is not the best thing to line my stomach, given the perilous nature of the ocean voyage we're embarking upon.

For some it's a simple five-minute ferry ride across Victoria Harbour to The Peninsula Hotel. My faith in water-based transport, however, has diminished. Gone out with the tide. I wasn't always this way. It's just that with the birth of my daughter, the death of my wife and a number of other watershed experiences under my lifebelt, I'm increasingly aware of my own mortality. I don't like forfeiting the controls of my fate.

Victoria Harbour is a cymophobic nightmare. Boarding the Star Ferry is the Chinese equivalent of a log roll. It lurches to one side when everyone dis/embarks. It's chaos out there. Each voyage threads a sea-camel through the eye of an aquatic needle. And there's all the unidentified diseases being cultivated in its murky petri dish. If we have to swim for it we wouldn't survive even if we did make it back to terra firma.

I try to convince Mei it will be more fun to take the train. Go *under* the water, even though that doesn't thrill me either. Likewise the bus. On a day like today, with no air-con, we'd suffocate on carbon monoxide before we made it to the other side. The promise of a visit to Toys R Us in Ocean Terminal fails to sway her as well. The romantic in her is having none of it. She loves the ferry. For all the reasons it scares me.

I insist on sitting in the middle of the deck, where it teeters less. Fortunately it's not too rough. There's a gentle ostro to loosen the knot in my stomach. We cross the pond without incident. And are soon standing in the shadow of greatness.

The Pen is an institution for the insanely wealthy. Five-star elegance and sophistication rising out of Tsim Sha Tsui's madness. It looks down its nose at the Central metropolis and neon clutter across the watery void. Quite happy, no doubt, to put some distance between it and the postcard cliché guests view from their rooms. What goes on in those highly priced and prized suites, of course, is no different to what goes down behind it in the less salubrious hostels of Chungking Mansions. People just pay more for their indiscretions. And get their towels changed daily. Money can buy a lot of forgiveness too. I'd enjoyed the best and worst of times there.

The doorman greets me formally. Mister So. Mei thinks this is hilarious and repeats it all the way to the elevator.

Mister So. *Mister So*. Mister *So*.

I ask her to tone it down. People only whisper in places like this, June-bug.

The Pen is luxuriously calm. The clatter of Kowloon intimidated and suppressed. Shushed. Apart from a string quartet and well-heeled shoes clicking across the marble, there's barely an audible murmur from the tourists, business travellers and ladies-who-lunch in the lobby lounge.

The gravitas is infectious. By the time we exit the lift, padding our way down the thick carpet, we're both conscious of our breathing patterns. To reduce the growing trepidation with which we approach our appointment, I count-off the room numbers.

Mei repeats them after me. Quietly.

She's a lanky, meretricious minx. Embarrassingly thin. My apodyopsis says she must be over six-feet tall in the nude, which she practically is. Standing barefoot, smoking, in that short ebony chemise. The black lace gloves that gather loosely around thin forearms are a weird, albeit elegant, touch. A thick slick of black hair, extravasated above the slits of her eyes, bleeds across her crown and seeps down around her shoulders, framing aquiline features. On the Scoville Scale, I rate her a Habanero. Maybe a Scotch Bonnet, verging on Pure Capsaicin. Somebody should alert the authorities. One of the lascivious beauties from Peking's notorious Eight Lanes is missing.

I'm beginning to think Angel underestimated Madam Wu's age and appeal. Except she's not at the door of The Marco Polo Suite but, rather, the room next to it. Maybe police are cracking down on vice in Kowloon and forcing predators of her ilk to the high ground. Until the feeding grounds and watering holes of Tsim Sha Tsui are safe once again.

Maybe she's one of the new mainland faces of Fashion Week I've been reading about. Legend has it secret tribes of warrior women inhabit the Emei and

Wutai Mountains. Hidden from civilisation for thousands of years, no western male has ever seen inside. And only now, with Deng's Open Door Policy, do we occasionally catch glimpses of them on the catwalks of the world. And milling about open doors. Great policy. This is one of the best applications of it so far, albeit somewhat loose and literal. Of course, she could be an emperor's concubine, on a rare excursion outside the walls of the Summer Palace.

Qi The Consort farewells me with a prurient curl of her lips, as she turns and glides into the darkness. An elaborate tattoo crawls up her back, slips under the spaghetti straps of her négligiblé and entwines her neck, like a lace collar. Somehow it manages to simultaneously depreciate and strengthen her Scoville rating.

Mei is equally impressed. She's never seen art like this before. I want a painting like that, she says, as the gate to the Forbidden Kingdom closes.

No you don't, I say. And knock on the door of The Marco Polo Suite. The heavy oak swings open. We're met by an ill-disposed, yet familiar face.

Surprise! cheers Mei on our behalf.

24. ENTER THE DRAGON

YOU DARING LOUSY GUY.
BEHAVE, OR I SHALL
REMOVE YOUR MANHOODS.
AND LEAVE THEM IN
THE DESSERT FOR YOUR
AUNTY TO EAT.

My aunty has manhoods for breakfast. Is the lady of the house in?

Madam Wu is waiting. Be respectful. You do want to tarnish my instep with your thick face.

He's right. I don't want to tarnish his instep. I thank him for the heads-up, take Mei's hand and enter the finely appointed anteroom.

A brightly lit testament to colonial indulgence, the suite is tastefully appointed with the best of East and West. Large sofas and lounge chairs are clad in lush fabrics. A burnished coffee table and matching side-stands punctuate the room. Antique cabinets display a variety of ethnic vases. Shutters and curtains frame the windows. Crystal chandeliers. There's even doilies on the dining room table. Coppola could use it as a set for *The Godfather Part III: The Corleones Take Macao.*

Across the room, sliding doors part. An elderly woman, more aged than she is attempting to look, takes a moment to compose herself. She casts her eyes around the room. Soaking up the nostalgia, or waiting for an invitation to enter. Maybe she's allowing time for her hair to acclimatize. It's hard to tell if that enormous Joan Collins perm is real, or a shaitel. She's not quite the mackabroin Micki painted her to be but there is a shistaceous quality to her face. An effect exaggerated by an oversupply of glow-in-the-dark foundation. None of which can conceal her most prominent feature.

The Mole.

It squats on the prime real estate of her forehead like a toad. Ugly, venomous and threatening to reclaim the territory before '97. If the face is the soul of the body, Madam Wu's is cancerous. Those leading the investigation into her husband's death should take her tumour in for questioning. The size and colour of an unruly blackberry, it'd give Gorbachev's stain a run for world's most prominent birthmark. Look up the Seven Ancient Wonders and you'll find it there between The Temple Of Artemis and The Mausoleum At Halicarnassus. If maintenance work had indeed been performed, as Micki suggested, the mind boggles as to what she might've looked like before. It's possible, of course, The Mole had been deliberately left alone during the renovations. It could be one of those lucky moles.

I'd hate to see an unlucky one.

Maybe it threatened to go after the surgical team's family if they went anywhere near it. Anyone wanting to get this indigenous bastard out would have to call in an air strike.

Mei tugs my arm. She probably wants to discuss the insurgent Coco-pop. I'm waiting for smoke to billow out from behind The Empress Dowager. And someone to strike a large gong. Like a boarding school housemother, she smooths the front of her grey Armani twin-set. Shifting the crosshairs of her sights from me to Mei and back. Her mouth an emotionless flat line.

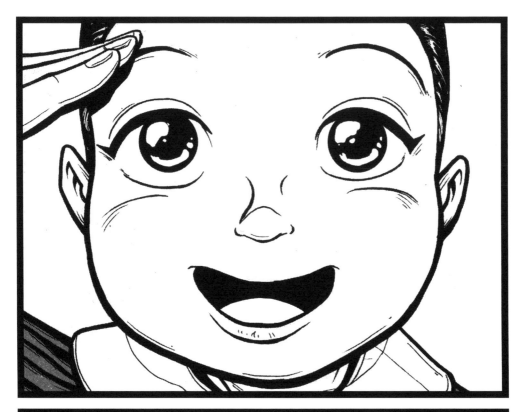

Wu frowns upon Mei, and my channelling of Dick Cavett, as only someone who has ascended the 33° of Freemasonry can. From the strong came forth sweetness, she remarks. Thank you for coming. She extends a heavily jewelled hand. The Beau Sancy diamond sits uncomfortably like Marie de Medici in King Henry's court, amongst the rings, bracelets, racklettes and liver spots.

Thank you for the invitation, I reply, clasping her scaly claw. Welcome to Hong Kong. I trust The Peninsula has been making your stay enjoyable. The Admiral and I usually opt for The Garden Suite. But this is nice too. Crash-proof as well. You can't even hear the market plummeting from here.

If she is attuned to the sarcasm she gives no hint. The Garden Suite was unavailable, she replies. I've been told the Kobayashi's are in residence. Perhaps next time.

Let me know. I'll have a word. See what I can do. Who handles your bookings?

The invitation was extended to you, Mr So, she says irritably. We were not expecting a companion.

No need to apologize. She's quite low maintenance. This will do fine.

It is considered polite to inform hosts when bringing a guest.

Oh. I see. Sorry. It's just, well, you know, we're kind of an item.

So I have been made aware.

Then it shouldn't come as much of a surprise.

Wu motions to the sofa. I assume this means we've passed the entrance exam. And I glance at The Weed triumphantly as I sit. Mei busies herself with magazines.

Perhaps my son can occupy your daughter while we talk, suggests Wu, sitting in the large chair to my left. The full implication of this revelation dawns on me as her son moves to collect Mei.

She spawned *him*?

Perhaps not, I say, staring her offspring down. He looks to his mother for approval. What a crushing disappointment he must have been to his father. Maybe that's what killed him.

Nobody puts baby in the corner, I add, doing my best Patrick Swayze.

As you wish, she affirms, swatting him away with a wave of her hand. A drink to shake the dust from your feet? she offers. It's an attempt to sound with-it, like a terminally hip aunt that says things like *cool* or *groovy* when she shouldn't.

Tonic water. Lots of ice.

How British of you.

For The Admiral, I correct her. She's a stickler for tradition.

Culture without tradition is like destiny without history, quotes The Mole, like a transsexual Albert Camus.

I'll have Ribena. In a fat glass. With a splash of vodka.

How-

How about we dispense with the courtliness.

The Weed takes an angry step in my direction. And is waved away, again. Perhaps you will permit me to offer you some tea? suggests Wu.

How Chinese of you.

There is a small ceramic pot with cups neatly arranged around it, atop the coffee table. I thought it was ornamental. She pours two cups and places one before me, ceremonially, then raises the other to her cracked lips. The deep rouge of her lipstick bleeds into the crevices. This is Longjin tea, she informs me. From Hangzhou. The English, I believe, call it Dragon Well.

Well, well, well. I thought I recognized the fragrance.

Yes, prosperity, Wu echoes, carefully placing her cup on the table beside her chair. To that end, you are in a position to assist us with the acquisition of a certain *objet d'art*. Something that would be of mutual benefit to us?

To that end, if I knew what all this was really about, I might be. Looking around, however, I get the impression prosperity is the least of your concerns.

Wu takes another sip of tea, as if waiting for me to continue.

The urn, Madam Wu. What does it really mean to you?

To the point, Mr So. Thank you. Allow me to respond with the same respect for your time and intellect, she says piercing me with narrow eyes. Do you represent your own interests or Ms Wong's this afternoon?

I don't know, I say. And down the remainder of my tea. I've encountered so many people acting in the interests of this relic, I'm still not sure who's acting in whoms interest. Or on whose behalf. Are you as confused as I am?

You do not strike me as one who hides his light under a bushel, Wu observes for no apparent reason. You know why you are here. And your motivation is probably one of self-interest, followed by concern for your family.

You're half right. I'm looking out for Number One. In the Venn diagram of life, however, I don't see my family and myself as mutually exclusive groups. Although, having met your son, I can understand why you might.

I appreciate your candour. One doesn't meet many honest men, or women, these days.

Honesty's over-rated. The truth is the cry of many but the game of few.

A thin smile creases cracked lips. Your directness is refreshing.

Glad you like it. Have some more. What's the deal with the urn?

It is as old as Methuselah.

Friend of yours, was he?

Do you know its worth?

I know what it's worth to some people. I know the price others have paid for it. I want to know what it means to you.

The whited sepulchre is one of a kind. It's value incalculable.

Nirawattapattanasserarat said you'd pay quarter of a million, I remind her, wondering when and why she began misappropriating so many biblical references.

Did he? That figure suggests neither of you truly know what you are dealing with, she replies casting an accusing eye at her son.

I don't know. At all. That's why I'm here. I know it's a valuable *objet d'art*, as you called it. An *idée fixe*. Your *raison d'être*. I know its value seems to be increasing the less I know about it.

Ms Tse hasn't told you its history?

Ms Wong, I correct her. She's given me its recent history. Although I suspect that's from a somewhat jaundiced point of view. Why don't you enlighten me?

I'd like to hear from you.

Okay. *Quid pro quo* it is then, with the accent on the *quid*. I know where it is. You know what it is. To get my end, so to speak, you need to give me yours.

I'm not sure we can do business that way.

Then we can't do business. And I thank you for your hospitality.

I stand, take Mei's hand, sling her backpack onto my shoulder and tell Madam Butterfly to enjoy the rest of her stay in Hong Kong.

Don't be so hasty, she implores.

I've had all the tea I can stomach. And I've sat here long enough to know my time would be better spent elsewhere. You should move on too. They may only charge you for half a day. Be sure and stop by Lamma Island on your way home, and try the seafood. It's to die for.

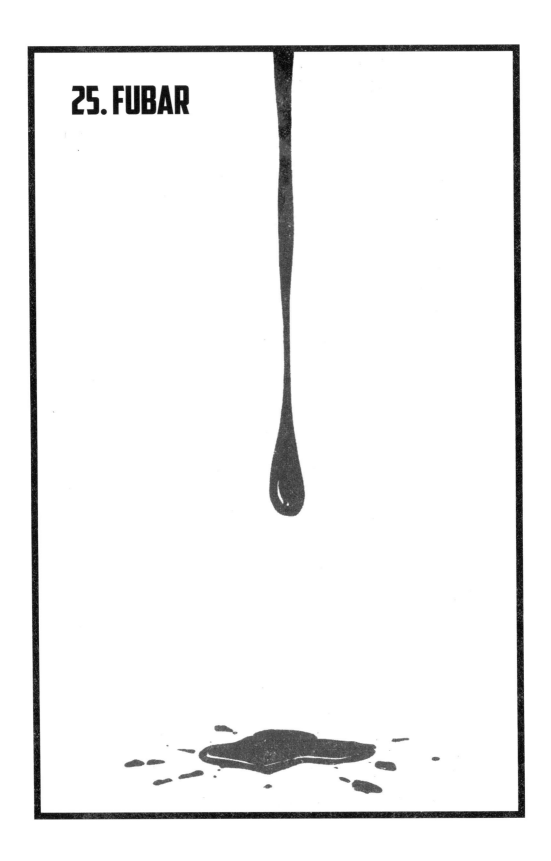

25. FUBAR

MEI RUBS THE TOP OF MY GULLIVER. Asks if I'm okay. I tell her I'm fine. But I'm not. I'm shaking. An agitating combination of post-stoush adrenaline and emotion. I'm angry with myself for snapping in front of Mei. I'm worried I might have pushed The Weed's nose through the back of his skull. Not very Confucian of me at all. Laozi would be disappointed. I console myself with the fact that even Han Solo shot first, sometimes. I just have to think of The Pen as Mos Eisley cantina. And The Weed as Greedo.

Unfortunately the Star Ferry is no Millennium Falcon. The roll of the vessel on an unsettled harbour exacerbates the churning in my guts. It's not just because my actions were gratuitous and excessive. Almost everything here is. The whole city. Its architecture and geography. The demographic disparity. The wanton pursuit of wealth and status. Moments like this, when you realize that, can make you feel sick. Nauseous. Your world seems to spin and drift.

The wind has shifted.

A stiff ponente charges up the harbour from Macao and China.

WE DISEMBARK IN CENTRAL. I ask Mei if we should call upon Eric Tsoi at Callett, Crambazzle, Dratchell & Feaque. Given I may have just killed a man, in one of Hong Kong's most celebrated luxury hotels, she is of the quiet opinion that it probably wouldn't do any harm.

Ars longa, vita brevis, occasio praeceps, iudicium difficle.

I kind of agree. The Mole wouldn't want the police involved in current events any more than the rest of us. If I had inadvertently snuffed The Weed, however, even The Pen would find it difficult to look the other way. And sweep something like that under the rug.

I lift Mei to my shoulders and walk along the harbour to the Shun Tak Centre. Grey clouds rush to greet us. She wraps her arms around my gulliver, hands across my temple. A dull pain introduces itself. I wonder if a bruise is on its way. And send my fingers to the area, in search of a bump. Mei asks if it hurts.

Only when I laugh, sugarpop.

What you laughing about? The man falling down? That was funny!

Not for him, sweetpea.

Why you hit him with your head?

I didn't hit him sweetheart. I tripped. On the carpet and sort of fell into him. He just kind of kissed my forehead.

He kissed you? Eee-yew!

It was an accident, cupcake. A Liverpool kiss.

Like the kiss you give me, before I go to sleep?

A bit different to that.

He fell asleep after you kiss him too. Like Snow White after the apple.

Maybe a handsome prince will give him another kiss. To wake him up.

Mei thinks this is hilarious, all these men kissing each other. Princes don't kiss princes, she insists. Maybe a princess or a queen will kiss him and then he'll wake up.

I check my reflection as the lift climbs to Tsoi's office. A small contusion is evident. I can see where he kiss you Ba-ba, says Mei giggling.

The receptionist shows us to a conference room. Mr Tsoi will be with us soon. Mei passes the time by drawing a hieroglyphic of me head-kissing The Weed. I look across the harbour to The Pen. No red and blue flashing lights. Yet.

Eric arrives. Shakes my hand. Says hello to Mei, enthusiastically. And asks her what she's drawing. Ba-ba kissing his friend, she says. He raises a brow. I roll my eyes. And tell him it's a long, twisted tale.

Is there an Esther Wong in it? Thanks for that Jack. She really made the junior partner's day.

Didn't injure herself sliding down the barrister, did she?

He was disappointed to find out she's spoken for. When's your big day?

Knock it off.

She has a special place for you in her heart.

We've got *our* work cut out, my friend. What else can you tell me?

I don't know where to start.

What did she give you, Eric?

Goosebumps, for a start. And a lot of *sub rosa* about you and her, her sister and that guy they pulled *de profundis* from the harbour.

I know all that. What did she tell you not to tell me?

That's *ex officio*, lawyer-client privilege.

I'm your client. You're my lawyer. And this is where you pay for that privilege. Where was she the night Player got torpedoed?

She says she was with him.

Why is she alive and he's not? Did she do him in?

I don't think so. She's as *non compos mentis* as she is *corpus delicti*. Maybe she could kill you, by accident. Or with her biological arsenal. She was following him. Player had something that belonged to her sister. She wanted to get it back.

For her, or herself?

I didn't ask. It all sounded a little *ex post facto*. I think she wanted to see if he was having her sister too. She said she lost him, around North Point. So she went back to the hotel. In case he was looking for her. She thought he might be jealous. She's been seeing someone. A doctor.

Doctor who? I think to myself. Or should that be Doctor whom? Either way it's a change of pace and out of character for Esther. Unless it was a plastic surgeon or gynaecologist. Then I could see something in it for her.

I probe Tsoi for clarification. He presses his lips in a tight smile. *Corpore sano conundrum.*

She's no paragon of virtue.

Paradigm. It's a *paradigm* of virtue. A paragon is a large diamond. 100 carats. Perfect.

She's not one of those, either.

Exactly. And there the defence rests. She thinks you killed her boyfriend too. That's the kind of thing your love for her would inspire, apparently.

Jesus Christ.

Jesus Christ, repeats Mei.

Jack, I'm *ultra vires* a million ways on this.

So you should be. You're a lawyer. This is why you earn the big bucks.

And why I'm paying for the privilege.

What's your professional opinion?

In legal terms, we call it *fubar*.

Fubar! echoes Mei.

Ah, yes. Fubar. Now I remember. It's Latin for *snafu*.

Snafu! shouts Mei.

Ita vero certe, says Tsoi. Which means, until you or her or the police get me into a position where I have to discriminate, it stays that way.

Cogito ergo sum fubar. Got it. Speaking of fubar, I add matter-of-factly. You'll never guess what happened at The Peninsula this afternoon.

26. PAPER ROUTE

ANGEL IS BEHIND HER DESK. She should be home with Micki. They should be writing in each other's diary. Braiding hair. Painting nails. Playing dress-up. Talking about whom they're going to marry. How did it go? What happened? she enquires, before I can adopt a similar line of questioning.

Daddy gave the man a kiss, declares Mei, taking her turn to pre-empt me. I usher her into the office. She flicks on the TV. Presses play on the video machine and jumps into the beanbag.

Angel's eyes ask more questions. I tell her I'll explain later. Explain now, she demands. I know it's difficult for you to form relationships with women. But there's no need to switch teams. You kissed a guy?

I relate the altercation at The Pen. How The Weed tarnished my forehead with his face. And was on the business end of Liverpool Kiss, as it's known in the trade.

How did Madam Wu react to that?

I don't know. Where's Micki?

She never showed.

Where'd she go? She's supposed to be with you. At your apartment.

She's not.

How do you know she's not there now, waiting for you?

My mum would call me if she was.

Did you call her portable phone?

My mum doesn't have one.

I mean-

I know what you mean. Of course I called her. No answer.

Why didn't you page me?

I did.

I take the pager from my pocket. And apologize. Fuck, I think out loud.

Fuck, concurs Angel.

Fuck! repeats Mei, in the adjacent room.

So it's unanimous then, says Angel.

MEI AND I TAKE A CAB to Micki's place. The radio reports that someone slipped twenty minutes of porn into a mainland news broadcast. This amuses the driver no end. He makes a comment about it being footage of China screwing Hong Kong and Taiwan. Duran Duran chant *Notorious*. Bananarama sing *I Heard A Rumour*. By the time we arrive at the mansion on the hill I'm happy to put it all behind me.

MaryGrace politely informs me that Mam is not here.

I figured as much. Looking over her shoulder I can see the portable phone on the dining table. The rest of the place looks the same as it did last time I was here, minus the two people fornicating on every available surface.

I ask MaryGrace if she knows where Mam is. She doesn't. Mam was here at lunchtime. Had a shower and went out. Didn't say when she'd be back.

Did she have anything with her?

A newspaper, Sir. Mam had a newspaper.

She shows it to me. There's a few pages missing. MaryGrace apologizes, says she was peeling vegetables.

I realize, at this point, further questioning would be fruitless.

Peelings. Nothing more than peelings.

I sift through the paper as the cab winds its way down Stubbs Road. Three gunmen got away with two million dollars worth of watches from a shop in Causeway Bay. US Secretary Of State, George Shultz, thinks Hong Kong is a model of what human energy and talent can achieve when free of unnecessary restraint. I'm not sure if this is in response to the robbery in Causeway Bay or something else. I suspect it probably has more to do with the impending Handover. And China reaffirming its vow to take Taiwan by the turn of the century too.

There's more than a few pages missing from the front. And I make a mental note to check this edition against a complete one when I get back to the office.

27. ROOM SERVICE

MEI IS WEARY. And there's an increasingly familiar look of worry on Angel's face as we approach reception. Opening the agency door I can see why.

The Weed is propped against the wall. Nose bandaged to his face. A smudge of bruises beneath piss-hole eyes. Still, I'm kind of glad to see him, alive.

Stand by your bunks!

I told him this is not an outpatient clinic, says Angel as she collects Mei. But he insisted on waiting.

This is the man Ba-ba kiss at the hotel, Mei tells her. He fell down.

I bet he did, Angel replies before disappearing into the office.

The Weed tells me it's time to re-meet with Madam Wu.

Again? Tell her I'm flattered but I think we're moving too fast. I'm still recovering from our first date. So are you it seems, Venerable Grand Master And Scottish Knight Of Perfection. Of course you always did have a nose for trouble. Does it sting? I ask staring at his snout. It looks painful.

You will come. Or find yourself with an ass dent in the morning.

You watch too many movies.

Porno movies, suggests Angel. Are you the ass-denter, or the ass-dentee?

Silence evil spider woman! Or I will take you by the short rabbits and deliver you violently to the gynaecologist for thorough extermination! he spits. And then turns to me, lowering his volume. We have hated each other too long. Now I want to borrow the hatchet. Please, come. And leave your women here.

I raise my hand to assure Angel that everything is doobie-doob. It's all part of the plan, I tell her. According to The Code, seconds are traditionally bound to attempt reconciliation before a meeting takes place, or after sufficient shots have been fired. Lay on Knight Of The Sun, Prince Inept, I say with a sweep of my arm.

Angel is not convinced. I ask her to take Mei to the apartment. Close the office. I'll call later. Page me if our errant houseguest puts in an appearance.

THE WEED USHERS ME INTO HIS MERCEDES. Rising humidity creates some discomfort. This is augmented by manifest levels of disquiet, in anticipation of the journey. I've seen the way he traverses the motorways. *Going to the other side* is suddenly flush with alternative meaning. Instead of chauffeuring me across the harbour to Madam Wu's lair, I could end up being escorted to Abraham's bosom.

I buckle myself securely into the back seat. To The Peninsula, driver. And don't spare the horses.

He slips behind the wheel. Eyeballs the rear-view mirror. Please fasten your seatbelt. To prepare for crash.

I comment on his remarkable use of English. He takes this as a compliment. And a mirthless smile of the damned creases his lips as we pull away from the curb. I ask if he'd mind turning on the radio. He responds by pushing all the buttons in random order, eventually landing on a station devoted to loud static. And continues to fumble with the device. I realize this simple request is too much of a distraction for him, as he weaves across lanes. Much to the consternation of other drivers. I tell him not to worry. Remind him that in Hong Kong we drive on the other side of the road and suggest he concentrate on that. He returns both hands to the wheel, his eyes to the path ahead.

The static plays on.

At the tunnel our movement is reduced to a crawl. The Weed adjusts the rear-view mirror and studies me. I tell him I think the swelling is going down.

There is no need for you to be my biggest enema. We could enjoy a fruitful partnership getting in bed together.

I tell him it's not my intention to be anyone's enema. I have enough assholes in my life without getting into bed with another. He laughs inappropriately and almost rear-ends a truck. I express my desire to get to Kowloon without incurring an ass dent.

Do not worry. We will not have intercourse. Li Dan is an excellent driver.

Oh really. And where is this Li Dan when we need him?

I am Li Dan, he says proudly. Or you can call me names in English. I have taken Daniel before.

I bet you have, Danny boy. I bet you have, I reply absently, looking out the window in search of answers to this existential puzzle.

You look sad. Do you want to expose yourself to me?

Not really.

You are waiting to expose yourself to Madam Wu?

Yes. I will expose myself to her.

All your privates?

Pardon?

Your privates. Your secrets. About the urn. You will expose them to her? She is looking forward to this.

Yes. Of course. I will wave my privates in her direction.

And those of the Wong woman?

Ms Wong's privates are her business.

She has given you her business end. You know her privates?

You could say that, Li Dan. Although a gentleman should never kiss and tell.

You will tell Madam Wu, Mr So. It is in our personals that you pleasure her. She is very unsatisfied. If you do not pleasure her it is not attractive for you.

The thought of pleasuring her activates my gag reflex.

You should be worried. Last time I was not erect. I am not impotent this time, he says patting the pocket of his jacket, smiling confidently. Do not give me the reach-around in front of Madam Wu again.

I'll do what I can to pleasure her. And don't worry about reach-arounds.

She is not worried, Mr So. She knows I can harden myself. It is you who should worry about your backside if you rub me aggressively.

The car is on its final approach to The Peninsula. We park the conversation while The Weed attempts to traverse a number of lanes.

Welcome back, Mr So, says the valet, opening the door of the Mercedes.

The Weed sits on my wing as we cross the lobby. He taps me on the elbow, indicating the elevators, as if I might need some assistance with directions. Part of me feels obligated to warn him he's violated my personal space for the last time. The other part of me, however, believes he'll take much more from the experience when he discovers that all for himself.

You still look sad, he says as we enter the lift. Are you sure you don't want to expose yourself to me? He sounds concerned. Sincere. As if the journey across the harbour has washed away the opposing dynamics of our relationship.

The doors close.

I decide to correct his misunderstanding.

A seam or two gives.
Nothing they can't fix,
around the corner,
at Sam The Tailor.

The Weed looks like he's trying to work out where he is and how he got there. He'd probably have trouble recalling his name at the moment. He's taken a couple of big hits. I may have given him Parkinson's Disease.

I drape The Weed over my shoulder and assist him from the elevator. The British keep their end up and stand aside. Sorry folks, I say. A few too many Mai Tais. You know us Orientals. Can't hold our liquor. The distinguished gentleman nods in agreement, as if he knows this to be true from personal experience.

I probably should've bullied rather than belted Li Dan. Hauling his dead weight down the hallway, however, I'm amazed at the lightness of the malenky bastard. I'm equally surprised his aftershave hasn't revived him. There are less execrable smelling salts. Still, if I suffocate on the fumes, at least I'll save on embalming fluid. He regains his sea-legs as we approach The Marco Polo Suite. No longer needing my support, I thrust him ahead, recalling another aspect of The Code.

Any wound that agitates nerves, and makes hands shake, must end business for that day.

I take a little creative license with my interpretation. And end Li Dan's business for the day. Pushing him face-first into the oak. Then ringing the bell impatiently.

The door opens slowly.

The porcelain doll, previously seen soliciting business at the entrance of adjacent suite, is there to greet me.

Consort Qi has squeezed into a short, tight cheongsam. Black silk with double-happiness prints catching light in the right places. I'm not sure if it's the outfit or constipation that's responsible for the severity of her gaze. A lace glove caresses her willowy thigh. Another strokes the frame of the door.

The Weed falls in a heap at her stilettos.

She's not stooping to pick him up. Even if that outfit allowed her to bend, there's only one form of manual labour devotchkas like her lower themselves to perform. And they demand more than minimum wage for the effort.

Room service, I announce, stepping over Li Dan. Is Madam Bovary about?

28. HIGH TEA

MADAM WU OCCUPIES THE LARGE CHAIR at the centre of the room. She doesn't appear to have moved since this morning. Her disapproving expression is the same. Steam still drifts from the teapot. It's like I've slipped through a vortex in time.

Déjà Wu.

Even her final words are fresh in my ears. Maybe she thinks I've changed my mind about leaving in a huff and have returned moments later. Certainly her son is in much the same state as I left him. She gestures to the sofa without saying a word.

Keep an eye on your loin-fruit, I warn her. They can get into all sorts of trouble.

If they do not sin they will not know salvation, she replies. And thanks me for bringing him back, albeit in somewhat less than original condition.

I found him like this, I inform her. I think the big kids were picking on him in the playground. Children can be so unkind.

Indeed. This is Taiping, she says pointing The Mole at the amour-plated seductress who greeted me. My daughter, she adds.

Consort Qi is dead, I think. Long live Taiping. Wasn't the One Child Policy supposed to stop people like Madam Wu making these kinds of mistakes twice?

She sits beside me. I'm not sure how. The cheongsam wraps her form so tightly it would haemorrhage at the seams if she farted. Would that smell of Dior Poison and sultry afternoon sex too? She crosses her legs disinterestedly. Says she's pleased to meet me, in clipped English. Her flowing, sable tresses have been corralled into a bun at the back of her gulliver. Two stainless steel chopsticks hold it in place. I didn't realize you had a full house, I say to Wu. This must be your ace in the hole.

She is my daughter-in-law.

She married *him*? I ask, watching The Weed pick himself up and head to the bathroom, bowed in a cocktail of sorrow, shame and sickness.

I hadn't picked The Royal Arch Of Eunuch as the marrying kind. Least of all the kind to marry this breed of shikseh. I had him jumping broomsticks of a whole other genus. Surely they're as objectionable to each other as they are unendurable to any friends they have in common. Hera and Juno must have lost a bet to create such a pairing, or been off with Aphrodite that day.

The wolf shall dwell with the lamb, Wu says in their defence.

And the leopard shall lay down with the goat, I reply in a state of suspended disbelief, trying to work out whom all these animals are. And questioning where The Rat fits into the menagerie. She married him?

Taiping and Li Dan will be wedded, yes.

Will be wedded, I repeat. So she hasn't put her prospects for happiness completely behind her then. She's his fiancé?

If that is the term for one's intended.

One of them. I'm not sure what the biblical expression is. There are less formal ones. But modesty, manners and good breeding prevent me from mentioning them.

Thank you for your consideration.

Flaneusse.

Excuse me?

Flaneusse would be a polite idiom for fiancé, suitable for Taiping's position in the family. Check out Deuteronomy, First Epistle To The Thessalonians, and Book Of The Maccabees. They'll have a couple of fun ones. Leviticus is good for a giggle too.

Taiping permits herself a small, laugh-like noise. Madam Wu threatens her with The Mole and the stoic, android demeanour snaps back into place.

Flaneusse, repeats Wu.

Bless you. Yes, flaneusse. You should get your story straight about the relationship. Daughter, daughter-in-law, fiancé, flaneusse... it could create all sorts of confusion. Look at what happened in *Chinatown*. Daughter! Sister! Daughter! Sister! I say, bitch-slapping the air, mimicking Jack Nicholson and Faye Dunaway.

Rest assured, Mr So, our relationships are clearly defined and of no concern to others, she says in a tone which suggests that is the end of that.

Wu raises her teacup, encouraging me to do the same.

Mazel tov, I say and take a sip. It scolds my lips and the tip of my tongue. The taste is different from this morning's offering. I share this observation with the group. Both are a little taken aback by the admission.

Very good, compliments Wu. Perhaps your tastes are more refined than we give you credit for, Mr So. It is a different blend. Tie Guan Yin, or Iron Goddess in English.

In honour of Margaret Thatcher I presume. How *comme il faut* of you. Is it from Hunan or Yunan?

Fujian, she corrects, bringing the cup to her lips. She blows across the surface of the tea. You seem to have a small understanding of Chinese culture.

I was married to a small Chinese woman.

How much do you know of the urn's history?

As much as we discussed this morning. I was hoping for a more complete register of the crimes, follies and misfortunes surrounding it this time.

It's quite a story.

I'd better have another drink then, I say skulling the Iron Goddess.

Wu nods to her prospective daughter-in-law. Taiping stands and pours more tea. The way her tendons flex as she grips the heavy ceramic pot suggest there is hidden strength in those hands. This deuce is wild. It's not hard to imagine her ripping out your spine as she macerates you with her thighs.

Beside the teapot is an ornate wooden box. Taiping flips the lid and offers a cigarette from within. Her long, lithe fingers strike a match. I wait for the sulphur to burn off before drawing on the flame. And notice a few small marks on her translucent forearm. This *éminence grise* has been on the horse, riding the dragon to hell and back. All of a sudden The Flaneusse is not so desirable. Her Scoville rating falls to Jalapeño. A mere Peperocini.

She ignites a Davidoff. Extinguishes the flame, and her fuckability, with a pursing of rouge lips. Snuffs it with a sharp shot of breath. And returns to her place beside me. It's impossible to ignore her callipygian curves as she places a large glass ashtray on the table. Such a tragic waste of genetic toil as I have seen. All aces and spades.

A villain with a smiling cheek, a goodly apple rotten at the heart.

Madam Wu has been observing Taiping's movements, in a slightly more detached manner. She's waiting for this *nouveau* mating ritual to conclude.

My mother had a little Mongol in her. Which probably makes me related, to him. And to my mother, obviously.

I know all I care to know about your family, Mr So. Are you familiar with anything beyond the schoolbook history of Khan? Do you know what happened to him? And please refrain from making your *mordant* comments. They are tiresome and unnecessarily prolong our encounter.

I'm sorry. You're right. That's more-dant enough. My sense of humour is an acquired taste. Not everyone's cup of tea, you might say, in keeping with this evening's theme. I don't mean to be a party Pu-er. You're obviously more of an Iron Goddess woman. I'm guessing Taiping goes for the Silver Needle, or a Fur Peak blend. As for your boy, well, he probably fancies a Big Red Robe.

Thank you, Mr So. That is enough. Temujin was the oldest son of a tribal chief. A vassal of Ong Khan.

A vessel or a vassal?

A vassal. A subordinate. Might that be a term you're familiar with?

I'm familiar with it. I'm just surprised that you are. The vassal with the pestle has the pellet with the poison. The chalice from the palace has the brew that is true. Or was it the flagon with the dragon? RIP Danny Kaye.

Please do not interrupt again. My patience wears thin.

Mine rides up. I know how you feel. Although patience is really just a minor form of despair, disguised as a virtue. A fantastic disguise, in your case.

May I continue?

I'd be disappointed if you didn't.

When Temujin was born a large clot of blood was clasped in his right hand. His father saw this as a great portent to his son's destiny. And named him Genghis. After a Tartar chief he had captured in battle.

More tea, Tartar? I ask, blowing through that last comment, stabbing out my cigarette and raising the pot.

Both women ignore my comments, although Taiping sees some of the humour in them. Or in something. Whatever it is she's not telling. I pour another libation and wonder if it's habit-forming. Wu continues almost as if I'm not there. A big part of me feels like I'm not.

His father kept the clot.

In a pestle? The pestle with the plasma has the-

He sealed it in a small glass vial, she interrupts, tone escalating. Temujin wore it under his tunic every day.

Temu-jin... and tunic. Short glass with an extra squeeze of lemon please, I pun despite her warnings. I can't help myself. I'm making a conscious effort to stifle these thoughts. My lips, however, are decidedly loose. Maybe it's a side effect of the tea. Am I overdosing on Iron Goddess?

He wore it under his tunic every day. It was said to be the source of his power. Making him invincible. Protecting him. Until his death in 1227.

Maybe he forgot to put in on that day.

The cause of his death is unknown. Only that it was shortly after his subjugation of the Xi Xia and Jin Dynasties.

Coincidence? I think not.

He was buried in the shadow of Mount Burhan Haldun.

Madam Wu. Thanks for the history lesson and all but, at the risk of sounding disrespectful, what's your point?

My point, Mr So, is that the history of Temujin does not end there. His body was exhumed and cremated. Some say by those he humiliated in battle. Some say by his descendents. There are many who would have desired his spirit. To possess it for themselves. Many still do.

Necrophilia is alive and well. He lies in darkness but others see light in his ashes.

His ashes, and the blood of his mother, were placed in a white jade urn.

Butter in a lordly dish. The flagon with the dragon...

White jade. From the Qin Dynasty. Even with your limited knowledge of history, Mr So, you should be aware of the importance of this period.

Oh yes, The Mighty Qin. Bob Dylan wrote a song about it. Although he seemed to think they were Eskimos. Still, it was the sixties, a pretty confusing time for all.

The urn also contained the ashes of Qin Shi Huang, the emperor who unified China, says Wu. Her tone has risen to a shrill level.

The Mole throbs with anger. I'm not sure whether to keep pushing or stand off. It's a confusing time for me as well. I think I see where you're going with this, I offer as a kind of verbal cease-fire. One good *urn* deserves another, I add, changing my mind.

Kublai Kahn, Temujin's grandson, went to great lengths to secure this urn. With it in his possession he united China, again. He completed what his grandfather had set out to do. And created the Yuan Dynasty.

Yuan good urn deserves another.

Madam Wu raises her hand, palm out, signalling me to stop. So I do. Having gained my undivided attention, however, she issues a sharp slap to my face with a speed most would consider inconsistent with her age. It appears I have indeed underestimated the widow's might. I was cautioned about this. I turn to Taiping. Partly due to the force of the blow. Partly to see her reaction. Something that suggests I didn't just imagine it. Her malignant smile, and the sting on my cheek, confirms it was no hallucination.

This is your final warning, Wu rebukes me.

Or what?

The urn was buried with Kublai Kahn. And, soon after, the Yuan Dynasty collapsed. The Ming Dynasty that followed flourished for almost three hundred years. A vast army and navy were created to facilitate trade and communications. It made the country wealthy beyond comparison. It was a true *belle époque*, you might say.

If I was French, I might say that. If I were German, I'd probably say *gute zeit*. Or *hermosa época*, if I was Spanish.

Many attribute the advances to Ming's retrieval of the urn from Kahn's tomb.

No rest for the weary. No peace for the wicked.

It passed from generation to generation.

Wu pauses to refill my tea. Taiping lights another cigarette. So do I. We're developing quite a nice little collection of ash between us.

By the sixteenth century, Wu continues, China's success and influence was so great many had forgotten from what it was born. As is often the case, each generation sheds a little of its past. Rural culture and commerce became influenced by urban trends. Society embraced a bourgeoisie scholarly class. It became gentrified. A civilization unlike any other.

Let's hear it for civilization, leading contributor to the demise of culture and the human race, I toast. And infuse myself with more tea.

You're right, in a way.

Don't thank me. Thank Emerson.

Social class, commercial behaviour, philosophical factions and government institutions were affected. Art. Literature. The urn was lost. Consigned to history and a museum collection. At the same time the country's success opened the door to its demise. There was an influx of silver, replacing copper and paper banknotes. When the value of silver was diminished the whole economy was undermined.

I see what you did there. Silver. Under-*mined*. Nice.

The Little Ice Age compounded this damage.

Little Ice Age? There was another, smaller one? How did I miss that?

It is a colloquial term, Mr So. It refers to the natural disasters that beset the country at the time. Crop failures. Epidemics.

Pestilence, flies, frogs, grasshoppers, I add, completing her apocalyptic list. Rivers of blood. Fire. Hail. Death of the first-born. Weeping. Gnashing of teeth.

Not quite. People did, however, lose their faith. In authority. Which continued to grind the faces of the poor.

Keeping their noses to the grindstone.

This paved the way for Li Zicheng's rebellion. And the Qing Dynasty.

Qing Dynasty. Not to be confused with Qin Dynasty?

Qing was the last imperial dynasty of China. It was plagued with international interference, rebellions and apathy. The Empress Dowager Longyu had no choice but to abdicate on behalf of Emperor Pu Yi in 1912.

I saw that one. Great movie. Ten thousand years to The Emperor! I exclaim getting a little carried away. Wu frowns. I check myself and ask if she expects me to believe the Qing Dynasty was really forsaken for the want of an urn.

You can laugh, Mr So. It is, however, supported by history. Whether you believe it is irrelevant. Scepticism, as your Oscar Wilde said, is often the beginning of faith.

You do not need the wisdom of Solomon to see it has political currency.

By political you mean manipulating public affairs for private advantage? It sounds like the Ark of The Covenant. Did you see Raiders Of The Lost Ark? I ask, starting to feel like the titular hero and wishing I'd worn my brown Fedora. Come to think of it, didn't he recover the ashes of Nurhachi for Lao Che in Temple Of Doom?

I am not familiar with this legend, confesses Madam Wu.

Really? It's probably available on laser disc. You should rent it. If you're into this type of thing, and you obviously are, you'll love it.

The Qing Dynasty has also been called the Manchu Dynasty.

I can see how people get them confused. They both have a dynasty in them.

The Qing Dynasty, she states with a knowing smile, as if revealing the secrets of The Ark itself, has also been called Later Jin Dynasty.

I nod sagely as if I now understand how this ties everything together. I'm actually just too scared to make another Jin joke. I'm also dying to know how the story ends. How did her husband come to be in possession of the urn? He might have been old but I'm pretty sure he didn't put one through the concubines of the Imperial Court. I'm not getting any younger either. Maybe I should ask about it before we all expire. She could gloss over the bit about him tea-bagging the Empress Dowager. How did Mr Li come to be Sublime Prince Of The Royal Secret?

The fall of the Qing Dynasty-

You mean the Manchu Dynasty.

They are the same.

Which is the one with Joan Collins and Tracy Scoggins in it?

Mr So...

Sorry, I apologise. Do go on.

The Republic Of China was formed in 1912. And ruled by the Kuomintang. Sun Yat-sen and Song Jiaoren began the difficult task of unifying China.

I bet the urn would've come in handy.

They sent many in search of it. But their plans for the nation were interrupted. Renegade warlords. The rise of the Communist Party. Conflict with the Japanese.

These things always come in threes.

After the War Of Resistance with Japan differences between the Kuomintang and the Communist Party intensified.

Out of the fire. Into the frying pan.

The Kuomintang were defeated, of course. Heralding the rise of Communist China under Chairman Mao.

And we all know how that turned out. Yet another society condemned to live behind walls. Built to stop people getting out and besieged from within.

Mao was also obsessed with the urn.

He didn't strike me as a superstitious kind of guy.

With age comes wisdom.

No fool like an old fool.

The Chairman was a man of many contradictions. Like numerous Party leaders he publicly eschewed feudal superstitions and beliefs in favour of nationalism.

By eschew you mean attempted to wipe out. More hypocritical than contradictory, don't you think? Jingoism out the front. Credulity in the rear. Why not employ a little science? That's usually the best antidote for old hooey.

You do not have to be credulous to believe in the power of a symbol, Mr So. What it could represent to his people. And to his administration. He pursued it relentlessly in the interests of patriotism and nationalism.

Good old nationalism. Culture of the uncultivated. Last refuge of the scoundrel.

When Chiang Kai-shek fled to Taiwan, with the urn, the Chairman was furious. To the end Mao believed it crucial to a truly unified, prosperous China.

Some people don't give up their convictions until they see the Yellow River and have no place left to retreat to, I say employing a little axiom-fu. Throwing some Mao-ish pearls of wisdom back at her.

All did not share his beliefs. It was a source of dissent amongst the old guard of The Long March and emerging Party leaders.

This is thrilling stuff and yet I'm having trouble concentrating. Could be the rigours of my nefarious activities catching up with me, or the diuretic qualities of the tea. I'm not the only one who's noticed it either. Wu asks if I am okay.

Yes. History was never my strength. But don't let that stop you.

Deng Xiaoping was a counter revolutionary. His open-door views affronted The Gang Of Four. A faction that included Mao's wife, Jian Qing.

May she rest in pieces, I say. The old battle-axe had fallen to cancer this year.

This group was responsible for Deng's banishment, Wu continues. With Mao's health in decline they were planning to seize control of the country. Removing Deng was vital to achieving this. Unknown to many, however, they were also in talks with the Kuomintang. To have the urn returned to the motherland. In exchange, Taiwan was to retain its independence - publicly - and profit from lucrative economic ties. Some say Mao's final wish was for his ashes to join those of Temujin and Qin Shi Huang. The triple pillars of China joined as one. He'd spent so many of his final years pursuing ways to extend his life he was sure this would ensure his immorality.

I giggle at her Freudian slip.

It is also possible Jian Qing saw a way to honour her husband and her personal goals. With this symbol in-hand she believed The Gang Of Four would have the will of the people and, more importantly, the support of the army. They would be free to continue with the Cultural Revolution, shaping the country in their image. There is also evidence to suggest they would default on their agreement with Taiwan and take the country by force. They came close to succeeding. When Mao died, however, Premier Hua was named Chairman of the Communist Party. And before Jian Qing could take possession of the urn Hua had won the support of the military. A *coup d'etat*, as I believe you call it in English, was executed within a month. Deng was retuned to power.

The Cultural Revolution was over. And the modern history of China began.

Where does your husband figure in the *mise en scène,* as I believe you call it in Chinese, of this Shakespearean drama?

Li Longji was a collector of antiques, she says in a tone that suggests she wants to distance herself from her spouse. On trips to Taiwan he would arrange for inspections of the treasures that reside beneath the national museum. It is fair to say the Kuomintang escaped with more than their lives. Thousands of years of Chinese culture remain there, hidden from public view. Some are rotated through the galleries. Few, however, would even be aware of their existence. Li came over the urn by accident.

Eww. I know that feeling. I came over the cushions by accident once. But who among us isn't guilty of something like that? I turn to Taiping. What have you come over by accident?

She exhales a plume of smoke in my direction. Wu continues her story.

The attendant charged with escorting Li through the collection was ignorant of the urn's pedigree. And, for a modest sum, it was liberated. It took pride of place in his Shanghai office. Business flourished. He attributed much of his good fortune to it. Given its precious nature few would have been told its true history. His secretary, maybe. And perhaps one or two of his… mistresses. She bristles with this last word, as if merely thinking it causes bile to flood her mouth. Old men often cast their pearls before swine, she says as if offering the wisdom of Buddha. They believe young women are impressed by such stories.

Not just women. I'm aroused. And I think your young Princess Of The Libanus here is a little moist too, I remark, attempting to solicit a response from mummies little robot.

Taiping remains uninterested. Crosses her legs away from me, exposing a healthier portion of thigh. This seems to displease Wu, if I correctly read the narrowing of her eyes and brief, mole-ward surge of blood. I'm sure its diameter just increased. I ask it why she thinks Micki liberated the urn from her husband.

I was aware of all my husband's affairs, Mr So. Every woman is. Men cannot live on bread alone, particularly in their advancing years. I knew of his preference for fleshpots, his dealings with Ms Wong, the strengths and weaknesses of their relationship. He often referred to her as his little warrior. *Mulan* was a favoured term of endearment. I believe he may have innocently given the urn to her as a gift, as your client suggests.

Then it is hers to do with as she wishes.

Madam Wu spits her reply. This is not a trinket to buy the affections of some-

The venom renders her incapable of completing her thoughts.

Flaneusse?

Some *jezebel*, Mr So. The woman is not worthy to fix the latchet on my shoe. Perhaps I was generous in suggesting Ms Tse had acquired it by legitimate means.

Ms Wong, I correct her.

Ms Wong had been in his office many times.

According to you she had been had in his office many times, I counter, warming to the subject. I take another swill of Iron Goddess.

Either way, and by whatever means, she learned of the urn's history.

Orally, perhaps?

She saw financial gain in possessing it. I don't need to remind you of what depths a woman will sink to attain something they desire.

I'm getting a Master's degree in Conniving Depths.

She acquired it illegitimately.

Not if it was a legitimate gift, a *bona fide* gratuity or an honest mistake.

I can prove otherwise. Again, Mr So, I remind you of the urn's significance. Not just its value in terms of history, but its value to the future. The reunification of China is at hand. It is a powerful, priceless symbol. Not a trophy for a mistress.

Madam Wu, perhaps it is time for me to enlighten you and the rest of your Grand Elected Knights Of The Kadosh, I say, sitting forward. Had you simply asked for it to be returned, Ms Wong might've handed it over. Had Player not taken it from her, she might've gone so far as to sell it back to you. Now, however, she is riled, frightened and confused. You don't back women like that into a corner. It starts a war of attrition. A conflict even your revered Temujin would have found daunting. She can be like the flail of God. Sometimes you catch yourself wondering what sins you have committed for Him to have sent a punishment like that upon you. Pleasure and joy for her lies in conquering the enemy. Taking what they have from them. And hearing the lamentations of their families. You know the feeling.

My interest lies with the urn. That is all. I sent my most trusted staff to retrieve it.

That was your first mistake. You should've erred in favour of competency rather than familiarity. And the *faute de mieux* of Simon The Zealot here.

I had to ensure they could be trusted. Not only with the task but with the knowledge of what they were retrieving. You don't have to be as unscrupulous as Ms Wong to be tempted by the financial gains the urn represents. All would seek to optimise their earnings when armed with the truth. I had to limit the possibility of it coming to harm. Should it be damaged in any way the loss would be incalculable.

Let me help you with the math, Grand Chevalier Of The Brazen Serpent. One dead guy plus one comatose guy equals life in prison.

Perhaps they over-reacted or misinterpreted my instructions. It's unlikely they would admit, or anyone could prove, they were acting in anything but self-defence. Particularly when dealing with people of such immoral character.

Self-interest is not the same as self-defence. And judges know the difference. They see quite a lot of envy and hate carried out under the guise of virtue and moral indignation.

Your history, and presence here, tells me you wish to avoid unnecessary complications too. Does Ms Wong have it?

I don't reply. I've lost my train of thought. And found a cigarette. I light it. Maybe I'll find it there. It's where all my headlines used to hide.

You don't know. And again you waste my time, Mr So. She stands. The sudden movement startles me. She's taller than I remember. The mole towers above me like The Grand Inquisitor Commander.

Taiping rises. And suddenly I feel very small and insignificant. Outnumbered. Outgunned.

Wu tells me she is a patient woman but even Job would grow tired of my hollow words and games.

I respond to her biblical references with something more contemporary, from *The New Testament. The Book Of Cary Grant* and *Gospel According To Alexander Haig.*

Madam Wu, I say apologetically. In the world of advertising, there are no lies. Only expedient exaggeration, terminological inexactitude and tactical misrepresentations. 85 percent confusion, 15 percent commission. Sit down, please. I am not one to clipe. I can get the urn.

Wu concedes to my request. The Royal Hatchet And Croix Of Heredom remains on standby. Your time is running out, Mr So. When can I have it?

By the end of the weekend. Think you will have half a million by then?

I believe the offer was two hundred thousand.

And I believe…

My words trail off. I'm finding it difficult to articulate my thoughts. I blink self-consciously, twice. And try to focus. On something. Anything. I rub my weary eyes. Madam Wu smiles. I squeeze my lids together and try to shake the haze from my head. Wu's tea remains untouched, on the table beside her. I rise uneasily and swivel to face Taiping. She stands, legs slightly akimbo, hands behind her back. A malevolent grin slices across her face.

Wu clears her throat. The Mole draws a satisfied breath and cackles with quiet glee. We have reached an impasse, it says.

I stumble like a newborn foal. Outside, the neon on the harbour smears across the window.

THIS COULD'VE
BEEN SO MUCH EASIER,
HALF-CASTE BASTARD.

She swings a billiard-table leg back
on its aging hinge, as if it were
a baffing spoon. And pitches my
testicles into my throat.

Like a private exhibition of pointillism,
the lights above become tiny dots.

And take rapid flight across my
consciousness, into the black.

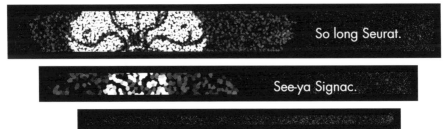

So long Seurat.

See-ya Signac.

29. CHECKING OUT

THE ROOM IS DARK. My mind is hangover-grizzly. And about to give birth to a noble brain spasm. I feel like I did after Ling died. When I slipped into the space between. Maybe I'm having a flashback.

Is there carpet in purgatory?

I collect myself, slowly. Take inventory. My tongue is made of cotton wool. Eyes are dry. Soft light leaks from behind curtains. I draw them back.

Central beckons across the harbour. The iridescent noise of the neon screams and shouts. I'm probably still in The Pen. Although, looking around, the room appears smaller than the suite I was poisoned in.

The game has been adjourned. *J'adoube*. How had I allowed myself to become *en prise*? How long had I been *en passant*? A clock by the bed says ten-thirty. Angel will be wigging out. Where's my pager?

I stumble around like a thief in an empty house. Each step reminds me of the divot Wu took out of my fairway. *Ground Under Repair*. It'll be a while before I'm able to play a round again. I enter the bathroom. Drink my body weight in water from the faucet. I'd use the glass by the sink, except it might be designed to explode when it reaches my mouth. I soak my dial and try to rinse away the paranoia.

Good news. I need a piss. The international sign that vital organs are functioning. Must be the diuretic effects of all that tea. Hard to believe my dehydrated body has a drop to spare. According to Mao's doctor anything less than 300ml was cause for concern. Relief is sweetened with the knowledge that my micturition passes muster. Even if it does feel like someone's rubbed Tiger Balm on my bilge. That Iron Goddess really had a kick to it.

A scorched spoon rests on the cistern. Someone's been cooking up a storm. There's a syringe in the wastebasket too. With a couple of soiled tampons for company. On the vanity basin sits half a tube of Little Black Sister, Guangzhou's answer to Darkie toothpaste. Make-up. Perfume. Dior. Poison.

Taiping.

I give the bedroom the once-over. She travels light. Heavy on the underwear. I've seen lingerie shops with less options. Half a dozen variations of her cheongsam fetish hang in the wardrobe. I could bust open the room-safe except all I'd find is her stash. They may have left me unattended but they wouldn't leave me any souvenirs. Li Dan might be a clusterfuck but the women in his family struck me as a little more disciplined, judging by the way they struck me.

They didn't want me out of the picture, just out of the way. Like a buried piece or a bad bishop, *sans voir*. Wu may be a bad mother and Taiping a bad motherfucker, but they wouldn't deprive my daughter her father.

Entering the hallway, I sidle up to The Marco Polo Suite. No light bleeds under the door. And there's no sound from within. They must be taking in the sights. Maybe they took my advice and went to Lamma Island.

I aim for the Star Ferry. A lungful of sea air might clear the soup in my mind. The late evening heat sucks me into the sidewalk before I advance one hundred meters. This city can be a real bitch when it wants to be.

I hail a cab and ask the driver to crank up the air-con. He bemoans Black Thursday and the price of petrol. A late bulletin mentions the execution of two Hongky heroin traffickers in Kunming. Axel Rose launches into *Paradise City*.

I think about Taiping's appetite for destruction. Welcome to the jungle, rocket queen. Anything goes.

30. CHECKING IN

POR-POR IS GLUED TO THE TELEVISION. She doesn't even look at me. Does this means she's angry, or is *Firewalker* one of the better films in the Chuck Norris oeuvre? Angel lies on the other end of the sofa, cradling Mei protectively. Both seem to be asleep. Although Angel may be faking it. And projecting a little mute indignation.

Bing exits the kitchen and threatens me with the wok. Do I want any dinner?

I decline with an appreciative smile, hoping to conceal just how crap I feel. And approach the couch.

I unhook Mei from Angel's arm. Carry her down to her room. She valiantly attempts to open her eyes. Morpheus, however, has her in his grip. I kiss her forehead. Lower her to bed and pull up the blanket.

Here's lookin' at you, kid.

Angel is perched on the edge of the sofa, looking straight at me. She pushes sleep from her face, washing her palms across her eyes. You're late, she admonishes, wagging her index finger like an angry wife.

Sorry. Tough day at the office.

How was The Pen?

Horrorshow.

High tea?

And then some. Even had my cucumber sandwiched.

Beats jerkin' your gherkin. You look like shit.

Thanks.

What happened?

Just another Friday night in the world's greatest city. One too many gin fizzes from Madam Gruzinski's private collection, I say. And extend my hand. Come on, let's get you into a cab. You could've gone home.

And miss Firewalker? Not likely. How was the party?

She goes by the name of Taiping. Not quite as effeminate as Junior but definitely plucked from the same tree. There are some strange fruits in that family, I can tell you. She's a more compelling mix of form and function. Her rack is well in tune with her pinion. She stamped this QC tag on my bumper. And then her old lady put a dent in my tadpole tanks.

I'll take you to The Adventist, Angel insists as we leave the building. You should get a doctor to take a look.

I've looked. They're still there. I wasn't planning on using them this week anyway. You can rub something on them. If you promise to be gentle.

I mean the rest of you, numbnuts.

The rest of me has suffered worse hangovers.

A taxi pulls up. She asks the driver to wait a couple of minutes. She wants to know what I found out.

Everything you need to know about Chinese history but are afraid to ask. Oh. And Wu could take all of England's penalties at the next World Cup.

Micki?

She could manage the squad I guess.

Don't make me hurt you, Angel says balling her fist and swinging it in the general direction of my ruptured repositories.

No idea. You got anything?

Oldham wants to see you.

Uh-huh.

Jack?

Angel?

Stop fucking around Jack. There's been a murder. Benny's been half-beaten to death. You've been doped, assaulted and kidnapped. How is this all going to end?

I don't know. In tears? Micki's got a line on some febrile property. Ditto her sister. I'm fast developing an opinion that it's too hot for either of them to handle. The Imperial Court figured they'd get a fairer shake at it if I wasn't running interference for a while. So they put me up in a suite at The Pen.

Nirawattapattanasserarat?

Co-opting, coercing and double-crossing any or all of the above.

For what?

Fortune and glory, kid. Fortune and glory.

Be specific, Dr Jones, she says picking up on my *Temple Of Doom* reference. Or I'll sap your cobbler's awls myself.

I'll give you a hint. It's not my Sankara Stones.

The ashes of a Ming Dynasty emperor?

Close enough. The ashes of Genghis Kahn, or Temujin, as he's known at the club. And a certain Qin Dynasty emperor who may or may not have unified China. He liked all outdoor sport and meeting people.

Qin Shi Huang?

So you were paying attention in history class.

The ashes of Genghis Kahn and Qin Shi Huang, in the same urn?

Together at last, if you can believe it. And it doesn't matter if you can't. They do. And they don't balk when it comes to conversion. So don't open the door to strangers.

I kiss her cheek and tell her no need to rush to work in the morning.

Try telling that to Carpet World, she says. They want an ad by noon.

You on top of it?

These days, Jack, that's all I'm getting on top of. I could fuck a doorknob, she says slipping into the taxi. And making it impossible for me to even look at a doorknob the same way again.

31. VACANCY

SATURDAY MORNING SLAPS ME around the head. I wake in my own bed. First time for a long time. Mei is staring at me. She wants to know why I'm not sleeping in her room. I tell her I was up late watching TV. And didn't want to wake her with my snoring again. She says she doesn't mind. It's not that loud. I steer her toward breakfast and let her know that, when she's finished, we'll be going on another adventure.

I love ventures, she says. I want a big venture.

We brush our teeth, twice. Pack her bag. And visit the *dai pai dong* on the corner. Mei has macaroni, with a rubber sausage and fried egg. Thick toast drowned in condensed milk for me. Washed down with *yin-yeung*, a blend of tea and coffee in the same cup. It's an odd combination but it somehow works. Given the adjuncts my body has endured lately, a straight cup of tea would probably kill me.

Let's roll, doodle-pop.

MIDIAN IS WORKING THE DAY SHIFT. What gives? he asks.

My balls. Seen my boyfriend about?

Not for a night or two. I've been dog-watch to dawn mostly.

Anyone else work here?

Mike engages the concierge and learns The Rat's room has been empty since yesterday afternoon. He made a brief fly-by and picked up something from a deposit box. Went upstairs for a change of clothes. And left immediately after. Maybe he's soiling someone else's sheets, I say. Would it be okay if Mei and I played housekeeping for a while?

You going to tell me what the rumpus is?

I already have. It's two parts of sod-all. And you can have the rest of the dirty details on the way up, if that's what yanks your chain.

He walks us to the elevators. Has a discreet word with the girl who did me the favour the other night. She'll page us if Miss Thailand returns before we're done.

That's very decent of her, Mike. What will you have to do in return?

Something indecent, between shifts.

She the only member of staff getting a security clearance from you?

You should be telling me the nature of your business, Jack. Not digging into mine. What do you care about my rigorous screening process?

Maybe you should stay down here and spend some quality time with her. Keep an eye on the door. In case she's not as sharp as her looks. Occupy Nirawattapattanasserarat if he fronts before we're back.

Mike hands over the key. He'll page me if I need to vacate the room in a hurry. I tell him I've lost my pager. He should just call the room. Let it ring once and hang up. This'll cost you, he says.

It already has.

Then maybe your fortune's about to turn the corner and things are looking up, he quips as the lift doors close.

Maybe. We make it all the way to room 17-11 without assaulting anyone.

DO NOT DISTURB.

The sign might have kept housekeeping away but it's no deterrent for Mei. She hasn't learned to read. Surprise! she shouts, barging in as soon as I unlock the door. Shhh, I beseech her. Or you might spoil the surprise.

She points to the other end of the room. What's in that box over there?

Atop the coffee table sits a cardboard carton. A foot-and-a-half long, one-foot wide and the same deep. It has erupted. Spewed crushed newspaper onto the floor. Soiled the brochure-perfect appearance of the suite.

Mei runs to inspect it. There might be a severed gulliver or beating heart inside. I sweep her up and place her on the sofa by the window. The view isn't bad but the box still commands all her attention. I flip the flaps.

Empty.

I unfurl a piece of balled newspaper. I'm no authority on Chinese dailies but I recognize this one. *Wen Hui Bao*. The mouthpiece of New China. Keeping us loyal comrades informed of developments on the other side of the fence. It was media of choice for The Gang Of Four too. They took a double-page spread to celebrate the start of the Cultural Revolution. I'm sure Wu knows all about it. I must ask her next time. This sheet dates back a couple of weeks.

Over against the wall there's broken glass. Thick, crystal shards strewn on the floor. A gouge in the plaster five feet above. Someone didn't get what they wanted for Christmas. I examine the expensive shrapnel. Baccarat? Waterford? Swarovski? Is that bufar, Ba-ba? asks Mei, from the sofa.

Fubar, sugarpop. Yes it is. Don't play with it.

I head to the boudoir. An empty Louis Vuitton suitcase is open on the bed. The wardrobe has four pressed white shirts. Two Armani suits. Midnight blue and grey. Damp, bloodstained towels lie on the bathroom floor. The basin is bedecked with toiletries. Moisturizer. Eye gel. Lip balm. Preparation H. A bottle of Iquitos by Alan Delon. I give it a squirt. The Rat and The Weed have the same taste in lighter fluid. Did they get a volume discount?

Puh-yew! You so stinky, Ba-ba.

I pour over the writing desk. Davidoff and Marlboro butts clog the ashtray. Two have rouge lipstick smeared across them. A notepad offers some mindless doodling. And two words. *Bengal Cat*. A page from the *South China Morning Post* is in the waste basket.

We're out of here, pooter-scooter, I inform my harshest critic.

Let's roll, stinky, she replies.

MEI RETURNS THE KEY TO MIDIAN. I ask if he was on deck last night.

All night. And the night before.

All night? You didn't take a break? Put your feet up, between shifts?

Well, yeah. Around six bells on the middle watch. I had to attend to a small matter on the fifteenth floor. Half an hour or so. Why?

You weren't the only one pulling a swifty. And getting your chain yanked. Our mystery guest had a couple of mystery guests. I don't suppose you could look into that. And some recent copies of the South China Morning Post.

He delegates the task to the innocently titled Cherry Chan. The way she smiles intimates Midian will soon be making a deposit in the favour bank. Mei reminds me how hungry she is. I pull a packet of Garden Pop Pan biscuits from the backpack and sit her on a couch. We watch Mike intercept Cherry Chan, and depart with what appears to be a promise of reward for effort. He returns with the papers. Anything else? Something's come up.

Keep it in your pants for just a second, I suggest, flipping the pages. There's an article about the dispute over the Waglan Islands. Lu Ping and the drafting of the Basic Law. And a column reporting that, due to its size, Bengal 1 had to find a new mooring. It's now sits off North Point, sandwiched between Canis Minor and Canis Major, two other nautical jewels in Hong Kong's crown. I hand the paper back to Midian. He wants to know if I got what I was after. More than I bargained for, I tell him. But no less than I deserve. Kobayashi.

Gesundheit.

Bengal 1, I clarify, unamused.

I know who Kobayashi is. He was in the teppanyaki bar the other night. Cleaned out the caviar. Drank the Krug dry. With Liu Pang, and Darius Man's new wife. Koko. You ought to see the keel on her. Talk about a couple of ships that go bump in the night.

I thank him. Tell him to take the rest of the morning off. Go see what floats Cherry's boat and ring a few bells for me while he's there.

Mei and I stop by the phones. Dial Oldham's portable. He picks it up on the eighth ring. I can hear him straining under the weight. Meet me at the Luk Yu Teahouse on Stanley Street, I tell him. Four-thirty. Mei gives a look that suggests, as a precautionary measure, I should call Eric Tsoi too. I'm not sure what she's anticipating, but it's probably not a bad idea.

The receptionist at Callett, Crambazzle, Dratchell & Feaque takes a while to locate him. This reminds me how much I hate telephones. Sorry, Eric, I say sarcastically when finally connected. Did I catch you in the middle of someone?

We have more than one client on our books. You might be *primus inter pares* but we don't all sit around waiting for you to ring.

I'm going to see Oldham this afternoon.

Turning yourself in?

No. I'm turning you in, Gordon Gecko. I got a call from one of your mistresses. She said you were inside 'er, trading. Anything new from Esther The Molester?

Nulla fides, nulla spes.

Okay. Do me a favour, *pro patria*. Call the agency at five-thirty. Find out who's *medias res*. We'll work it out from there.

Pax vobiscum.

I look at Mei. It hasn't been a very exciting day. Hopefully it'll stay that way. Still, I think I can put a smile on her face before the sun goes down.

Hey sweetheart, you want to see the boats?

32. ON THE WATERFRONT

I HAVE AN ON-OFF RELATIONSHIP with The Royal Hong Kong Yacht Club. Much of the early eighties was spent adrift on the South China Sea, getting off with all manner of flotsam and jetsam. Movie stars and rock gods, pumping the bilge of life, with a ship-shapely crew of perky pageanteers standing by their bunks. Ready, willing and waiting to be scuttled. Saluting whatever we ran up our flagpoles. Armed with Bollinger bubbles and Bolivian blow for ballast.

These days I'm only on deck if a client wants to meet there. Or Mei fancies a swim in the pool. I'm not a paid-up member. The staff know me well enough to turn a blind eye. And I've done sufficient favours for club officials to earn a few of my own.

We skirt the building and walk to the pens.

Amongst the billionaire berths and the millionaire moorings, the hidden treasure of the club trawls. Toiling from sunrise to sunset. Tendering the needs of the nautical, aboard dilapidated diesel sampans.

The Boat Aunty.

Skin as dark, worn and weathered as seasoned leather. Knotted hands, strong as the lines they furl. Few know as much about the tides of activity on the harbour. These crusty crones are the osteoporotic keel of the establishment. None are wiser when it comes to the ebb and flow of club members, or the undercurrents of their lives. You can learn a lot about someone when charged with loading supplies, cleaning quarters and hauling waste. Coleridge summed them up pretty well.

For all they knew, when the breeze blew and foam flew, when in reel and rout the death fires danced about, when at night the water like witch's oil burnt green and blue and white, they spoke only occasionally, to break the silence of the sea.

Which one is ours? asks Mei, searching the flotilla before us.

I whistle and wave across the marina's stagnant cesspool of oil-laced water, seeking the ancient mariner's attention.

I'm not required to know the answers to these questions. Or respond to them. All she's asking me to do is listen. Before she can concede to the request, she must give half a dozen reasons not to. It's the traditional type of preamble one must endure before getting to the true sport of the matter.

Price.

I tell her I'll buy a tank of fuel. She says it's a waste of fuel, her time and my money. There is nothing to see here, she declares. Only the follies of foolish men, or something like that. It loses a bit in translation. The sampan nudges the pier. Get in, she puffs with a dismissive grunt. And stuns Mei with a toothless grin. We climb aboard. Seat ourself on the wooden bench at the bow. And the leaky bucket retreats from the jetty. I ask if there's been much activity around the club.

Not so much. A lot of boats for sale now. Not a lot of parties.

What about Bengal 1?

They have too much money. Can't lose it all. Very busy. Always busy.

They load supplies here?

Load people here. Food at Wan Chai. Other things from North Point.

Is that normal?

What is normal for such people? They always do things that make no sense. Maybe dropping guests who don't want to be seen, or picking up some who shouldn't be known. Sometimes very late. Old Fung down there get angry. They interrupt his mahjong many times.

What happened?

I don't know about these things. Go talk to Ah-Fung. You see enough now, or you want to waste more of my fuel?

Without waiting for my answer she turns the boat to the landing.

I will get no more from her, save for a silent nod as I peel off a C-note for her fuel fund. Enough to support her for a month or two. Mei waves as the boat wobbles into the afternoon.

A thin smile creases Ah-Cheh's face. Is she looking back on her own life, or at the future of Mei's? Keep her away from these people, she calls out. They do not care for children. Or did she say they do not take care of their own children? The sputtering of the motor combined with her low Hakka intonation renders the words inaudible.

IT'S ALWAYS DARK beneath the expressway. This afternoon, with the sun hidden behind a sheet of grey, I can barely see our shadows. There's still police tape and Benny-stains on the pavement. Who was he here with?

Mei wants to know what happened. I tell her someone gutted a fish. Eww, she says, tugging at the blue and white tape. I ask her to leave it alone. And we cut through a small lane behind the wet market, to the harbour.

It takes a couple of minutes to find Ah-Fung amongst the madness of trucks, forklifts, laden pallets, cane baskets and labour intensity. I get the feeling his cohorts are wary of giving him up to a bastard stranger and his infant daughter. Persistence and my mastery of the vernacular pay off. We are eventually granted an audience.

Ah-Fung is a more loquacious and louder than his seafaring sister at the yacht club. Latrating responses when his attention is sought. He's one of those old men that look like an old woman who look like an old man. Tanned hide and barnacled bones. I let Mei work her charm on this sea dog for a moment then take an indirect approach to my enquiries. You didn't have much luck with the mahjong last night, I remind him.

Never lucky in mahjong. Or in life! Not since my third wife! he shouts. Maybe he was hoping she'd hear him. Everyone within six leagues thought it was hysterical. Which night are you talking about? he asks, going easier on the decibels.

I mention a late arrival from Kobayashi's yacht. A delivery? May have been accompanied by a couple of women and a perfumed man? I suggest his fortunes might change if he can remember.

He laughs derisively. A man who takes money for information will pay later!

Such affairs should not be conducted in the presence of little sisters, he adds. And extends his hand toward Mei. She is too scared to recoil. And yet, while the back of his hand is permanently stained with the grease and scars of a thousand years, his palms are worn smooth. They're probably cleaner than mine. He brushes Mei's cheek with a tenderness that belies his demeanour. No place for young hearts, he says quietly. It is all changing, he continues, raising his eyes to mine. They reclaim the land. The old woman hands Hong Kong to new emperors. Ill winds blow through the city. Fortunes are lost on boards of all sizes. A map. Stock market. Mahjong. Ha! I have been losing all my life but I am still here. Your brother from Macao is not here any more. Your friend was here. Left part of himself here. How is the rest of him I wonder?

Who was here?

Such affairs should not be conducted in the presence of little sisters, he repeats, ignoring my question. The harbour is no place for them. Bad luck they bring.

Women are unreliable on the shifting shoreline of mutual advantage. Your friend learned this. He is not the first to falter in these unstable sands.

Who killed him?

His confidence and ignorance killed him. For what? Ha! For what?

I don't know. I give up. For what?

Not my business to inspect cargo. Not yours. I am busy. Can't you see? You should also be busy. With other things. Not these things. Stupid. Like all dealings with women and men who smell like women. No good can come of it. I should have listened to my second wife. Go to die, she said. I should have listened. I would not have married number three. Ha! You should listen. One woman in your life is enough. Take this one, he says waving at Mei. This one is enough for you. No more do you need.

He's right, of course. I should listen to him. But I won't. So we both beat on, boats against the current, borne back ceaselessly into the past.

33 . SOUP & NOODLES

OLDHAM SITS UNCOMFORTABLY in a booth at Luk Yu Teahouse. The tables are twice his age and half his size, built to oriental specs. Don't get up, I say, knowing that even if he could he wouldn't. It probably took five minutes to wedge himself in there.

I sit Mei on a stool at a neighbouring, small table. Take a colouring book and some crayons from the backpack for her amusement.

A waiter, who decided against retirement just before the Boxer Rebellion, shuffles over. I order *char siu bau* and Yakult for Mei. A bowl of wantons and noodles for myself. Then slide into the booth, opposite Oldham. Back to the wall, a leg up on the bench for comfort. Neither of us are the type to play footsie under the narrow table.

The detective pours the tea. I tap my index finger on the table in the traditional manner, acknowledging his courtesy. Hopefully this will go a little better than my last tea ceremony. A flashback shivers up my spine as I bring the chipped china to my lips. I'm relieved to discover it's a run-of-the-mill Jasmine. And happy the cup didn't detonate in my face.

Oldham must have detected the paranoia in my actions. He asks if there's something wrong. I tell him it's kind of hard to tell these days. Wrong has a way of sneaking up on me. Chau wants to apologize, he says, unwilling to probe the tenor of my divulgence.

So he should. That clown suit of his was a crime.

The other Chau. You remember. The one who sucker-punched you.

Is that the official police report?

As close as I'll get to filing one. What can I say? He's a good cop, just a little overzealous in the execution of his duties. You know how it is.

Sure, I concede. It's a common disorder that afflicts the inexperienced. I remember the first time I got shot out of a canon. Took me weeks to come down. William The Conqueror had the same problem with Berdic. Henry The Eighth with Merry Andrew.

Oldham sighs. You had some information you wanted to pass on?

The waiter returns with a bowl of steaming wantons. He slides it across the table. It stops, with precision accuracy, in front of me. No less than I'd expect. He's had years to practice this disinterested approach to service.

I add a spoonful of chili to the concoction and let it sit for a while. For flavour enhancement. And for bio-health issues. You never know when you're going to discover a new, exciting strain of botulism. And the condiments here could sterilize a pig.

You should've told me you were going down to North Point, Jack. I could've met you there.

It's lovely at this time of year, don't you think?

What did you find out?

I grab a pair of chopsticks and try to capture a wanton, suddenly aware of how hungry I am. Still making me for a murderer, Detective?

Can't make chicken soup out of chicken shit. We think it was your Thai girlfriend, Nirawattapieceofwork. Gun in his room was a match for the giblet we dug out of Player. Found his fingerprints on it as well.

Case closed, I say. And spear another wanton.

We got other prints too.

Don't tell me. Mine?

A woman's. Unidentified.

How do you know the prints are female?

They've got wider hips, bigger tits and change their mind every five minutes. We found a hair in the trigger too.

Was it short and curly?

It was black.

Well that narrows it down a bit.

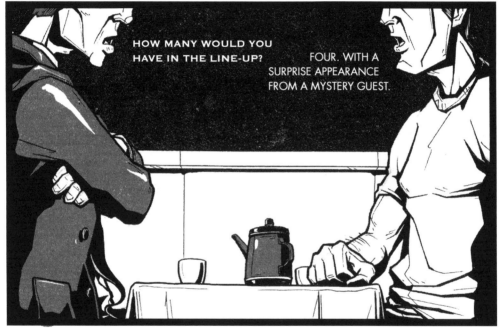

HOW MANY WOULD YOU
HAVE IN THE LINE-UP?

FOUR. WITH A
SURPRISE APPEARANCE
FROM A MYSTERY GUEST.

The Wong sisters and who else?

You haven't had the pleasure of Madam Wu, so to speak?

The one with the mole?

You noticed that did you? Not a lot gets passed you.

Kind of hard to miss it.

She's got quite a lovely daughter too. You'll like her, Oldham. Makes one hell of a first impression.

How well did you know Player?

Only by name. And even then I had help.

How about his reputation?

Ms Wong gave me the top-line.

Micki or Esther?

A bit of both.

I thought you would've learned your lesson. Once bitten, twice shy.

Third time's a charm. Are you sure you don't want some of these wantons, detective? Because, you know, I could stuff half a dozen down your throat. And you could eat them with the chopsticks I ram up your ass.

A bit testy aren't we, Jack? Don't get your balls in a twist.

You don't know half of it, I say, pushing the bowl away from me. All I can see now is testicle wantons floating amongst limp noodles.

Oldham pulls a stack of photocopies from beneath the table. And spreads them before me. We looked into Player, he says. Like you said. He's got a file. Multiple files. Might've been co-operating with a number of government agencies. The US and the Brits had him tagged. The Chinese too, probably. And the Cossacks. He was playing a lot of angles on both sides of the Great Wall.

Uh-huh, I grunt skimming the pages.

Drawing a lot of interest from above, Jack. A lot. I couldn't make this one go away if I wanted to.

Do you want to?

Doesn't matter.

Matters to me.

I got a murder that needs to be wrapped up in the tightest package you can imagine. And a local kid whose wife probably deserves some answers.

What are you saying?

Be clean. Or get clear.

I look at him for a moment. Then reach into the backpack, grab a moist towelette and call Mei over. Ask her to wipe her face and hands. Now that's clean! I say when she's done.

And fresh! she adds in well-rehearsed tones.

I ask Oldham if he's going to claim this one on expenses. His portable phone rings. We leave him to extract the rosewood furniture from his boxer shorts.

It takes an eternity for the cab to get out of Central. Stanley Street, Lyndhurst, Hollywood, Wyndham, Queen's Road, they're all at a standstill. I can hear fire engines bemoaning their place in the narrow arteries. The driver tells me there's a fire on Upper Lascar Road. Cat Street. Probably one of the antique shops.

There was a time, not that long ago, when 80 percent of stolen goods were fenced on Cat Street. That's how it got its name. *Thieves*, in Cantonese, were rats. Those who bought from them, cats. Cat Street. It's evolved since then, touting all manner of curios and remnants from Mao's Cult Of Personality now. Originals and reproductions, alongside genuine antiques, for those who know how to distinguish between the echt and ersatz. The cats toy with tourists these days. Still, it made me think of the *cat* I found scrawled on notepaper in The Rat's room. It didn't occur to me it might refer to dual destinations. I assumed it was merely an allusion to Bengal 1. Given Player's background and the object in question, I should've looked down this avenue of possibility earlier.

Coincidences were becoming a rarity as the week wore on.

34. INSPECTION

ANGEL SWIVELS IN HER CHAIR. Shifts from buttock to buttock. She coos energized tones down the phone and pulls at her left earlobe. You won't believe it! she exclaims cradling the receiver.

Fire on Cat Street?

How'd you know?

I can feel the heat from here.

Angel is keen to get home. More out of curiosity than concern for her family residing there. Her mother, twin brothers, younger sister and ailing grandmother are all in good health. An uncle, who owns a small antique shop at the other end of Cat Street, said a lot of people were evacuated. As a precaution. It wasn't much of a fire. I tell her she can finish early.

Not much point, she admits. Traffic is backed up and will take a while to clear. They're only letting residents with elderly or dependents into the area. And the only thing dependent on me is you, Jack.

There's no word from Micki. No sign of The Rat, The Weed, The Mole or The Flaneusse. I should be grateful. Although part of me is feeling neglected too. Angel agrees. What is it with these people? One minute they're all over you like a sexually transmitted disease. And then they just disappear. Leave you standing around with your dick in the wind.

I'm about to make a crude comment about dicks in the wind and never knowing which way they'll be blown when the air is awash with Poison.

Taiping stands in the doorway, as if at the end of a catwalk. Red cheongsam, trimmed with black piping. Right arm cocked on her hip. Left arm at her side, holding a small purse. Hands and wrists sheathed in ebony velvet. Patent heels put her close to nine-feet tall. A stiff breeze is sucked into the vacuum behind her.

Taiping, I say politely. Welcome. I was just saying to Ms Fuk how great if would be if you dropped by. Can I get you some tea? I have a pot of Gan Lu out the back. Actually, it's more of a Gan Lu Gua Pien blend. Of course, if you fancy something cheekier, we might have a little Bao Hao Yin Jan left.

She scopes reception like an 800-series endoskeleton. Skull rotating on immobile frame. Her eyes come to rest on Angel, who has risen to her feet, standing beside the desk. The women evaluate each other, top to toe. Angel bristles. Straightens her spine. Pulls back her shoulders and threatens the visitor with angry breasts.

Taiping steps off to her left and crosses reception. The click of her heels is like a metronome on the wood floor. A ticking time bomb.

Angel moves to intercept. I hold her off, extending my arm across her path. Part of me wants to see how the encounter would play out. Part of me is all too aware of the intruder's agility and knows what can happen when she goes on the offensive.

The point is rendered moot.

Angel stops to admire Taiping's artwork, framed within the heart-shaped void of the backless cheongsam. Close your mouth, I instruct her. One is not a codfish.

Remembering there is a couple of innocent children - and Mei - in the adjacent room, I follow at a safe distance. And watch from the doorway as Taiping strides through the studio to the bathroom. She pushes the door open with her foot.

Look! says Mei, daring to break the silence. The painted lady! Hello!

Taiping stops. Looks down. I wait for lasers to shoot from the narrow slits shielding her optical sensors. And my daughter to be vaporized. She smirks tightly. Then trains her sights in my direction. Traverses the room in three strides. And pulls up an arm's length from me.

Another thin smile creeps across freshly painted, moist lips.

She scans the room again. Pausing long enough to look down upon Angel and wind the steel spring of tension.

Anything particular you're looking for? I ask, hoping to stop this territorial dispute escalating into global thermonuclear war.

Yes, she replies succinctly, as if that's all that need be said. Her shoulders turn ninety degrees. Her slender hips follow a split second later. And she exits.

The phone rings. And rings.

Angel is seething. She's probably annoyed she didn't go toe-to-toe with the android. I call her name a couple of times, quietly, floating it by her on a gentle breeze, until the spell is broken. And she answers the call. It's Eric Tsoi, dialling in as requested but unsure why. She tells him I'm still here, safe and unsound. No change for fifty years. Pax vobiscum.

I retreat to my desk. And reboot the Macintosh.

Mei is watching Bert do *The Pigeon*. Our pubescent freelancers are conspiring on something at the studio table, pretending not to have witnessed anything unusual lately. I look at the layouts on my desk. Put my alignment-Nazi hat on. The kerning on one of the headlines is a couple of millimetres out.

You've got to find her, a little voice inside my head says.

Like my conscience, Angel has crept up on me. I don't look directly at her. She might try to hypnotize me with her eyes. I tell her I don't know who she's talking about. She tells me I know exactly whom.

I don't *got* to do nothing.

No one *has* to do anything, she counters, moving behind and placing her hands on my shoulders. Potent phalanges knead the muscles of my neck. We do them because we can. Because we *feel* it's the right thing to do.

I contemplate an appropriate response. One that doesn't involve gaffer tape and violating her in new and unusual ways.

The phone, bless its analog heart, rings.

Angel reaches over and picks it up. She smells like baby powder.

Mike Midian, she says hanging up. I attempt to swivel and ask her what he wanted. She holds me in place. She isn't finished with me yet. You know where she might be, she says continuing the dialectic. And the massage.

I think I know where she went, I confess. The harbour. Last night. And I bet she was at your barbecue on Cat Street today.

What are you going to do?

Nothing.

Her hands plough into my deltoids. Nothing?

You can only help those who want to be helped.

She wanted help, Jack. She came and asked for it remember?

Micki can take care of herself. She'll come to me when it suits her. When she's up to her neck in guano and needs someone to dig her out.

Jack, she whispers into my ear. You betrayed her. More than once. And you're probably still thinking of ways to make all this pay off, for you. Because you think she's playing you. Except you're the one who's playing. Everyone and every angle.

A man's got to keep his options open.

So does a woman.

She's keeping more than her options open, Angel.

I was talking about me. I'll go to the police. I'll tell them what I know. If you're going to do nothing, I've got to do something. You can't abandon her.

I'm slightly taken aback by Angel's allegiances. I shouldn't be. Women stick together. Part of their communal quest to repeal and restructure human nature. No sleep 'til spinsterhood.

What did Midian want? I ask, trying to get the conversation back onto something I can deal with.

He said to tell you The Rat's back.

35. HELLO SAILOR

THE DRIVER IS DOING HIS BEST with the peak hour traffic. Still, it creeps under my skin. The *Top Gun* medley isn't helping either. *You've Lost That Loving Feeling. Take My Breath Away. Dangerzone.* Fuck Berlin and Kenny Loggins.

Midian is at the entrance of the hotel. He opens the door of the taxi. And, before I can take my yellow sign from the rear window, he gives me the skinny.

Too late, Jack. Anurak just blew. Cleared out. Suitcase and all. A couple of minutes ago. I paged you.

I reach for my pager. And remember where I left it. Why didn't you stop him, Mike?

I got the girls to screw up his account. I billed him for damages. He dropped a wad of cash on the counter. And started complaining. Loudly. We're a hotel, Jack. Not a detention centre. Managers have to write reports. Staff need to account for actions and inaction. We're evaluated on how we handle these situations.

Cars are banking up behind us. Horns are honking. Civil unrest is mounting. I ask Mike if he saw who left with The Rat.

There were a couple of people in a silver Mercedes. I didn't get a good look at them. They were just heads in the rear window. Sorry I couldn't do more.

You and me both, I say, closing the door.

I point my Mandarin Maverick in the direction of Upper Lascar. Cat Street.

We take the introspective route around Central to Hollywood Road. It's like the journey of life itself. From Tung Wah Hospital to Man Mo Temple, via the morticians. When the coolies died they brought them here to rest, at the top of Ladder Street, before their final trip back to the mainland.

The radio is killing me softly, with *Songbird.* Fuck Kenny G.

Incense permeates my lungs as we alight. And walk down to Cat Street. Police, firemen and half a ton of voyeurs are milling about. The smell of wet, extinguished wood hangs in the air. I prefer it to incense but could live without either in the ether. I feel a headache coming on.

The damage to the char-broiled shop doesn't look too bad. Medium-rare. They must've arrested the fire before it really caught on.

I lead Mei to an adjacent store. Bring her attention to a couple of trays displaying jade pendants and bracelets. An elderly proprietor comes to the door. Assures me it's all real. No fakes. We're just looking, I tell her in Cantonese. She laughs. And says if I come inside she'll show me the real stuff.

We follow her in. Mei pauses to admire the statues and busts of Chairman Mao. I'm making discreet enquiries about the fire when she reappears beside me, holding a pair of silk slippers. Tiny ones. As worn by those lucky enough to have had their feet bound in the goode olde dayes.

Look at these shoes Ba-ba! Too small even for me!

The practice of footbinding has officially been abandoned. Although there are villages in southwestern China where examples of the practice can still be found.

If anthropologists had taken a look around our Happy Valley hamlet recently, they might also have caught sight of an aging adman with both his hands and feet tied, getting royally stitched up too.

ANGEL GIVES AN INQUISITIVE, CONTEMPTUOUS LOOK as I sign-off artwork. The Standard Chartered Bank Tax-pleaser promotion. *Get gold for your tax bill!* Waves cigarettes. *The wave of waves. The way smoking should be. Today's flavour.* Who writes these things? I think. And then remember that I do. The Boss Phone, from General Electric. *The future of mobile communications.*

Mei sits in her beanbag. Flipping through *There's A Wocket In My Pocket*. Don't tell me Dr Seuss didn't have grown-ups in mind when he penned a lot of this stuff.

Quimney up the chimney. Gherkin in the merkin.

I tell Angel to send the freelancers home. If Wu and her clan don't kill us, the over-time will. She should get on her way too. It's Saturday night. Go let off some steam. Soak in a tub. Karaoke. Whatever.

Right now I'd settle for a six-pack of Pabst and a tin dick.

I think I've got some beer in the fridge.

What's a tin dick? asks Mei.

Not a tin dick, sweetheart. A tryptic, I reply, tap dancing madly, stranded in the outer-reaches of Smartarsa Major. I'd engage the hyperdrive and blast out of here, only my flux capacitor doesn't have the 1.21 jigawatts to complete the jump to lightspeed.

What's a triptick?

It's an enzyme, cupcake. It catalyses the hydrolysis of proteins to form polypeptides.

Mei giggles. That's a lot of funny words.

I know. There's a tryptic in my triptych.

There's a yottle in my bottle, she rejoins with a laugh. And returns her attention to the good Doctor.

Angel saunters over. Wants to know if I'm going to tell her what happened. I tell her I will, when the freelancers leave. She immediately dismisses them with the brusque economy of the word that only Cantonese allows.

So?

Nothing, I reply. Nothing, on no one. The Rat's gone underground with miscreants unknown. Probably Wu and her charming family. Who knows? We spoke to a lady who runs the antique shop across the way that was torched. You probably know her. You're probably related. She says there was a woman hanging around the front of the shop for a while. Couldn't tell if it was Micki, Esther or the delightful Taiping.

There's a bit of a difference.

Not from a distance, when you have cataracts the size of fried eggs. She said a gweilo turned up. They went inside. A few others arrived shortly after. Probably Wu, her son and Anurak. There was some commotion. Maybe a shot fire-

A gunshot?

No. A shot of tequila. Yes, a gun shot. People started to gather. There was a bit more rumpus. Someone screamed. The gweilo burst out of the shop. The owner told everyone to move along. People went back about their business, slowly.

What about the fire?

Could've been a Jewish stock-take. A coincidence or an accident. No one really knows or wants to say much about it. Which means it's probably one of those things everyone knows too much about.

Which means we'll never know what happened.

I bet someone in your family knows, I say with a smile.

Where was Wu?

There's a noise in reception. Someone opening the door. I check my watch. A bit late for visitors. Although these days you can't rule anything out. It's probably just a courier, picking up the artwork. Angel takes the boards from my desk. I de-boot the Macintosh. And put the pager in my pants.

There's a wocket in your pocket, sings Mei.

And yeps on my steps. Come on, it's time to go home.

She closes her book and climbs out of the beanbag. I pick her and the backpack up. The latter is almost as heavy as she is.

What have I got in there?

I kill the lights and enter reception. Just in time to see a blond man collapse on the floor. He's dressed in navy whites. A parcel of newspaper, slightly bigger than an urn made from a single piece of white jade, lies beneath him.

Uh-oh, says Mei, with her usual capacity for understatement.

Angel is rooted to the floor beside her desk. Probably wondering how many more last-minute incursions she can handle. They're starting to wear thin on me as well. I step between her and the body. Thrust Mei into her arms. Tell her to go inside. Then lean down to roll the sailor over.

A solid six-foot-something, he attempts to raise himself on hands and knees. He looks up at me. And vomits blood onto the floor. Pushes the package out before him, smearing claret across the floorboards. Over the line. Touchdown. He scores in the dying seconds of the game. And expires.

I turn off the lights and gingerly retrieve the parcel, trying not to get blood on the floor. And quickly realize that's a redundant exercise.

I canter into the office, where Angel and Mei are trying not to be distracted by the corpse in the adjacent room. Someone to see you in reception, Ms Fuk, I say placing the package on the studio table. It's an ill-timed attempt at humour. I can tell from Angel's unstrung expression. I pull the screen from the wall, creating a temporary morgue.

Angel tells Mei to draw a picture of something nice. A castle. Flowers. Do you want to watch TV? Let's watch TV.

The body is still prone. Immobile. Torso neither rising nor falling under the weight of the interloper. I roll him over. His white shirt has some real problem stains. More than I'd expect from the preceding scarlet yawn. I can barely make out the Bengal 1 insignia over his left breast. There are richer bloodstains on his right flank. They're probably older. A belly wound of some kind. The coroner can work it out.

Remembering how important it is to lift heavy objects with your legs, not your back, I drag him inside. Lay him behind the partition. The fluoro Muppets on the television provide a post-modern soundtrack to this murderous comedy.

Mna-mna. Do do do do-do.

Mna-mna. Do do do-do.

Warm, burgundy syrup is matted in the hair on my forearms, pasted between my fingers and wedged under my nails. Mei asks what's that on my hands and shirt. I simulate ignorance. Pretend she's just drawn my attention to it. Oh, this? Don't worry sweetpea. Angel's boyfriend fell over. He's going to lie down here for a bit. I point to the TV. Is that Guy Smiley?

Angel stares me down, angry that I have soiled her name by dragging it into this mess. Her alabaster complexion has also gone a shade of grey. If she's more worried than she's letting on she's not alone.

I drop down to search the pockets of the damned.

Some keys. A few Hong Kong and US Dollars on a money clip. Mainland RMB. Micki's business card, with a Cat Street address and our office written on the back. In the other pocket there's a Swedish passport.

Andreas Bergman. Recent ports of call include Hawaii, Japan, Taiwan, Shanghai, and Macao. Poor Norse bastard probably thought he was going to see the world. Now he's gone the way of the Viking.

Fuck Abba. Fuck Ikea. Fuck their massages and their meatballs too.

Is he? enquires Angel, as to Bergman's unbearable lightness of being.

More than he'll ever know.

I invite her to open the pempe on the studio table. She declines. Aren't you curious to see what all the fuss has been about? I ask turning the package in my hands, peeling pages of *Wen Hui Bao* as I go. The guy who conquered half the world is in there. Wouldn't want to upset him.

I'm starting to feel like Indiana Jones. Just before he snatched that Peruvian idol off the pedestal in *Raiders Of The Lost Ark*. I give a quick look over my shoulder, half expecting Belloq and a horde of angry pygmies to charge in. The way this week is panning out it could still happen.

The last piece of newspaper falls way. And reveals...

Bubble-wrap.

I slice through the binding Scotchtape with a Stanley Trimmer. Roll the urn gently across the table, careful not to dislodge the lid. I can't resist the temptation to stop and burst a few of the bubbles. Who can? The popping startles Angel. And draws Mei to the table as I stand the urn upright for all to admire.

Mei's expression suggests she can't work out what all the fuss is about. Bor-ing.

Angel glances at me. I look at Mei. We all look to the urn.

Disregarding its hallowed place in the grand design of life, the remarkable contents and bizarre series of events conspiring to bring it to this point in time, the Great White Hope is actually quite ordinary. A fragile band of red cloth secures the lid, anchored by wax seals. There's a bit of grime in hard-to-reach places between the dragon's claws, the ridges of its scales and the feathers of the phoenix. But it would scrub up okay. If it's really as powerful as Wu says, it might even glow in the dark and grant three wishes when you rub it just right.

Can we go home? pleads Mei, failing to grasp the gravity of the moment. I'm hungry!

My pager jumps into gear. Like a harbinger of doom its reverberations can be felt around the room. Angel looks at the wocket in my pocket. Is that your pager, or are you just happy to see me? she asks flatly.

The phone joins in the hilarity. I tell Angel not to answer it. That infernal machine has brought mankind nothing but pain and misery. She picks it up anyway. The lines of communication are not so clear. Hello? Hello?

I check the pager. Micki's at The Pen. Needs to see me. Urgently. I ask Angel if she'll be my date. I'll have her home by midnight. Promise.

Maybe it's time to call the police, Jack. Really. Look at this mess.

First things first, I say picking up Mei. Let's get you some dinner!

I'm so hungry I could die!

Angel is not quite as dramatic. You can't leave me here. With *that*, she protests, indicating the corpse. What if whoever did that decides to come here?

They'd be here by now. And if they turn up later, they can talk to the police. They'll be arriving soon. To keep you company.

Jack-

If I don't get Mei home for dinner, she'll kill me. Poor choice of words, I know. And then Por-por will eat me alive. And not in the good way that you're thinking about. She's my mother-in-law for goodness sake. That's just sick. Phone Oldham. Tell him what happened. I got a call. And left. No names. Tell him we were here. You were in here with Mei. This guy comes in. Pukes in the lobby. I drag him into the office. Can't leave him in reception. How would that look to clients? He karks. You call the police. Be naïve. He'll believe you. Play it straight. But don't tell him about the urn, I say scooping it into bubble-wrap. You didn't see everything that happened out there. Just in here. The phone rang. I bolted. Got it?

Got it? echoes Mei, popping the life out of some bubble-wrap

Angel wants to know what I'm going to do about my clothes. I tell her they'll come back in style eventually.

The splooge, Jack. On your shirt. And jeans.

I look at my legs. A little blood has transferred to Mei's pants too. Bing will have to soak them in cold water. Or maybe we can just leave it for the police.

Give me a couple of minutes, I instruct. Then call Oldham. Keep the door locked until he gets here.

I kiss her cheek. Mei makes playful lip-smacking noises. Adrenaline is charging through my veins. I'm about to tear up the stairs. Then realize the folly of vaulting fourteen flights. And wait for the elevator. It's one of those awkward moments.

Angel tells me to be careful. Out there. And sends me into the night with a kiss.

Mei plants one on my cheek, for equal measure. I'm pretty sure the rest of the women I'll be dealing with this evening won't be as forthcoming with appreciation. Especially Por-por. If she's in a vendetta kind of mood, I may not have to worry about the others. I won't even make it out of the building.

Don't fiddle with the evidence in there, I warn Angel, entering the lift.

A wicked smile returns to her lips.

If I want seamen, Jack, I'll go down to Fenwick Pier. Like everyone else.

36. RIDING THE DRAGON

THE CAB DRIVER LAMENTS BLACK THURSDAY. If only he knew the answer to all our problems lay, swathed in bubble-wrap, on the back seat of his Nissan. Although he really needs to fix the suspension. One more bump and it's Ash Wednesday in here.

We pull into the Hilton. I locate Midian. He wants to know what's in the package.

The holy grail, I tell him.

Anything in it for me?

You'll get a piece of it.

When?

When it all goes according to plan.

So, probably never.

It's could pay off, like Prime Rate at Sha Tin.

I'd have a better chance of winning Mark Six.

Then think of this as your lucky number. I need to leave it here for a while.

We hand it to the concierge. I fill out a receipt. Slip one half into an envelope. Write Eric Tsoi's name and address on it. Post it on Monday, I instruct. If Angel or I don't come to pick up before then.

Who's Angel?

My secretary. You'll like her. She has a pulse. And breasts that smile.

They're all God's creatures, he says with a smirk. I love them all.

Mike Midian, Julio Iglesias and Willie Nelson. So different and yet so the same. You guys should go on tour.

Willie and I never play the same city at the same time, he says, like there's more to the story than I'll ever know. A brief moment of silence ensues, while he assesses my face and the weight of the situation. Watch your back, he warns.

I didn't know you cared.

I don't. I need the money. I've got a wife and two barmaids to support.

THERE'S NO ANSWER when I knock at The Marco Polo Suite. No light under the door. No sound within. I backhand it, sharply, again. Nobody home, a voice beside me says, so remote it needs its own area code.

Taiping is propped against the door. Eyes, barely visible at the best of times, strain against the brightly lit corridor. Pupils, at maximum dilation, look like they're about to give birth to her brain. It's crowning in her optical canal as she teeters on life-threatening heels. The bright-red cheongsam, so desperately clinging to her emaciated frame a short while ago, is open to the navel. Exposing a thin line of flesh across her chest. It slithers around a small breast, down her flank, to a place just above the bony handle of her hip.

Come visit with me, she commands, languidly rolling off the door. And returning to her dim room.

I follow, out of curiosity.

The curtains are drawn. My eyes are slow to adjust. Illumination comes from the glow of the television, loudly broadcasting *Vampire's Breakfast*. The latest Canto ghost comedy. A couple of idiots are investigating a morgue.

Taiping stands by the table. Her velvet-clad pincer lifts a cigarette from a packet of Marlboro Red. She invites me to join her. I accept, mainly to see if it blows the back of my gulliver off. Are you sure I should be in here? I ask loudly, competing with the television. What would your husband say?

Ha! My husband? My wife, she spits sourly with a side-order of bile.

What are you trying to tell me? That he's as camp as a plaid rabbit? I figured as much. Especially when I saw him on that float at Mardi Gras with your Thai friend, last time I was here. Something about the sequins. And the way they were greasing each other's buttocks. Quite a marriage of inconvenience you're going to have there. Still, as far as beards go, Taiping, you're the cat's whiskers.

Qing Yi, she says. Call me Qing Yi.

Why?

That is my name. Qing Yi.

My knowledge of Chinese Opera is rudimentary, to say the least. Purloined from pilfered library books. Still, I know that Qing Yi is one of the three female stereotypes. A noblewoman of quality and character. An ideal of the Chinese woman. Faithful, proper, shy, graceful and, in this case, laughably inappropriate. Her parents must have had such hopes for her. Qing Yi is dead, I think. Long live Taiping. I ask why there is so much confusion over her identity.

Taiping is the name Madam Wu has chosen for me.

I see, I say. And the whole wolf-lamb-leopard dynamic falls into place. It leaves me feeling like a goat. Or someone who just got caught rogering one. You're Madam Wu's mistress?

Yes.

I shouldn't be surprised. I'd read somewhere that all animals in the Celestial Kingdom were originally classified under twelve groups. They can look like flies when seen from a distance. Break water pitchers. Be drawn with a fine camel-hair brush. Be one of the masses. Shake like a fool. Act like stray dogs. Be fabulous. A siren. Or a suckling pig. Tame. Embalmed. And then there are those that belong to the Emperor. No doubt there were times when Taiping qualified for a number of these clusters.

This latest revelation from Her Royal Hetaeraness puts a neat spin on traditional feminine imperatives and The Three Obediences. *First to father, then to husband, and finally to son.* It makes a mockery of my flaneusse label too. She's obviously required to put her back into it from time to time. Nose to the grindstone. It's a dirty job but, hey, someone has to do it.

Beauty can be such a cruel mistress, I empathize. Why does she call you Taiping if your name is Qing Yi?

It pleases her. And that is my job. To please her.

I bet you do. Sort of like a lesbian Harold And Maude. Although your anililagnia is probably rooted in fiscal pleasure rather than physical attraction.

This is about as un-Qing Yi as it gets, theatrically speaking. What, only a moment ago, belonged to the Emperor would now appear to be a stray dog. A fabulous siren on the cusp of becoming an embalmed suckling pig. Her interpretation of The Four Virtues at this time would, no doubt, knock the critics on their asses too. Rarely has fidelity, physical charm, propriety and diligent needlework been embodied with such abandon.

I extend my palm to her cheek. Caress it. She smiles. I trace the contours of her jaw and neck across to her shoulder, to her breast.

Her velvet chela tugs at the belt on my jeans. It gives rise to thoughts of Curley, from *Of Mice And Men.* And the reason he kept his digits in gloves *fulla' vaseline.* I suppress the urge to gag when I think of the places this ranch hand has been, as she releases the buckle.

I push her firmly in the chest. And send her sprawling to the bed.

Surprise soon falls from her face. She's been in this position before. And remains on her back. Resolute. Elevating her torso, resting on elbows. Knees over the edge of the bed, she presents herself proudly. A crude smile daubs her parted lips. Further south, her inner thigh is festooned with two butterfly tattoos. The flux of images on the television gives them the appearance of flight, as if fleeing her cocoon. It suffuses her sinuous frame in unhealthy hues.

There's a litre of Watson's distilled water on the nightstand. A syringe. And a necktie. The latter belonging to her sharing and caring husband, no doubt. Darkness prevents me from seeing the track marks on her arms. I almost feel sorry for the gloopy bitch. Dragons are having her every which way. I pick up the remote control and mute the Cantobabble.

You going to fight me or fuck me? Taiping wants to know.

I'm still deciding, Fubuki. Where's Emperor Hirohito and Ms Wong? I ask stepping into Position A, between her knees.

With surprising speed for a junkie, she wraps her legs around mine. A deft swivel of hips sends me to the mattress. In the same motion she rolls over and straddles my chest. Pins me to the bed. Black Bess riding Dick Turpin. I glimpse a third butterfly, on the opposite thigh, beside the chrysalis. Richard Attenborough would be thrilled. A whole new species. Of course, if their home has been neglected for as long as she says it has they may not be butterflies at all. They could be moths.

I take a swing with my unpinned arm. She bats it away. Hits my face with a clenched fist. Hard. Your manhood so useless that I must beat you? This will be a fine service, she says, setting the agenda. And clocking me across the chin. My innards will make your little brother drive so hard my intestines will be scrambled eggs. You will blow up my throat.

It occurs to me Taiping has been renting movies from the same store as The Weed, although perhaps from the Adult Section. She might also be the only person who could match Angel when it comes to potty-mouth rhetoric such is her sophisticated command of litotes, paronomasia, periphrasis and metonymy.

That's quite a tongue you have Qing Yi. You kiss your mother-in-law with that? Or does she wash it out with soap before you get on with your chores?

Enough talk, she demands. And slaps me again. My pussy aches, Jack So. I hope you sex me better than you wrestle.

How's this for a trade? I please your uterus…

Yes. Now.

And you can kiss my ass.

What?

She's off-guard and too light to maintain the high ground. Fuck you, I say.

And swing my arm like a club, connecting between her elbow and shoulder. Knocking her off balance.

Springing upright, I slam my temple against her cheek. She falls away with a grunt, curling onto her side. And attempts to crawl up the king-size. I grab her leg. Drag her, face down, across the sheets toward me. Getting a good look at the artwork on her back. I drop my knee into the middle of her spine, crushing the belly of the beast. Then force one arm around behind her. The other flails, like a barracuda on the deck. She shakes like a fool, before giving up the fight.

Is she laughing, or just winded? Maybe I broke a couple of ribs or snapped her spine. She's gurgling blood. I release the pressure on her back. She lies still for a moment. Then feebly reaches for the bottle on the nightstand. Rolls over. Sits up. Issues a corrupt smile.

I pass her the water. She tries to kick me in the crotch but has lost much of her speed. The attempt is more playful than purposeful. I block it with my shin. Kick it out of the way. And throw the bottle at her. She catches it smartly but not before half the contents splashes over her thighs, between her stirrups.

The water pitcher, as they say, is broken.

I don't know. I do what I'm told. Madam leaves, I please myself.

You can get back to that when I go. What did she tell you to do?

Wait here. For you.

So here I am. Now what?

I don't care, she says, as if suddenly resigned to defeat.

Maybe she's done all that was asked. Maybe she's coming down from whatever she's on. I feel like I've been screwed. Fucked over. Maybe they didn't want me here at all. Maybe they just didn't want me over there.

I grab a robe from the closet and toss it at Taiping. Tell her to put it on before she catches cold. She drapes it over her shoulders. Reaches for the nightstand. I push her arm away.

My head aches, she says. I need medicine.

I pull the draw. See a couple of plastic straws. Ends sealed. Filled with heroin, I guess. That's how they sell it at Southorn Playground. There's an orange vial of pills too. I don't know what they are but it's a safe bet it isn't Panadol.

Knock yourself out, I say, like a disappointed parent.

She washes a couple of Dilithium Crystals down. Flops back into the darkness. Staring at the TV. How long will it be before she finds her light in ashes? What would her father say? Did he sell her into this?

I bin the syringe, smack and pills. Sit on the edge of the bed and call home.

Por-por answers. Mean as hell. She hands the phone to Angel. I ask her how things are going.

The police came. Wanted to know where you were.

What did you tell them?

That I didn't know.

Did they believe you?

Probably not. Oldham told me to wait around. I said I'd rather wait up here.

Mei?

In bed. Asleep. You?

In bed.

Jack!

Don't worry. I put up a fight. You would've been proud of me.

Micki, Taiping or Madam Wu?

Qing Yi.

Who?

Qing Yi. It's far-qing complicated. I'll explain when I get back.

Taiping doesn't seem too worried about my departure. Goodbye Jack So, she says from a distant planet. I leave the door ajar. Put the basket of contraband by a room-service trolley. And stop by the concierge. Tell him to send security and a doctor to the sixth floor. There's a nymphomaniac in distress.

A COP SITS BEHIND THE WHEEL of a paddy wagon. I get the taxi to circle around the back. And I take the service entrance to the first floor.

So Fuk Yu is dark and empty, except for the uniformed officer on the sofa. Legs outstretched. Probably asleep. I call the elevator and catch my breath.

Outside the front door of the apartment all I hear is the TV. Oldham has either been and gone, or not come up for a fireside chat. Yet. Unless he's sitting there enthralled by *The Professionals*, *Moonlighting* or the episode of *Family Ties* where Alex is on speed. I open the door. Slowly

Bing is at the table. Hunched over a bowl. Armed with a pair of tweezers. She's picking black spots of caked blood and other impurities from a bird nest. Mei drinks soup made from this, every now and then. It's supposed to be good for you. And your skin. Por-por is addicted to it. And nowhere to be seen. Probably given up and gone to bed. I'll have to deal with her in the morning. I stick my gulliver in Mei's room.

Angel lies on the mattress by the bed. Even in the half-light I can tell she probably has a healthy regimen of bird nest in her diet. She cranes her neck to look at me. Raises a finger to her lips. Gets to her feet. And follows me into the living room. Crossing the floor I trip on Mei's backpack. I issue a few select curse words. And push it out of the way.

Before Angel can begin her inquisition I call The Pen. And ask the concierge if Madam Wu has returned. No, he says. And there wasn't a nympho in distress on the sixth floor either. The room was empty. What the fuck? I say to myself.

Not right now, says Angel. Maybe after you take a shower.

Pardon?

You said *want to fuck*. I said take a shower first.

I said *what the fuck*. But good to know you're up for it all the same.

Truth be known, I always feel a little toey after a stoush. And, given the three rounds I went with Taiping, there's still enough testosterone coursing through my veins to pique my interest. The correlation between sex and violence, in my observation, has always been strong and direct. A matter of degrees. From recent encounters, to the damaged doxies stacked on the furniture of my childhood, the line between the twin sisters of sin was as thin as a polyisoprene sheath. *Ribbed for her pleasure.* Live by the pork-sword, die by the pork-sword. Violence breeds violence. Families breed contempt. And so on.

Who's Qing Yi? asks Angel, reading my mind.

Taiping is Qing Yi. Or what's left of her. She's going to give you, Cleopatra and the Queen of Carthage a run for your money, when you get to the Second Circle Of Hell.

I'll be sure to pack an extra set of nipple clamps.

She has a close working relationship with Madam Wu. In a sapphic sort of way. Kind of a Gomorrah to Li Dan's Sodom. Think of her as a person of shallow learning, who has swallowed the lessons of antiquity without digesting them. And she wanted my love to be the knife that she would turn within herself.

Urgh. She reads Kafka too?

She probably killed him.

I never finished The Castle.

It's okay, neither did Kafka. I think he left a lot of things undone, I say, feeling a bit Kafka-esque at this point in the time-space continuum. He's lucky he died of tuberculosis. This whole thing would've done his head in.

I can't believe Madam Wu's a rug-muncher. And gets Taiping to clean the carpet. Dante would have to come up with a whole new Circle of Hell just for her.

It's quite a gerontocracy she's running over there. I'm going to need at least a barrel of mind-bleach to wash the catachresis away.

Is everyone gay? Who do you blow to get an old-fashioned knee-trembler?

The Weed, I guess. What about the police?

I dated a cop. Handcuffs were great. Nightstick wasn't up to much.

So you had to restrain yourself. I meant the police downstairs, copulator, but thanks for sharing. How'd it go with Hong Kong's finest this evening?

They had questions. I didn't have the answers.

I thought you had an answer for everything. They didn't give you a ride in the car? Let you turn the siren on?

I tried to turn it on but it ignored me. They wouldn't even let me buy it a drink. It's probably gay as well. They're quite keen to speak with you though.

Really? I wonder what about?

No idea. Parking fines?

Maybe they're onto all those library books I lifted.

Now that you mention it, they were from the Special Branch of The Library Police. They probably want to revoke your lending privileges.

What did you tell them?

I said I'd seen someone that looked like Anurak, or the runt of Wu's litter, waiting out front of the building this afternoon. But mostly I tried not to say anything that would lead to more questions.

You're getting good at this.

At what?

Subterfuge.

I've always been a fast learner. I know which way the wind is blowing.

I bet you could teach it a thing or two.

I could make its toes curl.

Bing giggles. Like all domestic helpers she has the invis-ability to make you forget she's around. Amahs are the audience sitting in the dark, while the circus of our life plays out before them. *We make our exits and entrances, mewling and puking, whining and sighing, full of strange oaths, sudden in quarrel, until the last scene ends our eventful history.* The house lights come up. They make their way to the lobby and mill about until another amateur production invites them to opening night. Or, to look at it from a more Buddhist perspective, if a tree falls in the forest and there's no amah around to hear it, who's going to clean it up?

The doorbell chimes. *Song Of Joy.* Bing rises to answer it. I tell her I'll go. And she disappears with her bowl of bird nest into the kitchen. I wish you'd tell your boyfriends not to come over at his hour, I caution Angel. People are sleeping.

Maybe it's one of your paramours, she replies as I open the door.

Micki leaps in, *risvegliato*. One arm, thrown around my neck, crushes my windpipe. The other, swinging low, plants a Gucci purse in my goolies. I'll be needing a new bag myself, at this rate. I hold back a tear, breathe deep and ask how she got past the police.

Same way you did, says a familiar, ill-equipped voice.

The Rat steps into frame, pushing a small revolver before him. Hope you don't mind us dropping in, he says. The sweetness in his tone is so sickly it could induce diabetes. The Mole and a pistol-wielding Weed follow in his insignificant wake.

Actually, could you guys come back later?

The Weed pokes his weapon into my stomach. He's too close for me to relieve him of it without something going horribly wrong. I step back, slowly. And draw them all into the living room.

Well, I hope you brought enough bullets for everyone.

37. HOUSE CALL

BING WALKS OUT OF THE KITCHEN, sees the guns, inhales a Hail Mary and drops a bowl of bird nest to the floor. Not quite the distraction I was hoping for. The Weed, having learned a few hard lessons this week, remains focussed on the dynamic between his weapon and me.

Now you've done it.

At the opposite end of the room, Por-por stands in her nightshirt. It's a kaftan type of thing with a batik print. Her perm is bent out of shape. And her glazzies squint against the light as she surveys the new arrivals. They're really going to get it now. I've never seen her so angry. And I was there when she found out I knocked up her daughter. If she's conscious of the potential threat to our existence she doesn't show it. She wants to know what's going on. And berates us all for being so noisy. So late. So rude. Then, aware of the mess on the floor, she seeks out Bing. And scolds her. Does she know how expensive bird nest is? At this point, I think it's fair to say, Bing doesn't care what it cost. She'd renounce her faith if it meant being back in Baguio.

I attempt to bring some order to the proceedings. Ask everyone to settle down. Then introduce Por-por to Wu Zetian and her extended family.

The Mole, gracious as ever, with a large Louis Vuitton handbag in the crook of her elbow, speaks formally. She apologizes for the intrusion. Assures Por-por the matter will not take long to resolve.

Por-por huffs a sceptical response. More mainland tourists, she says. Don't you spit on the carpet and steal the towels from the bathroom.

Mei appears beside Por-por, in Ewok pyjamas. She charges into my legs. I lift her chest-high. She clings to my neck. I do my best to assure her that everything will be okay. And instruct Bing to leave the mess on the floor for the moment. Bring refreshments for our guests.

That will not be necessary, corrects The Rat. Why don't you and your family take a seat? he recommends, motioning to the couch.

Por-por takes a place on the black vinyl two-seater. She mutters something about just having the rug cleaned and our guests dragging bird nest into it at their own peril. Angel sits beside her. I take an arm of the couch. Mei clings to my shoulder, a panic-stricken Ewok. Put the pistols away girls, I request. Unless you're planning to shoot all of us.

I will only penetrate you if things get raunchy, says The Weed. I threaten your ass. And if you move I will explode all over you until you are limp.

We better take it outside, Li Dan. To the roof. What you're proposing is hardly suitable entertainment for a child, I say, lowering Mei between my legs and sliding the backpack to her. Besides, Por-por just had the rug cleaned. You think she's angry now, wait until you see how she reacts when you blow my beans all over it.

A duet on the roof would pleasure me, he replies with a disingenuous smile. I bet he's soiled his shorts already.

That will do, snaps The Rat. Nobody has to get hurt.

Nobody else, you mean.

Por-por grumbles about mainland tourists and The Handover coming early.

Yes, agrees The Mole. Let us get on with it, shall we? The urn please.

What makes you think I have it?

Mr So. We all want this concluded quickly. If it is not here it will be close by. There has not been an abundance of opportunity to secure it, since it came into your possession.

Since Micki's silenced partner made a mess of my office? Since Junior made a mess of him? I warned you about keeping an eye on your kids. They've been running amok. Sending boys to do a man's job, what were you thinking?

Oh. And that reminds me, I add, turning my attention to her son. Dan, tell your fiancé I've changed my mind. I'd be more than happy to finish what we started earlier.

And what was that, Mr So?

She wanted me to compensate her for your shortcomings. Those butterflies on her thighs, were they your idea? You need directions down there?

I'm not sure who's more ruffled by this. Angel, The Weed, The Rat, Micki or The Mole. I hope I haven't deployed the daisy-cutter too early. Por-por watches their feet on the rug. The Weed shifts in his shoes, impatiently. And points his gun. At me. Wu raises an authoritative hand and negates him.

Yes, remember your place, Junior. Save your energy. You'll need it.

I look at Micki, standing tacitly in the shadow of Madam Wu's mole. What role is she playing in this little drama now? She moves her weight to another leg and I notice the black cheongsam she's wearing. I knew something wrong. The outfit doesn't match that handbag. Or those ridiculous heels. Is she going to a wedding or a funeral? It might even be something from Taiping's collection. In the wrong light you could almost be excused for mistaking the two. Although Micki gives away a few inches in the buff.

Li Dan has a lot to learn, admits Wu. He may be a weak vessel, but-

Faults and defects every work of man must have? I interrupt, employing some Johnson and daring to complete the arc of her thoughts. The boy must love it when people sing his praises in public like this.

He is obedient. You could learn from him. Obedience is the path to survival. Stubbornness leads only to trouble. Where is the urn?

Maybe you should have her spayed, suggests Angel.

I'm sure they have already. Li Dan has been neutered.

The Weed squeezes the handle of his shooter, knuckles whitening. Wu's hands remain clasped before her on the strap of the LV bag. One thumb, however, grinds against the leather. I'm getting to her too. Enough! she commands. Is this talk appropriate in the presence of a child?

I know it's not as G-rated as the death threats you bring to the party but I'm at a slight disadvantage. You've had all day to come up with your move. And you're still suffering from Kotov's Syndrome. I'm cobbling this Blackburne Shilling Gambit together as we go along. Where's the money?

Wu takes a step in my direction. Opens her purse for my inspection. And reveals a substantial sum of US Dollars.

Looks a little light. Feels light too. I put the corner of a wad to my mouth and pretend to take a bite. Mmmm. Light. And yet filling. I drop the cash inconsequentially into Mei's backpack. I'll probably feel like some more in a little while, I add. Are you sure they're US Dollars? Maybe it's Renminbi. Chinese never really fills you up.

Wu pulls an envelope from within and holds it out to me. A cheque, she says. For the balance. You can cash it on Monday.

What a coincidence. That's when you can pick up Temujin. Give that envelope to Miss Wong. For safekeeping.

Micki opens her eyes wide. Wu hands her the husk of the remittance, reluctantly. Monday?

Do you all want to come back on Monday? Or shall I get the mahjong table out? We've got time for quite a solid session. Hell of a kitty up for grabs too.

The urn, Mr So, Wu demands with inarguable finality.

It's closer than you think. But first, let me see if I've got this right. You get two dead emperors and a priceless piece of jade?

Yes, confirms Wu.

I get rich?

If that's what a quarter of a million dollars makes you, then yes.

And Miss Wong gets?

To carry on with her immoral practices. I don't believe she needs the money. If I am incorrect in that assumption, however, you and her will come to some arrangement with regard to the riches she now holds.

I can't help but smirk at the pot-kettle nature of the immorality issue. Good lord. Caligula would be envious of what goes on in the Wu household. Larry Flynt could guarantee global distribution for their home movies. Madam Wu preaches morality but lives in a night-cellar in Admah and has a summer cottage in Zeboim. It's like talking about wisdom when you're in Bedlam.

Behold now, I have two daughters which have not known man. Let me, I pray you, bring them unto you, and do ye to them as is good in your eyes.

And our Siamese Princess, over there? What does he get?

He has played his part. And will get what was promised to him.

Uh-huh. And the police?

The police, Mr So?

They, to borrow your term Mr So, get to keep their obsession for you. The money is more than enough to compensate you, or them, for that.

The cash will become evidence if they don't get something or someone else. I could lose that and a whole lot more. Money's not enough. You'll leave. I have to live here. I don't have the right of abode anywhere else. None of us do. The police need to wrap this up in sparkly Hello Kitty paper, put it in an oversized pink box, tie it off with a purple polyester ribbon and glow-in-the-dark organza bow. Oldham needs to go to his boss and the press and say *case solved*. Hong Kong's in safe hands. Mainlanders can't come over here and shoot the place up just because it's been restored to its rightful owners. The people need to know stuff like that. They need posters, tent cards and coasters. Bunting. T-shirts A full blown the-media-is-the-message campaign.

If nothing else, Mr So, you have proven to be a resourceful man, says The Rat with misplaced confidence. You'll figure something out.

Maybe I already have. Madam Wu knows what I'm talking about too. Don't you, sugar tits? Wu's silence and set features tells me she knows exactly what I'm talking about. She's probably not too happy about my reference to her breasts but, well, fuck her if she can't take a joke. What was it Deng said about arresting some of China's problems? I don't care if it's a black cat, a white cat or fucking Garfield, so long as it catches mice.

The room is focused on The Rat now. Even Por-por has him in her sights. He's starting to look nervous. Casting his eyes in Wu's direction.

The Cat In The Hat! shouts Mei, pulling Dr Seuss from her backpack. Angel puts a calming, containing arm around her. And opens the book.

I sat there with Sally. We sat there, we too.

And I said how I wish we had something to do.

I shift my hypothesis into overdrive. She's not going to surrender Little Lord Fauntleroy here. You know the old proverb, I remind them all, switching to the vernacular. All men, good or bad, rarely ill-treat their own children.

Por-por corrects my Cantonese. And repeats the maxim in Mandarin, for Wu's benefit. Or maybe she's just showing off.

Blood is thicker than water, I continue in English. Really thick, in Li Dan's case. Look at him. He's more confused than you. Maybe you think Taiping will roll over and take one for the team? Or should I say Qing Yi? Doesn't matter anyway. She doesn't have the profile. And she's a valuable commodity. Protected by a higher power. It won't be Micki or her sister either. They're going to look like victims.

The penny drops. Anurak lifts his gun. Points it at me. I could just give them you, he says. Dead or alive.

Hardly, Soi Cowboy. You think everyone here is going to tell it that way, the same way, when they get down to Old Bailey? Pull that trigger and you won't even make it out of the building. The police will be up those thirteen flights before Wu can even get out of the sofa. Imagine how happy she'll be about that. No, however we cut it, you get fingered and fucked. Any move you make is disadvantageous. Zugzwang. The urn will stay where it is, of course. Probably for twenty-five to life. If Wu sticks a fork in your ass now, however, she can turn you over. And you're done. We all get paid. Everyone gets laid. Especially you. Nightly. By fifteen guys and a mop handle, for a packet of menthols. If you're lucky. You're dead, Anurak. Get yourself buried.

He's stunned. The Weed is looking a little green around the gills too.

I stand for my closing remarks. Raise Mei's backpack. Hold it before my chest. Easy tigers, I warn them. The urn's in here. You don't want an itchy trigger finger to make this all for nothing, do you?

The Rat and The Weed look to each other. Then to Wu for guidance. She nods. They lower their barrels. I put my right hand into the backpack. Wrap it around the Ruger I've been keeping in there for special occasions just like this. Ever since a late night visitor dropped it in the office. Does the condemned man have any last requests? I ask The Rat. He doesn't seem to grasp what I'm saying. I make it crystal clear. And pull the weapon, levelling it at him.

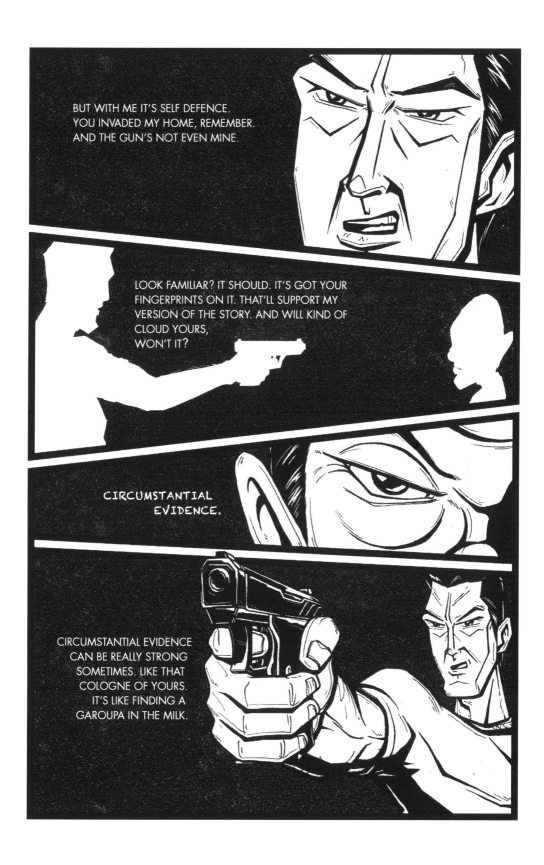

Tympanic membrane ruptured, The Rat howls like a wounded banshee.

Two down, Temujin to go.

Strict observers of The Code would regard my actions as less than honourable.

The challenged chooses the weapon and the ground. The challenger chooses the distance. Their seconds fix the time and terms of firing. Any disagreements to be resolved at the same time, at right angles to the principals, with five-paces interval.

Ai-ya, complains Por-por, more worried about blood soaking into the rug than my contravention of The Code.

Micki moves catatonically to a position beside Por-por. Bends to collect The Weed's weapon. Angel beats her to it. And drops both guns into the backpack. Then takes it to the other side of the room. I'm pretty sure this is another of the things Fisher-Price didn't have in mind when they designed it.

Perfect for school use, weekend trips or spend-the-night parties, and more!

Bing, on auto-pilot, runs to the kitchen, wondering what she's done for Zita, Patron Saint Of Domestic Helpers, to have forsaken her like this.

Amongst it all Madam Wu stands motionless. Expressionless.

Bing returns with a dustpan. Attempts to sweep the bird nest into it. Por-por tells her not to throw them in the bin. That stuff is expensive.

Mei, unable to keep up with the rapid turn of events, trades concern for bemusement. She points at the two bodies on the floor. Fubar, Ba-ba?

Snafu, I confirm, as Por-por takes her to the dining table.

I suggest Madam Wu might be more comfortable sitting down. And take her by the elbow to the sofa. Don't worry, I tell her. The vessel with the vassal wasn't in the bag with the fag. In case you were wondering.

Obviously, she replies coldly.

I sit The Weed next to his mother. He's still dazed and bleeding heavily from the wound on his cheek. I might've broken his nose, again. Re-broken it. Maybe I fixed it. He should thank me. I pull the silk tashtook from The Rat's pocket and give it to him. He says thank-you, meekly. Maybe I knocked some manners into him too. Although a change of fortune often has the same affect on manners. It probably goes both ways. Almost everything in this opera does.

The Rat attempts to stand, perforated eardrum playing merry hell with his sense of balance. The constant ringing must be a bitch as well. It doesn't take much effort to push him down. Stay there, I instruct. I don't want to keep hitting you. And you don't want to look any worse for when you meet the press tomorrow morning. I pop the other one and you're going to find question time a little difficult too.

Swelling has all but closed one eye. He turns and gazes monocularly upon The Weed. Maybe it's the physical pain or the emotional duress, but he appears to be on the verge of tears. All right, all right, I say. Get over there then. Breaking up is hard to do, I know. Enjoy each other for a few moments more.

The Rat hauls himself across the carpet.

Normally, when I split a pair of mop squeezers, I double down. You'll understand if I pass this time. The deck and the odds are stacked in the house's favour, wouldn't you agree, Madam Wu? How do you see this one playing out?

The Mole looks across at her first-born. Perhaps he has been spared the rod too many times, she admits, passively. They are both yours.

And with that she consigns her son to the past.

Buy one, get one free? Now there's an audacious zwischenzug. Does that get me two entries in the lucky draw as well? It's tempting, but a deal is a deal. Anurak for the urn. You can set thine own house in order.

38. EXCHANGE RATES

SO, NOW WHAT? asks Wu, from the couch. Angel and Micki would like to know the answer to that too. I can tell. They're standing in the doorway that leads to the bedrooms. Por-por couldn't care less. She's in the kitchen with Mei and Bing, castigating the latter for her indiscretion with the bird nest.

Worst-case scenario, I begin. The police find me holding intruders at bay. Some or all of which are linked to a spate of homicides, attempted murders and maybe even arson. That puts the onus on you, Madam Wu, to improve all our situations. Especially your own. Your time starts... now. Angel, dial Oldham's number.

Anurak makes one last appeal to Wu. Madam, please. You can't.

Just watch her. She's a true friend Rak. She's going to stab you in the front. Besides, a little time apart will do you good. Absence makes the heart grow fonder and all that. I just hope it doesn't go the other way. Out of sight, out of mind. By the time you get released Li Dan could be stabbing someone else from behind, if you know what I mean. He might have a big hairy chest on his back too.

No! he begs, rising to confront me. I push him back into his place. Subconsciously, or maybe even consciously, he's resigned himself to his fate.

Micki. Join your friends on the sofa over there.

Wu sighs. Mr So, where is the urn?

Yes. Back to business. Good idea. Nothing like a little enterprise to distract you from the pain of letting go. The urn is on its way. Hopefully you can arrange to have the rest of the money arrive at the same time.

You have the cheque, Mr So, she says, regaining her headmistress composure. And, as we discussed-

Cheque schmeque. I'll cancel it myself, if you haven't already. I can tell you're the cash-and-carry type. Probably don't even have a credit card. With your kind of money, Madam Wu, you don't have to worry about opening and closing times. That kind of moolah gets complimentary side-orders of shrimp, free hats and a happy ending. Arrange it. Angel, give her the blower. Anurak, while she's doing that, tell us why you drilled Player, how the Swede copped it and why Benny got low-balled and cold-cocked.

You're the one with the gift for stories, he says, wincing at the continuous 1000Hz test pattern tone that must be oscillating in his aural cavity.

I want to hear your side of it, I tell The Rat, while Wu spits military commands into the phone, in Mandarin. Or maybe I'll change my mind. And you can all tell your versions, Rashamon-style, to a captive audience on Old Bailey. In about six-and-a-half minutes.

The urn should be motive enough. You know its value. And our commitment to getting it back.

Two people died for it. That's a tad excessive. Even if you only believe half the shinola. Benny didn't know any of that. His crime was one of passion and stupidity.

Your partner isn't the only one guilty of that, he says, turning to Micki.

A lot of people wanted Player gone, she responds, *con anima*. He'd shafted dozens. A good percentage of the female population in Macao. And Shanghai. There was a bonus for seeing him off. It was part of the attraction wasn't it, Anurak?

My reasons were just the mercenary nail in his coffin. The means to a self-prescribed end. Even he knew it wasn't a matter of *if*, just when, where and by who. Your reasons, Ms Wong, and those of your sister, were a little more personal.

Micki says nothing. Her eyes search the carpet for an answer. Eventually they find mine. A tear slides down her cheek.

She has AIDS, says The Rat.

I look at Micki. I want her to deny it. This was the type of news you heard on the radio, saw on TV or read about in the paper. Not that walked and talked in your living room. And you banged on the banks of Acheron.

Micki stands. Pride returns to her bones. Not me. Esther. The money is for her, Jack. Doctors. We don't know how long she's got but you've heard the stories. She's going to need looking after. You've seen the pictures. Player knew. He killed her. And others. I did the world a favour, she says staring out the window.

You knew where the urn was?

Micki is somewhere beyond the building at the moment, *patetico*. The Rat continues, in absentia. We worked out who it was entrusted to.

Whom.

What?

To *whom* it was entrusted. Not who.

They needed someone whom could provide discreet, private passage. From Shanghai, to Hong Kong.

Actually, in that context, you're better off with who. But let's moor that to one side and get back to your private passages. It had to be someone, say, from Kobayashi's crew, aboard Bengal 1? Why bring it here? Why not sell it in China?

That is our country, says Wu, proudly. The urn and any news of it would have found its way to me. It's a big nation but there are even less places to hide than here. And even less protection. In many respects, I can be a law unto myself there.

But you're not there now are you? Why didn't you just lean on The Swede? Surely he wasn't heavily invested in the charade. It wouldn't have taken much to buy or frighten him into capitulation.

We attempted to, says The Rat. But his motivations and rewards were of a personal nature, he contends. And looks at Micki, transfixed by the window.

You know what a hard habit she can be to break. How persuasive Ms Wong can be when she wants something. She came to you for a number of things, didn't she? And you were quite forthcoming too, weren't you, Mr So?

Angel grasps the innuendo. Her disappointment is obvious. Her suspicions have been confirmed. I can feel them looking down on me, shaking their head and walking away, shoulders low.

The way these women share their secrets, Mr So, perhaps you should get yourself to a clinic. Along with anyone else you may have known since then, he says eying Angel.

She lashes out at him. It's a sharp slap that was probably meant for me.

You're copping it from all directions, Anurak. Best watch your mouth. The monster-in-law will unload on you next. Why didn't you make a deal with Bergman? With all of them. Player. Benny.

Ms Wong did. Of that we are sure. Although she hasn't said as much about it. We believe many deals were done. It's apparent, however, most were trading off stocks they didn't have. Your arrangement was just the most pellucid.

I should tell Angel to hit him again, for unauthorized use of *pellucid*. Instead I ask who took a piece out of Benny and why. He knew nothing.

That, it would seem, was his undoing. Perhaps Player thought he was you. Maybe he was trying to find out what you knew.

I place a hand on Micki's shoulder. You were playing both ends against the middle. Me against them all. The whole time. Cat Street?

That night Esther and I went to the yacht. Bergman was supposed to meet Player in North Point. Deliver it. Player never showed. I guess we know why, now. Maybe Bergman got some entrepreneurial ideas of his own.

Maybe you gave Bergman some fresh ones.

I knew Player's fence on Cat Street. Bergman called me the next day. I said his end of the deal still held. Convinced him to make the switch.

We weren't surprised to find him meeting Ms Wong there, says The Rat. Only a few places would be willing to exchange it quickly and quietly. We'd canvassed most of them, offering gratuity for information.

They had me, counters Micki, as if that were some kind of excuse.

So why didn't Bergman just hand it over?

I don't know.

Yes you do.

I told him that if I didn't make it to Cat Street, or something happened, he should come to you.

Even when you were standing there next to him? In the shop?

When dickless pulled the gun he panicked. And ran.

I'm not sure which dickless she is referring to. I'm hoping one of them will oblige me with a response.

To chase after him would have drawn attention to us, confesses The Rat.

Not to mention how hard it is to imagine Madam Wu hitching up her skirt and taking off in hot pursuit. Why torch the shop?

We were as surprised to hear about that as anyone. Although, given the ill fate that seems to have befallen many of those keeping the urn from its rightful owners, perhaps we shouldn't be.

You sent Taiping to the agency to see if The Swede had made it to me?

While we went to the harbour to see if he would return to the yacht.

With a bullet in his belly?

We weren't aware of his injury, he says in a tone that suggests he might be trying to convince himself. Our timing and thinking, like my aim, was off.

The Weed stirs. No it wasn't. I was right. You didn't listen.

The Rat warns his lover. Li Dan. Don't. It is not-

No, he says shrugging off a consoling arm. I am unsatisfied to be finished in this way. Who do you think gave him the nerve to be killed here?

I have no idea what he's saying but it's been so long since he said anything I can't wait to see what he comes up with next. Neither can Madam Wu, who has finished making her arrangements on the phone.

You think I am nothing, Li Dan continues. You all think I am impotent penis. But I can be a monk with an umbrella too. Without hair and sky. Without law and God. I would have finished him in Cat Street if you had not stopped me. And I would have put dents in this ass too. I would not have failed like your fondling Taiping, he says to his mother. I would have taken your breath away too, Jack So. If they had let me.

So you do have it in you Danny boy. Congratulations. You killed a man. I hate to disappoint you though. No I don't. I live to disappoint you. That umbrella you're holding, so proudly, it leaks. And the heavens are about to unload. If I were you I'd shut-up and take cover behind your mother's skirt.

Por-por, Bing and Mei return to the table. Bing has a tray of glasses. And thinks now is a good time to offer everyone a glass of Ribena.

I ask Micki about the bogus call she made from The Pen. She doesn't respond. I ask her to give me the cheque. She hands me the envelope.

I open it.

Empty.

I look at her. Accusing her.

Jack, I didn't, she protests.

At this range, I can smell the Poison on her. She stares me down. I open the bag. Retrieve the phone. And realize I have no idea how to operate it. I scan the buttons for something that might enable me to pick up the call, or at least stop it from ringing. It's like death by Moog. I pass the phone to Angel. Hello? No answer. The connection is terminated.

Mei is buzzing from her sugary Ribena libation. She wants to know why all the people are here. I tell her they'll be going soon. And apologize to Por-por. She says it's not good for old women or little sisters to be up so late.

The Rat asks if he can go to the bathroom. I tell him to hold it. And if he needs a hand with that, maybe his boyfriend can hold it for him. I'm waiting for Madam Wu to spend a penny. If she wants to make bail and get out on a good behaviour bond.

She demurs a beat or two, before deciding to end the Manchurian standoff. She opens her bag. And presents me with a Thomas Cook Traveller's Cheque.

I didn't know they came in XL sizes. I count the zeroes. And stuff it into my jeans. Here's those Mark Six numbers Midian was looking for. I wonder if the moneychanger on Lockhart Road would accept this?

Micki walks to the window, *nobilmente.* And gazes into the night. I tell her I'm sorry. She says she is too.

I give Angel the receipt from the Hilton. And tell her to pick up the urn. This charges the room with anxiety. She turns to leave and puts the portable phone on the table. Take it with you, I suggest. In case you get waylaid.

Waylaid? These days I'd settle for a feel from a taxi driver.

Well, there's no time for any more dirty deeds tonight. We have guests in town for the weekend.

I'm saving myself for someone special anyway. Don't forget Tuesday, she reminds me chirpily. And pulls the door tight behind her.

I wait for her heels to recede down the foyer, then face the room.

Tea anyone?

Por-por convinces Mei it's time for bed. And leads her down the hall. She warns me not to make any more mess.

I dismiss Bing. She retreats to the cupboard in the kitchen that doubles as her bedroom. To pray, most likely.

Micki sits at the table, thumbing local gossip magazines.

I turn on the television. Robin Parke is recounting the day's events from Shatin racetrack. I'm taking a punt on a trifecta of a whole different breed at our place. And I doubt he'd be any more enthusiastic about our chances. I flick the channel over to Benny Hill, who's starting to look quite sensible in the light of my escapades.

The Rat repeats his request to visit the little boys room. Little boys room is just a euphemism, I remind him. There's not any little boys in there. He winces. In pain. This could be derived from any number of afflictions, my attempts at humour chief among them. I send The Weed in to freshen up with him, while I stand in the open doorway. Don't forget to flush.

Li Dan washes his face. Inspects the wound on his cheek. Anurak combs his hair into place. Smooths his jacket. Probably wondering what colour prison suits come in.

I'll have them dry-clean that for you. By the time you get out, if you watch what you eat and get some regular exercise, it should still fit.

He ignores me. And I usher the unhappy couple back to the couch.

Wu appears to have fallen asleep. I don't know how. I can hardly stand the excitement. Maybe she's narcoleptic.

I try to mend the bridge to Micki. She ignores me. Was she down at the harbour when Bergman delivered the red herring? No answer. She even regards the compliment I pay her outfit with suspicion. My enquiries as to Esther's health are rejected silently. I'd count the money except that might be considered vulgar. So I take a few belts of Ribena, to get my sugar levels up.

It's an uncomfortable thirty minutes that becomes the best part of an hour.

I offer Wu a copy of *Life And Death In Shanghai*. She declines. Already read it? What am I thinking, you're probably in it. Bonfire Of The Vanities?

Por-por wanders out. Informs us Mei is asleep. And starts to clear glasses from the table. She notices Wu nodding-out on the couch and asks if I hit her as well. Then disappears into the kitchen.

A knock at the door gets everyone's attention.

Wu snaps into consciousness. Micki braces in the chair. The Weed and The Rat drag their eyes from each other. Even Por-por returns from the scullery. The beanfeast builds with intensity.

What's behind door number one?

It's Angel. Short of breath. Miss me? she asks, shaking the rain from her hair. And giving me a great idea for a shampoo commercial. All other eyes, however, are on the ancient amphora swaddled in her arms.

I take it from her. Remove the bubble wrap. And place it on the table. Bing immediately salvages the packaging. Unable to resist popping a few plastic pimples as she takes it to the kitchen. Who can blame her?

Wu, Li Dan and Anurak stand. They skulk toward the urn like hyenas upon wounded prey. Micki exhibits a flicker of interest, circling the room, a wary hawk. Ever the opportunist. And the unofficial Handover Ceremony begins.

Angel, you can be The Queen, I say, distributing roles. I'll be The Governor. Madam Wu can be Deng Xiaoping. Or would you rather be Zhao Ziyang? And you, I say to The Weed and The Rat, are concubines of the Imperial Court.

The room is silent as I lift the urn and hand it auspiciously to Madam Wu. Is it everything you thought it would be?

She regards it regally, aware of its full weight. And the critical mass of the moment. Anurak and Li Dan part as she walks to the sofa. And sits. The Mole quivers in anticipation. She runs her hands up the urn, studying the wax caulk and ribbon. She caresses the lid. And then, inexplicably, twists it.

The seal is broken.

I'm no expert on antiquities, yet, even with my limited knowledge I suspect that has significantly decreased its value. Others must also be of the same opinion, given the amount of air that was just sucked out of the room.

Wu removes the lid and peers in. I wait for supernatural spirits to fly out and faces to start melting. She holds no such fear. Recaps the urn. Turns the vessel on its side. And shakes it. Violently. Then bends her ear to the jade and listens. For what? Voices of dissent? She rights it in her lap and removes the lid again. A small cloud of dust rises from within.

Bing and I brace for the Apocalypse.

Madam Wu? asks The Rat quietly, as if fearing reprisals.

The Weed approaches his mother slowly, looking more confused than he did when I slammed his head into the elevator. He halts as she empties the contents of the urn onto the floor, sifting the ashes through her open talons.

Wah! shouts Por-por and starts complaining about the carpet. She takes two confrontational steps toward Madam Wu. Angel has to hold her at bay.

Sandcastle! erupts Mei from the doorway. She runs to the cocktail of Mongol warlord and Qin Dynasty emperor being emptied onto the rug. I bound across the room and gather her into my arms.

Wu looks at me, her mole full of menace and anger. Where are they?

Where are what?

Where are they?

Where are what? I repeat. And look to her cohorts for help.

The diamonds? Wu shouts, standing. Where are the diamonds?

Diamonds? I repeat *sotto voce*, appealing to Micki, who's taken a much greater interest in the proceedings.

Por-por tells Bing to get the dustpan. She crosses herself twice and disappears into the kitchen. Maybe the vacuum cleaner would be easier, suggests Angel.

Diamonds? I ask again. In there?

Wu fixes the venerated vase in her gaze. Worthless, she says. And drops it.

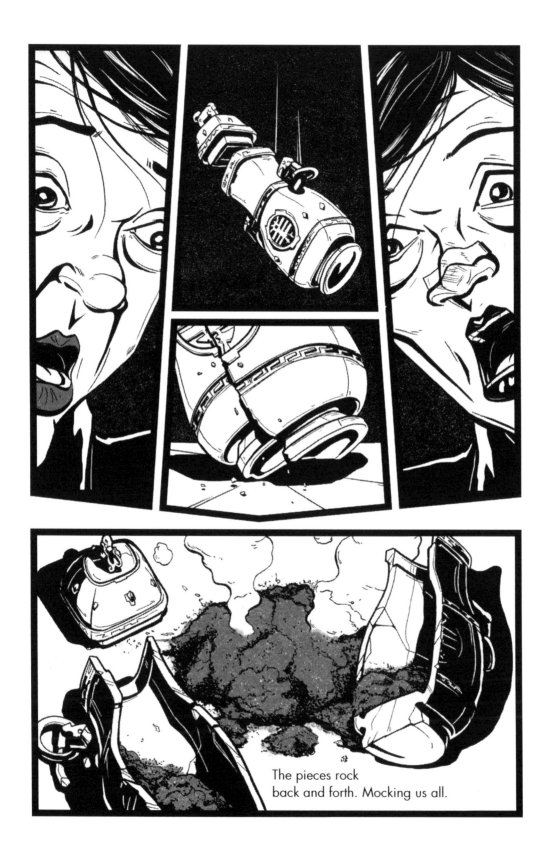

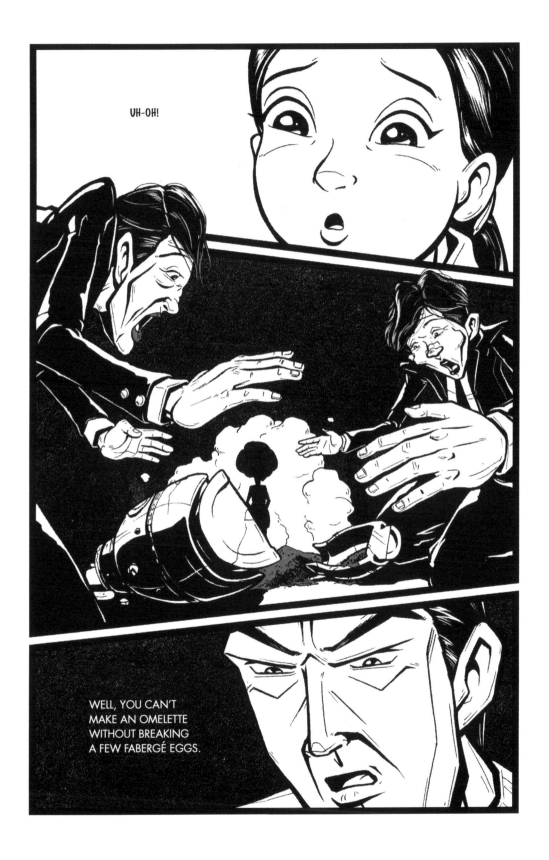

Por-por storms in with the dustpan. Anurak tries to push her out of the way. I kick him in the ribs. He topples over. Bing, hot on Por-por's tail, fires up the vacuum cleaner. Except, in her panic, she's switched it to blow instead of suck. And thousands of years of dead history are blasted around the living room.

Ai-yah! exclaims Por-por. She scrambles to turn off the machine. Berating Bing with a wide variety of Cantonese endearments. Angel finds great humour in the shituation. It's okay for her. It's not her rug. And she doesn't have to live here with a raging warlord. Or the spirits of Temujin and Qin Shi Huang for that matter. I suggest she take Mei into the kitchen while we clear the air.

Diamonds? I inquire discreetly, sidling up to Micki.

I had no idea. I knew her husband was invested in gold and precious metals. Gemstones. Antiques. I didn't know he'd consolidated them.

A nice little urn-er, I quip, for my own amusement.

Wu steps through the chaos in the centre of the room, instructing her pawns to leave the remnants on the floor. They question her. Leave them! she snaps.

Even without the diamonds it must have had value, Micki continues. As an artifact. The jade alone-

Without the diamonds it is worthless to me, asserts Wu.

Worthless? And what about the cost?

As you said, Mr So, you can't make an omelette without breaking eggs.

But I was only yolking when I said that. Where's the omelette? This isn't even scrambled fucking eggs.

The doorbell chimes. *Song of Joy*. Hold that thought. I wonder what's behind door number two?

An omelette, shouts Angel, from the kitchen.

They're half right. The visitor is from a broken home and all mixed up.

Taiping. A picture of innocest. As pure as the horse galloping through her veins, in a brilliant white cheongsam with ivory print, matching velvet gloves and pleather heels.

Qing Yi! I exult. I didn't recognise you, with your clothes on. Do come in. Let your hair down. And allow me take that for you too, I add, reaching for the case. She blanks me. And looks to her benefactor for approval.

Mr So, says Wu. You don't think I'm going to hand that over, do you? The urn is worthless. You may keep it.

Gee thanks, I reply appreciatively. And pull the cheque from my pocket. According to you, however, this is worth something. So I'll just cash it now. It'll save me going to the bank on Monday. Wu looks at the cheque. And back to me. No? Well, okay. I'll just keep it then. As a souvenir. We can frame it. Put it on the wall of the office. We don't see a lot of paper for that kind of money.

Li Dan! We are leaving!

So soon? But Taiping just got here. She must be tired after the night she's had. Take a load off Qing Yi. Take a load for free. And you give the case to me.

Mr So, the money comes with us.

No it doesn't. You don't check out of this hotel until you settle your account, in full. You've forgotten about the items you put on your tab. Your son's freedom. His boyfriend's incarceration. My partner's rehabilitation. Esther Wong's hospitalization. Por-por's dry-cleaning. And, remember, I did reunite you with Temujin and his imperial friend. Just because they're not the guys you thought they were doesn't alter the fact that I delivered them. As per our agreement. *Caveat emptor* and all that. Of course if you'd like to take this to the Small Claims Tribunal…

Wu looks through me. Nods to Taiping. Give it to him.

I take possession of the case.

Wu calls for Li Dan again. He starts to walk as commanded. Then stops. Looks at the stranded Anurak.

Leave those, instructs his mother, referring to the broken pieces of the urn in his hands. And the wreck of a man among the ashes.

The Weed gingerly places the two halves of the urn on the table. I put guilt on her, he informs me. I will put knife scars on her more than the hairs on your leg. I might be a dead pig. But a dead pig is not afraid of boiling water.

So long, Danny. We're going to miss you around here.

Madam Wu pushes the boy ahead. Before he can embarrass her further. Anurak makes a final bid for freedom. And reunification. I step to meet him in the centre of the room. Hit him in the chest with the briefcase. And knock him on his ass. A cloud of ancient dust engulfs him.

Li Dan gives an anguished shout from the hall. Wu tells him to be silent. Taiping pulls him into the elevator. By the testicles, it sounds like. The Rat scrambles to get off the floor. I kick him in the chest. Stay down. I could still change my mind.

About not handing me over to the police?

About not shooting you, I reply unemotionally. And pull the gun from my trousers, to underline my point. Angel, call Oldham.

Por-por wanders out, shakes her perm and looks at the rug. Then starts to roll it up. She prods Anurak. Tells him to get off it. Complaining quietly to everyone and no one. I tell her to leave it. To go to bed. Secure in the knowledge that I will have hell to pay in the morning. Fortunately I am now flush with enough cash to cover it. And any losses she may have incurred in the market.

Angel is still in the kitchen. I call out, again, for her to ring Oldham. She appears in the doorway, Mei on her hip. Already have, she says raising Micki's portable phone. Handy little things these, she adds, without a trace of irony.

I direct my attention to Micki. She's standing at the table, turning a piece of fractured jade in her hands, *dolente*. Thinking of all the things that might've been.

You've got fifteen minutes, I inform her.

39. YESTERDAY'S NEWS

We lie down in darkness and have our light in ashes...

MICKI AND I SIT AT THE TABLE. Broken jade between us, like days of future past. Visions before midnight and dreams out of the ivory gate. Etcetera. Etcetera.

All I have to explain is the corpse downstairs, I tell her. I don't have to do a good job of it. They don't have to believe it. I've seen the implausible truth and I still don't accept it. The way this pooch was screwed is barking mad. But it doesn't matter. The evidence is here, with the prime suspects. And the rest can be picked up before they pack their bags. All I have to do is tell the truth and I'm clear. I might even get to keep the money. You've nothing to lose. And everything to gain, if I believe what you tell me. So make it straight. And fast. The truth, Mick. Try it. You might even like it.

I got the urn from Li.

Junior, or senior?

Li Longji.

He gave it, or you took it?

Gave it.

Because you gave yourself to him?

I was going to give it back. I don't even like that ethnic shit. You've seen my apartment. You know my taste.

Sultry nectar at night. And bittersweet in the morning, I reply, unable to resist the opportunity for a final flurry of innuendo. You have, as some might say, swallowed the lessons of antiquity without digesting them.

I didn't want the old goat to get upset or lose face. He was a valuable client. I held onto it. After a while I was just going to tell him that having such a precious piece of history in my care made me nervous.

But he died.

Yes.

Between your legs?

Shortly after.

So he did get his dick caught in the mangle. At least now we can rule out Housemaid's Knee.

Elephants, buffalo, bizarre gardening accidents and pathological laughter too, she says austerely. Although he did curl up his toes with a smile.

You were Jessica Hahn to his Jim Bakker.

Yes, Jack. I defrocked him. Once.

Sometimes that's all it takes. And then what? As he lay down in darkness you saw the light in his ashes. You gave the urn to Player?

He was going to get it valued. Independently. I guess he did. And decided he wanted to be independently wealthy.

Did he know about the diamonds?

I doubt it.

He just cut you out.

Yes. So I got Anurak to-

You brought him into this? On your own? I look across at The Rat, smiling. Presumably at the ugly truth of her confession.

I knew Wu wanted it. I co-opted him.

Corrupted him.

He was already on that path. I don't make people do things they don't want to. You know that. I told him there'd be more in it for him if he worked with me.

You sent him after Player.

I sent him after the urn.

And Player, interjects The Rat.

You shut up. I still haven't decided what to do with you. And until that doorbell rings I can change my mind a dozen times.

I found out about Esther and her condition shortly after, confesses Micki. I was angry, with both of them. I figured Anurak could take care of Player too.

Sure. Why not? Your own little Four Cleanups Movement.

I FIGURED WE WOULD,
ESTHER WOULD,
NEED EVERY CENT.
I WANTED TO PUT
THE URN INTO
THE OPEN MARKET.
OPTIMIZE ITS VALUE.

BUT ANURAK HAD ALREADY
WORKED OUT A WAY TO
DO THAT FOR HIMSELF.
YOU KNEW IT
WAS ON BENGAL 1?
YOU SENT ANURAK
AFTER PLAYER. HOPED YOU'D
GET THE URN BEFORE THEY DID.

MORE OR LESS.

MORE, OR LESS?

I NEEDED HELP.

THE NIGHT YOU CAME TO ME?

I NEEDED HELP
TO KEEP PLAYER,
AND THE RAT, BUSY.

WHILE YOU GOT THE URN
FROM BERGMAN.

AND WE KNOW HOW THAT
PANNED OUT.

NOT REALLY. I DON'T. YOU DO.

I CAME TO YOU
FOR PROTECTION.

FOR A DIVERSION, MAYBE. FOR A
DISTRACTION. BUT NOT PROTECTION.

I NEEDED HELP, JACK.
YOU'VE SEEN WHAT
THESE PEOPLE ARE LIKE.

These people? You're *these* people, Mick. As stupid and selfish as they are.

I'm not like them. They're ruthless. Player, Wu, Anurak. They were all prepared to kill for this.

So were you.

He deserved it. The circumstances were-

You killed Player.

What he did to my sister...

You were down the harbour that night with Benny. Or you were following him, when he and Player went at it. Player wasn't there to meet Bergman. He went to meet you. Half the world was gunning for him. You're the only one he'd risk meeting down a blind alley. Hell of an opening move, dragging Benny down there by his 'nads. You sent him in to distract Player. And Anurak completed your Queen's Gambit. Nice execution, Xie Jun. Except I was supposed to be your Sicilian Defence. Not Benny.

He wasn't supposed to get hurt.

No. Just everyone else you were pissed-off with.

Jack. You're not-

Yes, I am.

Don't, Jack. Not again. Don't fuck me over. Again.

You fucked yourself, sister. So don't put this Fatal Attraction on me. The reviews are in. That bunny boiling on the cooktop is my family. Bringing this to me is one thing. Bringing it to my home? Two people are dead. Benny, as good as. You put my daughter in harm's way so you could unleash your personal brand of justice? Pay a few hospital bills?

You said you'd help.

I did help. I am helping. This is the best thing for you. Trust me.

But Esther. She'll-

She'll get by. She always does. And so will you.

No. Jack-

I'm not going away for you, Micki. And I will if I don't keep it straight with Oldham. I'm not like you. I can't slink off to another country and pretend this doesn't exist. I have to live here. Work here. I have to stay here. This is it for us. For Mei and I. All you're offering is a choice between you and her.

You loved me once.

Not more than her. Yesterday was good and today was fun. But today is done. And tomorrow is another one. She lost her mother. She can't lose me.

We'll work something out. We have more than this, Jack.

No we don't. This is all it is. As broken and worthless as that urn. I don't know if Ye Olde Curiosity Shoppe is even going to be interested in it any more. Let alone a museum. Or a collector. When did you find out about the diamonds?

I never knew what was inside, what was supposed to be inside, until now. Li never told me. Maybe he didn't put them in there. Maybe it was Player. He could've resealed it. Maybe he stole them. And was getting them out of the country. He had debts. And his cost of living was increasing exponentially.

He found out about them, I venture. About the time he had the urn appraised, I'd say. Maybe he had it x-rayed. But Wu knew about them too.

Maybe they were there all along. Maybe that's where Li kept them. Old guys do weird things with their money. All I know is what the urn was. And that people wanted it. Really wanted it. And I know what people are like, what they'll do, when they desire something. I wanted them to pay for it. I wanted him to pay for it. For what he did to Esther. Who's going to take care of her? She doesn't deserve much but she doesn't deserve what's coming. That's the truth.

The insoluble truth of this was becoming clearer and clearer. It hadn't changed for thousands of years. Warriors can be dispatched and men can be eliminated, but they should not be dishonoured or humiliated. A woman can die, but she must never be defiled.

The truth, Mick? Or the opinion that survived?

The truth.

What kind of truth? A truth of reasoning or a truth of fact?

It's a fact, Jack.

Really? Because if it were a truth of reasoning then the opposite is impossible. And that might buy you some sympathy. But if it's a truth of fact, well, that's contingent. And the opposite is possible.

Leibniz knows more about those diamonds than me. I would've held out for more if I knew they were there. We need the money. More than anyone now.

Well, right now, you've got two chances of seeing any of it.

Two chances?

Slim and fuck-all.

Jack-

Save it Mick. There's nothing you can say that can make a difference. It might've, if you'd been straight-up from the start. We wouldn't be here. Or if we were we'd be naked and rolling around the floor and laughing about it.

I look at her. Waiting for an answer. Waiting. She stands. Walks to the centre of the room. Collapses to the floor. Sobbing, *morendo*. Don't get tears on that rug. If it mixes with the ash it'll set like concrete. And I'll never hear the end of it.

Jack? intercedes Angel quietly, carrying Mei.

What?

That's enough.

That's enough, Ba-ba, concurs Mei. Today is gone. Today was fun. Tomorrow is another one.

You guys believe her?

We think her warp is as good as her weft. She's got nothing to hide and nowhere to go. That's enough. A woman knows when a woman knows.

A woman knows, Ba-ba, confirms Mei.

I'm wondering just what and how much a woman knows when a woman knows, when there's a knock on the door. Fuck me, I think. How'd the police get here so quick?

I look to Angel. Maybe she knows.

40. CLEANING UP

AS A TEENAGER, I endured a brief tenure as towelboy in a Mong Kok sauna. One of our regular customers was a *gweilo* professor. I made the mistake of asking him what I should read if I wanted to improve my English. Thomas Browne, he replied. And limped off to his weekly handjob.

It was one of the first serious books I ever stole from the library. The compendium took almost two years to finish. And nearly killed me.

Sir Thomas famously remarked that men were noble creatures, splendid in ashes and pompous in the grave. 330 years ago, he'd also debunked the myths surrounding an urn or two.

Now since these dead bones have already out-lasted the living ones of Methuselah, and in a yard under ground, and thin walls of clay, out-worn all the strong and specious buildings above it; and quietly rested under the drums and tramplings of conquests.

What Prince can promise such diuturnity unto his Reliques? What Song the Syrens sang, or what name Achilles assumed when he hid himself among women, though puzzling Questions are not beyond all conjecture. What time the persons of these Ossuaries entered the famous Nations of the dead, and slept with Princes and Counsellours, might admit a wide solution. But who were the proprietaries of these bones, or what bodies these ashes made up, were a question above Antiquarism.

As they say in literary circles, Browne really knew his shit. Although, needless to say, Angel did challenge his views on the trivial and vulgar act of coition. It's only vulgar if you're doing it right, according to her.

It is the foolishest act a wise man commits in all his life. Nothing will more deject his cooled imagination, when he considers the odd and unworthy folly he has committed.

I'm sure Madam Wu would have agreed with this. In fact, a similar notion might even have been the last thought that went through her mind. As her deranged son pounded her gulliver into the tiles of our lobby.

Turns out the police were already down in the street when Wu's coterie was leaving. Angel had executed a Lucena Position of her own. She'd called them when she went to pick up the urn. She was worried things were getting too gonzo. People with guns in the house. Mei in the middle. Por-por in danger of going off at any minute. She figured it could get real ugly real quick.

It's hard to be angry with someone when they take that kind of initiative. I knew there was a reason I'd hired her.

Angel had told the flatfoots to stay out until Taiping arrived. Then they could pick up the whole freak show at once. Just give The Flaneusse fifteen minutes. Or wait until they get a call.

Turns out Oldham got impatient. He entered the building, with his band of Chau-huahuas, just in time to see Li Dan doing a Jackson Pollock with his mother's medulla oblongata. Said it made the mess in my office look like a finger painting. Some would say she had it coming. Browne would've said every man is his own greatest enemy, and as it were his own executioner. Taiping just stood there, apparently. Watching. Waiting. Didn't raise a finger. Until they tried to take her away.

It took four of them to bring her down.

Buzzcut Chau copped a couple for his troubles. Alas, poor Yorick, he lost an eye. She stuck the pig with one of the stainless steel chopsticks from her hair.

Turns out destiny had its dick firmly planted in fate's cheek. And is not without a sense of humour.

According to Angel, a thousand years ago, the original Wu Zetian was a fifth-rate concubine who killed her son and daughter to get to the throne. Then had another of her children deposed and exiled. You can imagine what she did to those outside the sanctity of family.

My tale, according to Oldham, was impenetrably twisted. That's the beauty of the truth, I told him. It doesn't have the same problems as fiction. Fiction has to be credible. The more incredible something is the greater the chance people will actually believe it.

In the end, leaky as my version of the truth was, Oldham conceded it held just enough water to bail me out.

The Mole is churning burly with Player and sleeps with fishes. The Rat, The Weed and The Flaneusse are sunk. They're going to do Anurak for The Swede. Li Dan for his mum. And Taiping, well, for being an accessory.

Micki is drowning. She waxed Player and had a hand in Benny's fate.

Then there's Esther. Poor broad. Maybe they'll find a cure. It wasn't all that long ago that smoking was good for you. Doctors change their minds about things all the time. They're worse than pregnant women. Getting a general consensus of opinion is a Herculean task. One I would never undertake. She came by the office on Black Monday. All Hallows Eve. Wearing some kind of baggy designer jump-suit. Gold, with a big gold belt around the middle and more pockets than a pool table. She looked like one of Drax's henchmen in *Moonraker.* Maybe she was trick-or-treating. Maybe she had just parachuted in. Or maybe she was going to do a spot of welding right after.

I sympathy fucked her to the tune of fifty grand. That's what Angel calls it when guilt or pity kicks in, and you bestow largesse upon someone. A sympathy fuck. Esther will get another when she needs it. Who knows how long she has?

How much time do any of us have? It can't be long before we all lie down in darkness and have our light in ashes. Sir Thomas Browne said that. I'd always liked it. Now it had a whole new resonance.

I gave Angel a couple of days off and faced a few grim realities of my own. Starting with an AIDS test. The experience created more anxiety than anything I'd endured in the previous week. Maybe even my whole life. I'm more terrified of getting the results than I am of the actual disease. Fear of the unknown. It's not like you're going to be told you've got syphilis. Or Housemaid's Knee. Doctor Fleming and Saint Fiacre are out of their element when it comes to HIV. Doctor Salk too, no doubt.

Trying to eliminate the stench of death from the office was no picnic either. So Fuk Yu will operate out of new premises. As soon as we can afford it.

I did manage to hang onto the money. It wasn't reported stolen and a lot of my clients pay in cash. I have the technology and the typefaces to fabricate a receipt that proves it. Consultancy fees. After tax and a small donation to the policeman's benevolent fund, however, most of it will go to getting Benny back on his feet. Now that he's out of his coma. Typical of him to show up once all the work is done. Still, it's the right thing to do. I got him into it, I should pay to get him out of it. I'm going to sink some cash into securing a more extensive insurance policy for employees too. And by more extensive I mean actually having some coverage in the first place.

I guess the new computer I bought Angel could be considered a sympathy fuck too. For what I put her through. And her conduct under pressure. The guy from Gilman finally came down to replace my keyboard. I told him to go back and get her one of those Commodore PCs.

But you have Apple Macintosh, he said. You won't be able to talk to each other.

We hardly ever do.

The computers are not compatible. It will be like a chicken talking to a duck.

These things can talk now? Jeezus.

No. Files. Transferring information between them will be difficult.

I thought all this stuff was supposed to make life easier.

It will. In the future. If you have the same platform.

Someone should tell the manufacturers that.

I ended up getting her a Macintosh too, so we can share in the joy of rebooting. I'll even show her how it's done. Leisurely, of course. I've heard that's how she likes her intellectual improvement.

Por-por got a sympathy fuck too. In the guise of a new rug. She hated it. Said it was a waste of money. She got the old one cleaned for a fraction of the cost. And now Por-por has two rugs. What is she going to do with that? It will take up space. Space we don't have. I'm so irresponsible.

I tried to explain that, according to Schnitzler, the flight into stupidity was the least dangerous and most comfortable of all the flights one could take from responsibility. Even for clever people like me, the journey is never as long as we think. Por-por said Schnitzler was a stupid gweilo too. And that we should be thankful all the flights into death and sickness were full. Or cancelled.

Bing took a well-earned holiday. She went back to the Philippines, to see her family. And get closer to God. I hope He lets her come back. Good help is hard to find. On earth as it is in heaven.

Amen.

So now I'm sitting here, behind my desk. Waiting for Por-por to bring Mei back from her first morning at kindergarten.

Waiting.

They were courtesy of Mike Midian and his floral sexpert at the Hilton. A response to the five-figure sympathy fuck I sent his way.

Not sure I need a constant reminder of last week hanging over me, Angel says, observing at the urn. I guess I could get used to it. Like a lot of things.

Like what other things?

She raises an inquisitive eyebrow. Like I don't know what she's talking about. Except I don't. I don't think I do anyway. It could be another of those mysterious things that a woman knows when a woman knows. Like... that computer on my desk, she says with a smile. Thanks.

It's the least I could do.

I look forward to more.

You'll have to earn it.

The hard way?

Both ways. If we don't get some better budgets. Brokers aren't the only ones flat on their backs with their fiscal spherals in the grinder.

What are you saying? We're boracic lint?

Not quite.

We need some bigger clients?

Like a bitch on heat.

De Beers big enough for you? she poses. And drops a large, black velvet gonad on the table. Check out the size of these cajones, she says, emptying the contents on the desktop. Copious carats spill over the table. Paragon and on.

Fuck me, I say in disbelief.

Okay, she replies glibly, eyes gleaming.

How?

Any way you like. The lapidary makes the diamond, Jack. But it's the lover that makes the woman.

How *these*, Hugo? I demand. And grab a fistful of stones, some as big as a welder's thumb. Others like a nursemaid's nipple. We could set the golden hours of life with more diamond minutes than Mann could ever imagine.

There had to be more to this treasure hunt than everyone was letting on. So I opened it. The urn. No one goes to that much trouble for an old biscuit tin. And who believes that crap about power and unity coming from an idea? Political power comes from the barrel of a gun. Mao said that. Having a shit-load of money helps too.

The seal?

My uncle, on Cat Street. I called him when I found out what was really inside. And went over there. We sifted the rocks out and waxed it up again. Gloopy tourists and gweilo have been paying top dollar on faux antiques for years. That's one thing that won't change. It's easy to fake shit like that. Especially if someone is in a hurry to get at what's inside, or too ignorant to know the difference. I didn't think we'd have to worry about that pompous bitch examining the wrapping paper.

There comes a time when every Master concedes to his apprentice. You've taken the Lucena to whole new level, I admit.

That and every other position you can imagine. And maybe a few you can't. I've got a tabia that would bind Maróczy.

The ash?

Fuck knows. How many people do you know with a degree in carbon-dating? Could be whale dick for all anyone knows or cares.

Fuck me. With a whale dick.

THE MISADVENTURES OF JACK SO CONTINUE IN

SAYONARA BITCH

SHE'S GONE...

SAYONARA BITCH

...BUT NOT FORGOTTEN

RICHARD TONG

Jack So. Single father. Not-so-good   Samaritan.
When a benevolent beer spills   into a brutal
bloodbath, a wave of violence   washes over
the Neon Noir™ shadows of   Hong Kong
and dumps Jack in the deep end.   Again.

WHAT DO YOU WANT, JACK?

MORE THAN YOU'VE GIVEN. NOT AS MUCH AS YOU'RE OFFERING NOW.

YOU CAN HAVE IT ALL, IF YOU WANT IT BAD ENOUGH.

A sultry seductress.
An incendiary
    secret.

Rubbing shoulders with high society's most
celebrated, salacious and unscrupulous,
Jack discovers some home truths
are better left unsaid.

You can't bury the past
if it's not dead. And
sins of the father can
really be a bitch.

**DELUXE HARD-BOILED EDITION
170+ PAGES OF BOLD GRAPHICS**

HK$188

FOLLOW JACK SO

LIKE SO FUK YU

ALSO BY RICHARD TONG

THE DURIAN EFFECT

SECOND EDITION

An oriental oddyssey of epic distortion.

RICHARD TONG

In 1991, Richard Tong came home to a place he'd never been before. Hong Kong. With no money, no experience and absolutely no idea of what awaited, he embarked on a 10-year journey, exploring the alien corners of Asia and discovering the darkest regions of his soul.

"OH, EAST IS EAST AND WEST IS WEST, AND NEVER THE TWAIN SHALL MEET."

A BALLAD OF ONE MAN, TWO WORLDS AND THE SPINIOUS FRUIT THAT DIVIDES, CONQUERS AND BINDS.

Acerbic, poignant and witty. Raw like sushi, brutal like Bukowski and dry like the mouth of the Yangtze. The Durian Effect puts the odd in odyssey. It takes you swiftly to the edge of the great cultural divide... and throws you into the abyss.

ME&MY POTATO

One man, two worlds and a baby.

RICHARD TONG

Following in the acclaimed steps of The Durian Effect, Richard Tong's Hong Kong *oddyssey* continues with a look at the greatest adventure of all.

Parenthood.

Still wrestling with the local culture, while battling demons both personal and paranormal, he must now overcome a litany of bizarre customs, spectacular misconceptions and his own blinding ignorance in the quest to raise a bi-cultural baby.

Along the way he encounters a wily adversary, a confounding nemesis of uncommon cunning, and one of the most fearsome creatures known to humanity. The Chinese mother-in-law.

Tiger Nan.

Engaging, witty and absurb, Tong combines wry observations with a unique voice to deliver a brutally candid look at breeding in Beijing's backyard.

Printed in Great Britain
by Amazon